Sherlock Holmes

Consulting Detective

Volume Nine

AIRSHIP 27 PRODUCTIONS

Sherlock Holmes: Consulting Detective, Vol. 9

"The Adventure of the Failing Light" © 2017 I.A Watson
"The Adventure of the Three Strand Garotte"; "The Adventure of the Picked Pocket" © 2017 Fred Adams Jr.
"The Betrayal" © 2017 Erik Franklin
"The Adventure of the Brazilian Beetle" © 2017 Aaron Smith

Cover illustration © 2017 Zachary Brunner
Interior illustrations © 2017 Rob Davis

Editor: Ron Fortier
Associate Editor: Jame Ramos
Production and design by Rob Davis
Promotion and marketing by Michael Vance

Published by
Airship 27 Productions
www.airship27.com
www.airship27hangar.com

ISBN-10: 1-946183-14-8
ISBN-13: 978-1-946183-14-9

Printed in the United States of America

10 9 8 7 6 5 4 3 2 1

Sherlock Holmes
Consulting Detective
Volume IX

TABLE OF CONTENTS

Sherlock Holmes

in

"The Adventure of the Failing Light"

By
I.A. Watson

Aye: though we hunted high and low,
And hunted everywhere,
Of the three men's fate we found no trace
Of any kind in any place,
But a door ajar, and an untouched meal,
And an overtoppled chair.
Flannan Isle, Wilfred William Gibson, 1912[1]

The widow stood on the harbour's edge watching the ferry struggle across the sea-chop towards the old stone dock. January gusts whipped white snowflakes around her and billowed her black mourning dress, catching her dark bound hair out of its coils and whipping it behind her. She waited expressionless as the steamer from Ullapool completed its three hour voyage and it edged at last into the shelter of Stornaway's lee.

Holmes and I collected our bags and followed the handful of locals off the little boat onto the sea-front. The widow's eyes, grey as the winter morning, raked over the new arrivals and fixed upon us as the visitors she had awaited. She walked over to us, too young to be so bereaved, too fragile to bear such loss. "You will be the men from London, then?"

"Dr. Watson," I introduced myself. "This is Mr. Holmes. You are Mrs. McBride?"

"Yes." He voice caught on the identification. "I am the relic of George McBride."

"Our condolences for your loss," Holmes told her. Perhaps he too was unexpectedly moved by this fair, dark, wounded creature. "We are here to meet a Mr. Phearson?"

"The Superintendent? He is awa' the Post Office. I said you could bide him in my parlour. It's this way." She turned abruptly along the slushy harbour walk. We followed. The official buildings of sea-weathered stone gave way to timber warehouses and fishing sheds. Further along were simple hut dwellings for the men who harvested the seas around the Isle of Lewis.

Cobbled Kenneth Street ran inland from the South Beach jetty. A right turn took us up Church Street. Crowded terraced houses occupied both sides, humble but scrupulously clean, every doorstep scrubbed. The far end of the road terminated in a Presbyterian chapel.

---

1   Full text at http://www.potw.org/archive/potw230.html

Mrs. McBride brought us about halfway up and turned to her house. The door was not locked. The widow showed us through the narrow stair lobby into a tiny parlour with three chairs and a polished table. New flowers had been set on a hand-made lace doily. A modest fire burned in a modest grate. As was common here the front room was seldom used, always kept as the best room for when company called.

"You will be leaving here soon," Holmes observed to our hostess.

"The house comes with the job. George's replacement needs it. He has family of his own, due next week. The Board expects me gone by then." She spoke without bitterness, only with resignation.

"Where will you go?" I wondered.

"Back to my sister's, I expect, though she has little room. She's wed to a Hearach, one of the wardens at the Tarbert Penitentiary." Mrs. McBride saw our puzzlement. "A Hearach's a man from Harris. You ken that Lewis is joined to the southern part of the Isle of Harris by a thin isthmus? One road. They're in Inverness-shire but we're part of Ross and Cromarty. They're different to us, but Jack Gallett's… alright, I suppose. Anyway, that's where I'm going. I'll be making a pot of tea now."

"Please don't trouble on our behalf," I urged the widow.

"I'm not helpless!" she answered defiantly. "I've lost my man, not my hands. Will you take tea or no?"

"We would be pleased to, Mrs. McBride," Holmes assured her. He doffed his Inverness coat, hung it on a wall-peg, and settled into one of the armchairs.

I watched the widow move off to a tiny thin kitchen at the rear of the house.

"Your sympathies are predictable, my friend," Holmes told me. "A woman in distress always awakens the Perseus within you."

"Is it certain that her husband is dead?" I wondered. "The cable only said vanished."

"That is what we are here to determine, Watson. Be sure we shall do our best for the lady."

The front door opened and there was the sound of someone knocking their boots on the step. A bluff moustached fellow in an Edinburgh greatcoat pushed his head into the room. "Ah, you're here!" he called as he hung up his things. He extended his hand. "Gabriel Phearson, Superintendent for the Northern Lighthouse Board. Pleased to meet you."

We greeted the inspector and made room for him near the inadequate fire. It was bitterly cold in the Outer Hebrides in mid-winter.

"Your Board informed us that you have been to the site of the tragedy and can brief us on the details," Holmes began at once.

We were interrupted by Mrs. McBride's return with a tea-tray. I sprang up to help her arrange the things on the little side-table. Since there were only three chairs I indicated that she should take mine.

"I won't stay," she answered reluctantly. "I ken that I'm not needed here. Just… find what happened to Georgie."

She hastened from the room. Phearson shook his head sympathetically. "Poor wee lamb. Married four months and now a widow. She met McBride when he came here to work and it was a swift courtship. A handsome couple, they made."

"You knew him?" I enquired.

"I knew all of them, Dr. Watson. Wasn't I the last man to see them all alive?"

Holmes rapped the table. "Come, come. This is no way to lay out the facts. Begin at the start, Mr. Phearson. Give your report as you would to the serious men at the Northern Lighthouse Board at George Street, Edinburgh."

"Iphm! Well, then, here's how it began. It was back in '96 when those 'serious men' of whom you speak determined there must be a lighthouse on the Flannan Isles. The Flannans lie twenty miles west of here, the far edge of the volcanic ridge that formed these stormy Atlantic archipelagos. There are seven main rocks there, the largest not so big that you couldn't walk it in half an hour, with lots of underwater promontories and hidden shoals. It's a hazard to shipping alright, with a dozen wrecks in recent memory and as many near-misses. So the Board determined to put a light there at last."

"At last?" I prompted.

"Iphm! The idea had been discussed from time to time but had always been deferred because of the cost. At last the loss in shipping and lives was deemed to outweigh it. They spent near to seven thousand pounds on putting that lighthouse there, and half as much again establishing the shore station at Breascleit here on the island.[2] The Board contracted David Alan Stevenson, of the famous Stevenson engineering family, to design the thing.[3] It wasn't easy."

Phearson held out his fist, middle knuckles downward, illustrating his

---

2   The actual costs were £6,914 and £3,526 respectively, which totalled and converted to modern money would be around £2.1 million or $2.8 million.

3   Writer Robert Louis Stevenson, who had died in 1895, was the engineer's cousin.

point. "Eilean Mòr—that's Gaelic for 'Big Isle', is shaped roughly like this. Massive cliffs on all sides, with only a couple of places where you can climb to the interior. A steep, windy tramp it is too. A stone's throw south, past two jutting sea-rocks, is Eilean Taighe, House Isle, so called because like Big Isle it still has stone hut ruins of the settlers who lived there a thousand years ago. The Flannans are rough, lonely places. They loom large in local superstition."

Phearson shook his head to clear it of hauntings. "But the NLB's concern was the danger to shipping—and the problems of establishing a light on the highest peak of Eilean Mòr. It was very difficult to haul building materials up there; hard enough to just moor delivery boats. Big Isle has steep cliffs on almost all sides and plenty of hidden navigational hazards just under the water. In the end the builder had to construct a couple of cast iron piers, one on either side of the island, so one or other could be used whatever the wind direction. And then he built an actual railway to get the bricks to the top."

I raised my eyebrows.

"No, really," Phearson assured us. "It's still there, a little narrow-gauge track with a steam winding engine at the top by the lighthouse compound. A Y-shaped layout so there are branches to both piers, with a points crossing the lads call Clapham Junction." He sobered. "Called Clapham Junction. Anyhow, the tower was hard to build. We needed a cliff-crane too, to haul some of the bigger parts like the lamp itself, and a steel staircase stapled to the cliff-side to access the shore. I mention this so you understand just how wild a place Big Isle is."

Holmes already had an Ordinance Survey map of the Flannans, which the cartographers had subscribed with the formation's other local name, the Seven Hunters. He traced his fingers over the layout: the tower and its support buildings on the peak beside an 8th century ruined chapel, a dozen remnant bothies from those pre-Viking inhabitants, some suspected tumuli, the little cable railway, the new landing piers.

"The light was first lit a little over a year ago, on 7th December 1899, I understand," he prompted the superintendent along.

"Yes. I was there. There was a small ceremony. We take our traditions seriously in the lighthouse service." Phearson opened his brief-case and passed four folders to Sherlock Holmes. "These are the four men who worked the light. All of them have been there since the start except for McBride. Their details are in their Board files."

Holmes held up an imperious finger to silence the inspector while he absorbed the details in the documents he had been handed.

"Head Keeper Adam Wells,"[4] he noted. "A man of twenty years experience, considered a safe hand to establish and maintain this new light. His reference here describes him as steady, careful, and conscientious."

"So he is—was," Phearson agreed. "As superintendent I visit all the lights up and down this coast. All are kept to a good standard, of course, but I have seldom had occasion to criticise any light managed by Mr. Wells."

"Assistant Keeper Angus Farrar. Formerly a merchant seaman with some years of experience keeping lights. He was studying to take his head keeper's examination."

"That's right. He was a promising man. A temperancer, too. He'd had trouble with drink in his youth and would not take a drop now. Not that alcohol is allowed in any NLB property."

"Second Keeper Thomas Balreith. Also a former seaman."

"It is a common career progression. Sailors have good rope skills, a developed weather eye, discipline to work unsupervised, and are used to long periods of isolation. I'd say two-thirds of our employees have been at sea."

"And young George McBride, described in this file as an Occasional."

"That refers to him being an occasional substitute. The other three were company men, confirmed in their posts. The fourth was MacLoke, who was Third Keeper but fell ill last summer and is still sick. An Occasional is a newcomer, a temporary replacement, the least senior and least tenured of the team. An apprentice, if you will. That's why he and Mrs. McBride were lodged in this rented house in Stornaway rather than in one of the keeper's houses at Breascleit. McBride was the new boy, promising but green."

Phearson pointed to the folders. "At any given time, three of these four men would be at the lighthouse. The fourth would be on shore leave. Every fourteen days, weather permitting, our service boat, the tender vessel *Hesperus*, would take supplies to Eilean Mòr and exchange one keeper for another."

"So each man spent six weeks confined to the lighthouse and then had two weeks liberty here," I calculated.

"Generally so. It's hard on the families. Farrar has a wife and three children, Balreith has a wife, one bairn, and another on the way, and Wells has a grown-up daughter swells with him. Or did. But they all learn to live with it, like sailor's kin whose man goes far away for long periods of time.

4   Those familiar with the real-life mystery of the Flannan Isles Lighthouse will note that our story here renames the four keepers and the Superintendent who investigated the incident. Dr. Watson seems to have often substituted names and altered details out of discretion, to avoid upsetting bereaved relatives or to maintain confidentiality.

The actual missing men were Head Keeper James Ducat, First Assistant Thomas Marshall, and Second Assistant (Occasional) Donald MacArthur (or McArthur). The fourth man, on rotational leave at the time, was James Moore. The NLB Superintendent was Robert Muirhead.

A month and a half's not so bad compared to that."

"Continue with your account," Holmes insisted.

"Just so. My job as Superintendent is to ensure on behalf of the Board that all is being done according to form. I must check each site, verify supply deliveries, give out wages and so on. I also look if I can to the wellbeing of the men's families." He shot a worried look to Mrs. McBride's kitchen. "I last visited Eilean Mòr on 7th December, scarcely three weeks since, when Farrar returned to duty and Balreith came back to Lewis with me. Everything was in order then. Wells walked down to the jetty with me to see us off. I shook his hand. I was probably the last man to shake his hand."

Phearson paused to collect himself. He had known the lost men and cared for them. "December 14th was the day of the big gale. It was an appalling storm, with high-force winds and thirty-foot seas. Here in Stornoway it broke through the old mole and ripped apart some of the fishing cobbles. It played havoc all along the coast and it kept on for two weeks.

"On the 17th I was sent a telegram from the Board, relaying the complaint of an American steamer that the Flannan light was out. The *Arctor* was voyaging from Philadelphia to Leith and had put in at Oban because of the weather. Her captain, a fellow called Holban, had made an official report that the light was quenched. He'd nearly had his ship on the rocks. Soon after we heard from the *Fairwind*, which had struggled past the Flannans in bad seas on the 16th and had seen no lamp."

"Is it common for lighthouses to go dark?" I wondered.

"Almost unheard of," the Superintendent assured me. "It is a point of pride within the service. Even when I received the reports I thought it more likely that the weather had obscured the light or that the captains had misjudged their positions. Indeed, we pay a small retainer to a gamekeeper in Ulg to spy the light each night and keep a record. When he and his sons failed to observe the lamp after the 14th for several nights in a row they attributed it to the dismal atmospheric conditions, not to aught else. The Board evidently thought so too, since no special instruction was issued to investigate. The supply boat was due to visit Big Isle on the 18th anyhow, to take Balreith back to duty and bring McBride home for Christmas with his new wife.

"As it turned out, the seas were too rough for the tender. Captain Harvie did not judge it prudent to risk the vessel in the ongoing storm, and Harvie is a man of integrity and experience. It was not until the 26th December that *Hesperus* was able to head out and relieve the men on Eilean Mòr. It was then that the island was found deserted, the lighthouse abandoned, and no sign of the missing men."

"There was a storm," Holmes pointed out. "Might not your crew have been claimed by high seas or fierce winds?"

"That is the most likely explanation," Phearson agreed. "Balreith found evidence of remarkable storm damage, and Wells' and Farrar's oilskins were missing from their pegs. But it is a strict Board regulation that one man must always remain inside the lighthouse at all times. McBride should not have left also, especially without his oilskins in that appalling squall." He smoothed his moustaches in bewildered agitation. "The whole affair has shocked us all. The people here in Lewis and Harris are full of speculation and wild theories about what really happened. The NLB—and I—feel that any help you might offer in establishing the fate of those three poor souls would do much to sooth the anguish of their grieving families. And…"

"And what?" Holmes enquired.

"And if there is some extraordinary explanation, some bizarre twist that cannot be… should not have happened, then it must be discovered and addressed. Please."

The sea was still brisk as the *Hesperus* left the shelter of Lewis and steamed west into the Atlantic gales. A hard sleet rattled on the cabin windows and kept us all confined there.

Holmes was pleased that the crew of the tender vessel were the same who had been aboard on the 26th when the deserted lighthouse had been found. He wasted no time in encouraging them to tell their story.

"I was one of 'em as went ashore in the end," First Mate MacDonald revealed. He wore a typical seaman's beard and a thick fairisle sweater and rejoiced in the title of Buoymaster. He hunkered down in the close quarters under the steering deck and sipped hot cocoa from a chipped mug. "But you'll want the story from the start, won't you, Mr. Sherrrlock Holmes?" He grinned at me. "I read all your stories, Dr. Watson. A proper treat, they were."

"Your account, then." Holmes had no patience for adulation.

"Right you are, sir. So it was the day after Christmas before the old man thought it were safe enough to take the *Hesperus* out. I don't blame him. Week before, the waves were enough to wash half-way up Stornaway and flood Breascleit, and that's sheltered compared to open sea. But Tom

Balreith was fretting. 'E'd heard about them cables from the company and about maybe the light was out, and 'e wouldn't settle. Paced up and down the deck despite the wind, peering out as if 'e could see over seven leagues from Breascleit to Eilean Mòr. Wouldn't touch his breakfast."

I didn't blame the man. The back of the cabin had a small gas stove where the sailors fried greasy bacon and slabs of fried bread but I was feeling distinctly queasy in the ocean chop. My appetite was not assisted by the odour of the two nanny goats sharing the cabin with us; the Flannan Light had not only lost three keepers but its milk-goats and chickens too.

"It were close to noon when we sighted Big Isle through a dull spray. We made to land on the east mooring, but there were something amiss. Balreith had his field glasses out and he called to the captain."

He paused for dramatic effect, a natural storyteller. I obliged by asking, "What had he seen?"

"Well now, normally there'd be empty lamp oil drums and supply crates stacked out for us to take off, and probably one of the lads standing by to catch our ropes. It's a tricky place to cast on, Eilean Mòr, and it 'elps to have someone on the pier. But there was no-one there—and no pier either!"

"The storm," Holmes surmised.

"The storm it was, Mr. Sherrrlock Holmes!" MacDonald approved, as if the great detective had demonstrated his legendary genius. "The whole cast iron platform was wrenched away, pillars bent like they were made o' putty. Naught but a few columns just topping the surf, and that was a'. Thirty foot of jetty just vanished. Certainly nowhere we could set in with *Hesperus*.

"So we set a northerly course and circled the island, trying to keep the wind off us as much as possible and not get blown onto the rocks. We gave a wide berth to Dearcna Sgeir, which is being the biggest of the hazards and a main reason for the lighthouse i' th' first place. We could see for sure that the light was out, and Balreith was nearly frantic, part for his mates but mostly because the lamp was doused. It's the way of lighthouse keeper, y'see sirs. Anyhow, we make it round the westward outcrops and we thrash the boat up to the western pier. That weren't in much better state, mind, all twisted and warped with the railing bent double. And that big iron staircase that was pinned up the side of the cliff to let us get to the top, it was 'anging loose all ripped from its brackets and some of it crumpled like foil. The sea can be deadly when she rises like that.

"In we takes *Hesperus*, as close as we may, and let out the jolly-boat. Balreith volunteers to jump ashore and see what's happened. Captain Harvie risks putting in alongside what's left of the west pier and Tom takes a leap for it. We push off a bit for safety and Balreith makes his way up the cliff, picking his steps very careful. I can tell you, I wouldn't 'a fancied being the lone fella who went to investigate."

"Stout chap," I agreed. "What then?"

"Well, we tries to hold steady about three hundred feet off, which was no easy thing gi'en the conditions. We could see up the cliff to where the crane pulley used to be, and it's gone, just some bits of metal stuck in the concrete foundations. And that apparatus was on top o' the ridge, 120 feet above sea level. The signal tower was still there, but the semaphore balls were just slumped down, disconnected."

"That was the only way that Eilean Mòr could communicate out," Holmes confirmed. "It signalled to passing ships who conveyed messages on when they set into shore."

"Aye, tower by day or torch by night. There's been talk of a wireless, but nothing settled. Anyhow, Tom Balreith scrambles his way up to the peak and goes out of sight. We're all a bit nervous by then. Eilean Mòr has a reputation, you know. In the old days farmers used to graze their sheep here but no shepherd would ever stay the night. Once a year the folks from Lewis would come out to raid birds nests and gather simples, but always with special ceremony and never biding after sunset. Too many ghost stories, maybe. Since the lighthouse crew vanished I've 'eard them all again."

"What kind of stories?" I couldn't resist asking, though Holmes was clearly unhappy at the digression.

"Oh, well we're near Lewis aren't we, where they still talk about the Blue Men of the Minch, the dwellers under the water, and of the Viking ghost-ship that strokes over the sea between the Flannans, crewed by men with faces of naked bone. In fact there's rumours that some ship or other sighted a small boat in the storm, and some say it were the keepers fleeing the isle which is rubbish because setting out in that weather would've been suicide, but others say it were the Danish phantoms stealing away the men's souls. And there's sailors who'll swear to a giant sea monster, a hideous vast squid maybe, that rose from the depths in the tempest to feed. Or else it was the Kind Folk."

"You mean the fairies?"

"Oh aye. There's still plenty round here who avoid the old barrows and are careful on the straight tracks. There's half a dozen tumuli on Eilean Mòr, and a ruined chapel they say was built by St Flannan who the isles is named for. Once they called them the Seven Haley Isles, Haley being an old saying of Holy, you understand."

"And there's sailors who'll swear to a giant sea monster..."

Holmes could restrain his impatience no longer. "Your testimony about the 26th!" he demanded.

The first mate shot me a grin. "You were right about 'im in your stories, doctor. Anyways, Tom's away for more'n half an hour. We're getting a bit leery and discussing whether we need to put another man ashore when we see the light go on in the tower. Another quarter hour and 'e waves from the top of the cliff and comes down to the landing. We take *Hesperus* close again and 'e shouts across that Wells, Farrar, and the Occasional are missing and there's no sign.

"Captain Harvie, 'e decides we need to get back to Breascleit while the weather holds and send word about what's occurred. He briefs me and Thompson—that's 'im on lookout in the prow—and McGarran there to go across and reinforce Balreith until the Board sends aid. Tollan rows us across without spilling us all into the foam and drooning us and then 'e nips back to the ship and they all steam away leaving us on shore with Tom.[5]

"First thing we do is go back and try a proper search for the missing men. We follows the railway track up to the compound. There's a fence round the lighthouse, maybe to keep the goats in so they don't jump their fool selves off the cliffs. We head up there and give the place another going over. Not that we're likely to 'ave missed 'em the first time if they were there. The whole place is just six circular rooms stacked on top of each other with a spiral stair between 'em.

"But we checked. Stores, kitchen, common room, bunk room, service room, lantern. Beds unmade, cold ashes in the grate, clocks wound down."

"How often did the timepieces require winding?" Holmes enquired.

"Two daily mechanisms and two needing a wind every eight days," MacDonald reported. "The lamps were trimmed, though—I mean the little lamps for regular light, not the big one at the top. Balreith reckoned that meant whatever happened was in the daytime, when they'd refilled the lamps ready for night. A morning job, he said. The dishes were all put away off the table as well. There's some as are saying there was an 'alf-finished meal laid out and that, but they're just trying to make it sound more mysterious.[6] Only thing in disarray was one kitchen chair knocked over.

---

5   This account abridges a genuine primary source document, the letter from the real life Third Keeper James Moore to the NLB that describes his actions. Captain Harvie and the Buoymaster McDonald have not been renamed, but the roles of First Mate Mr. McCormack and Buoymaster McDonald have been conflated.

6   This detail has entered popular folklore via Wilfred William Gibson's poem, an excerpt of which prefaces this story. It may have been inspired by a similar erroneous account of an unfinished meal aboard the abandoned *Mary Celeste*. That factoid was in-

"So we leaves Tollan to look after the light and me an' Tom an' McGarran takes a turn round the island. Easier said than done, the way the wind kept trying to drag us off. I can see as 'ow that might 'ave done for the lads. It's a fierce place, Eilean Mòr, and it don't want men on it. We find the mangled wreck that was the crane, and a bit further on there's one of them big container boxes been smashed to smithereens. A right mess. A bad, bad storm is what it was, Mr. Holmes, Dr. Watson.

"We looks over as much of the island as we can before it gets dark again about 3pm. You'd think walking that little stub of a rock would be easy, wouldn't you, but half of it's cliff and cleft and if a body fell down there you'd not see it till you'd fallen in on top of it. Anyways, we found naught, and for aye we know those men might have been taken by the Kind Ones or eaten by a kraken."

Holmes had a copy of the telegram that Captain Harvie had sent to the Northern Lighthouse Board:

> A dreadful accident has happened at Flannans. The three Keepers, Wells, Farrar, and the occasional have disappeared from the island. On our arrival there this afternoon no sign of life was to be seen on the Island. Fired a rocket but, as no response was made, managed to land Balreith, who went up to the Station but found no Keepers there. The clocks were stopped and other signs indicated that the accident must have happened about a week ago. Poor fellows they must been blown over the cliffs or drowned trying to secure a crane or something like that. Night coming on, we could not wait to make something as to their fate. I have left Balreith, MacDonald, Buoymaster and two Seamen on the island to keep the light burning until you make other arrangements. Will not return to Oban until I hear from you. I have repeated this wire to Phearson in case you are not at home. I will remain at the telegraph office tonight until it closes, if you wish to wire me.
>
> Master, *HESPERUS*[7]

---

troduced by "J. Habakuk Jephson's Statement", an anonymous story in *Cornhill Magazine* of January 1884 that offered a fictionalised account of the mystery and popularised the ship as the *Marie Celeste*. The account was actually authored by Arthur Conan Doyle.

    A document purporting to be entries from the Flannan Lighthouse log recording the degrading mental states of the keepers is likewise considered a forgery, probably first created in an American pulp tale, but is often reproduced in mystery books and websites as a genuine text in the case.

7   This is the actual message sent on 26th December 1900 from Captain Harvie to the Northern Lighthouse Board, except that the names of the missing men and Superintendent have been substituted.

"It all seems pretty clear to me, Holmes," I ventured. "Three brave men lost to misfortune in dire weather. I'm puzzled as to why we should travel so very far to visit the scene."

"There is perhaps more to this than has so far been suggested," my friend replied. "Nothing substitutes for primary research."

A cry from Tollan to Captain Harvie alerted us; Eilean Mòr was in sight.

The bleak fist of Big Isle loomed before the little supply cutter. It seemed menacing and foreboding through the driving drizzle and sea wash. I could well understand why shepherds of old had quit its shore before night and how a rough seaman like MacDonald could say that it had an antipathy to man.

We circled the rock and approached the patched-up western landing, where crude timber beams were lashed to remnants of the iron pier. Two men awaited us on the platform beside a dozen empty fuel drums and some packing crates.

"That's Balreith and the new Occasional Wilson," Captain Harvie told us. "I brought the new crew out here three days ago on New Year's Eve. The Board had trouble finding men who'd come." He turned into the gale. "I don't like this westerly," he warned us. "There's a new front coming. The weather's turning sour again. I'll stand off for as long as I can, three hours maybe, but after that you must either return with us or stay on Eilean Mòr."

"We understand," I assured him. He nodded and turned to pilot his vessel in to the makeshift dock.

Holmes and I were welcomed by Balreith as we climbed ashore. "You'll be the men from the Board, then," he greeted us. "Experts, they said."

"Consultants," Holmes corrected him. "We are here to confirm the conclusions already reached by Superintendent Phearson—assuming those conclusions are correct."

"Fair enough. If you'll just wait while we cross over the cargo I'll take you up to the light. It's a bit of a walk and a climb, I'm afraid. We daren't use the iron staircase."

While keepers and supply vessel crew were shifting oil drums and food crates, Holmes drew me over to examine the fantastically-twisted ironwork of the damaged pier. "Imagine the forces required to do something like this," my friend marvelled. "The sea is an ancient power and sometimes unstoppable."

Once the cargo exchange was complete, the *Hesperus* drew off a little to avoid the winds slamming her into the fragile pier. Balreith left Wilson to stack a first load of goods into the railway truck that stood at the terminus of the little line. A long pulley rope connected wagon to the winding engine on the hill top.

"We'll tramp up this way," Balreith told us, leading along a steep muddy cliff path. "When we're at the top we'll set the engine in gear to bring the stores along. We're lucky that the storm didn't do much harm to the railway or we'd really be struggling."

"The storm seems to have been an unusually dangerous one," I suggested.

"The Flannans get the worst of the weather," the keeper admitted. "Nothing to stop the winds and waves from the deep Atlantic. Nothing between us and Newfoundland. We get high tides and higher seas; but yes, it looks like the recent gale was unprecedented. A hurricane, maybe. Look at that."

We had climbed up two hundred feet by now. Balreith pointed to the clifftop. All the turf had been stripped away for a hundred yards from the edge.

"Fear the seas that could reach this high and suck away so much," he said. "Strong waves coming up the inlet channel where the pier is, pressing between narrowing walls, foaming higher... And there were crates stacked on the eastern ledge that the high waves broke open and scattered inland almost as far as the bothies."

"We heard something about there being ancient ruins and some saint's shrine," I recalled. "Odd place to put it, so far from civilisation."

"Oh, people lived here once," Balreith assured us. "There's quite a few mentions in the histories. They built those little round huts and squatted in sea caves." He gave us a sad smile. "There's not much else to do out here between duties except read. I like to know about a place so I looked it up. There was a settlement here for centuries until it was wiped out by Viking raids in the ninth century. Afterwards the locals remembered them as pygmies or little people, perhaps because their huts were so tiny. Of course, no-one's quite sure which St Flannan had a chapel here."

"There's more than one?" I was surprised to hear.

"Evidently. Prevailing opinion is it was Flannán mac Toirrdelbaig or Turlough. He was a son of the king of Thomand, a part of Ireland covering most of what is now North Munster. He returned from a 7th century pilgrimage to Rome to become the first Bishop of Killaloe—the greater part of County Clare. His feast day is 18th December which… well it looks like my friends didn't make it to the 18th."

"We'll try to find out what became of them, old chap," I assured the keeper.

Balreith disguised his emotion and carried on which his talk. "I came across a 1703 book by this weird old historian called Martin Martin[8] where he calls the place the Seven Haley Isles and describes strange customs such as removing one's hat and upper clothing and turning sunwise at the Blessing Chapel. We don't do that now."

I had thought we had reached the summit. My aching legs hoped so. Balreith pointed and now I saw that the lighthouse was still some way above us, jutting from a smooth-topped rise surrounded by wheeling seabirds.

Balreith pointed away through the grim drizzle at distant places we could not see. "Over there is Eilean Taighe, House Isle, so called because it also has remnant huts from the old days, that they call 'the bothies of Clan MacPhail'. In clear weather it's an easy short swim. Southward lies Soray, the Eastward Isle and Sgeir Tomain. West are outcrops called Eilean a' Gobha, Isle of the Blacksmith, Roaireim, with a natural rock arch, and Bròna Cleit, Sad Sunk Rock. The books say that once when the world was ice these islands were all one."

It occurred to me that Tom Balreith was happy to talk about anything to do with the island except what had happened to his fellows. I could not blame him.

We crossed that bleak frozen wasteland, under a loaded sky and screeching gulls, across frosted grass or exposed rock. I was curiously reminded of the Grimpen Mire of Dartmoor. Although the landscape was very different it had the same desolate, uncanny feel. I half expected to be pursued by a monstrous Hound, or perhaps by the many-armed sea monster of local lore. I was glad when we achieved the lighthouse.

The other Occasional, Blackhouse, was obviously glad of it too. He'd been hanging nervously by the door, forbidden by regulations to go outside, obviously concerned whether his fellow keepers might return. "All is well," he reported to Balreith. "I've entered it in the log."

"Yes, the log," Holmes interjected. "I shall inspect that now."

At a nod from his senior, the Occasional produced the black day-book where the keepers were expected to record their duties. A flick through

---

8 *A Description of the Western Islands of Scotland* (1703; second edition 1716)

the pages revealed the mundane minutiae of light-house keeping: weather readings, supply records, oil usage, sightings of ships, exchange of messages. The book also recorded occasional injuries, such as the back problem that had invalided Eric MacLoke and had first brought George McBride to Lewis and Flannan to meet, woo, and wed his pale tragic wife and to vanish with his comrades.

The last entry was a notation about bad weather, added at 12.15pm on the 14th of December.

"What special procedures would you undertake to prepare for a storm?" Holmes asked Balreith.

"We would batten the hatches, so to speak. There was a rowboat on the eastern dock. We'd pull it out of the water, well out of harm's way."

"That boat is missing," I noted.

"It obviously wasn't out of harm's way enough. We'd also clear the docks of any empty crates or barrels stacked there for collection. Winch it all to high ground. Secure the weather station. Lock down the crane and the semaphore tower. Pen the animals. Then get inside and stay inside if we could."

Next Holmes looked over the lighthouse, from foundations to the tip. "This place is kept clean and tidy," he observed to Balreith. "You have maintained it since taking up your shift here?"

"Of course. The NLB expects everything to be kept to a high standard, as neat and tidy as any ship of the line. If these Occasional lads want to stay on as confirmed keepers they know they need to impress old Gabe Phearson. We've given the place a good scrub down. And nobody fancied sleeping in the keepers' bunks until we'd given them blankets a good wash."

Holmes sighed. Any evidence had been tidied away. "Did you discover anything unusual while you were cleaning?"

"Not much. There was a bit of seaweed scraped on the stair there from kitchen to common room. And another bit in the tool locker, for some reason. The toolkit was gone, by the way."

"Anything else missing?"

"Hard to say. There's not much here in the first place. I had to bundle up the lads personal belongings to send back to shore. If they'd intended to leave they'd have taken them along, wouldn't they? Angus Farrar wouldn't go anywhere without that photo of his wife and kids, nor Wells without his scrimshaw and his pipe."

The detective turned to me in agitation. "Too late, Watson, we are too late! What signs the sea has not removed, these hygienic lighthouse keepers have. Now time and light are running out. There is only one other lead to follow."

"And what might that be?" I wondered.

"Why the most significant clue of all," my friend assured me. "We know that three men vanished sometime after 12:15 on the 14th of December. But what became of their goats?"

"We're hunting goats?" Balreith asked disbelievingly.

"Chickens too," Holmes instructed him, "although they are somewhat more difficult to track."

"Holmes…" I began, appealing to him to explain his chain of reasoning.

We stood outside the lighthouse but still within the compound fence. An oil store leaned against the side of the tower. A ramshackle wooden shed served as combination chicken coop and goat hut. It was newly stocked with the nannies who had shared our cabin on the journey from Breascleit and with poultry that had suffered in crates on deck. Holmes examined the latch on the rough shed.

"Was this door closed when you returned to Eilean Mòr, Balreith?"

"I don't think so. It was ajar."

I began to see why Holmes was intrigued. "No wave reached this high. And if it had, it could not have unlatched the pen and washed out goats and chickens without any other damage. Someone chose to remove these animals and birds."

"Exactly, Watson. And if there is one thing that goats can be relied upon to do it is leave a trail." He indicated frozen pellets on the ground with the tip of his boot. "Older droppings have been covered with snow. The high winds and frozen ice have preserved the newer excretions. Let us follow the goats."

It was not an easy task, but laborious endeavour by dimming daylight set us on a trail back down past the ruined chapel in the lighthouse's shadow. Holmes found frozen footprints too, some crossed over others suggesting that the path had been walked more than once.

Bare walls were all that remained of St Flannan's foundation. The unmortared stone stood bleak and grey out of the white drifts. Crosswinds had obliterated all further trails, of bovidae or men. Indeed, the gale plucked at our coats as we slithered down towards the ancient ruin, staggering us off course as if to warn us away.

"Wells and I used to call this the dog kennel, because it was so tiny a place," Balreith remembered. "Then Farrar would call us irreligious heretics and begin to quote Leviticus or something."

Holmes refused to be deterred by the wind or by the keeper's maudlin reminiscence. He trudged around the chapel's perimeter, seeking any trace of his elusive goats.

He paused and hunkered down in the remnant of the doorway. "Look here. Something has been disturbed."

Balreith and I came over as he scooped snow away from a fresh-dug hole on the chapel's threshold. "That big stone slab over there covered this," Holmes pointed out. "You'll see the lichen marks? It has clearly been overturned recently and laid to one side. Quite a feat given its size and age. Then this hole was dug and imperfectly back-filled. Before the snow, I'd say, or soon after it started. It was raining when the pit was opened. The sides were wet and have frozen in runnels. If I understand the weather reports correctly that would place this excavation on or soon after the 14th of December."

"Something was buried?" I recognised.

"Something was dug up. A box some two feet square, judging by the shape of the hole." He rose and strode about, seeking further enlightenment.

"Why would any of the keepers bury something here, or dig it up again?" Balreith puzzled.

Holmes followed the slope of the hill downwards, to where little bumps and an occasional shaped stone betrayed the long-lost bothies of the little people. A couple of shallow walls remained to catch the drifting snow. Holmes ventured further, towards the treacherous edge of the eastern cliff.

"Watson."

Holmes' grave voice jerked me to attention. I joined him beyond one of the half-fallen walls and looked at the place where he was pointing.

It was a natural ditch formed where the volcanic rock had split open. A man's body lay wedged in there under a covering of snow.

Balreith came over too. He caught his breath. "We've found one of them," he gasped. "But which?"

It was a difficult job hauling the dead man from the rift. In the end we had to send for rope and pulley. Wilson joined us in heaving the corpse out of the hole where it had fallen. Had it not been for Holmes' assiduous goat search it might never have been found.

We lifted the body clear of its cleft and turned it over to examine it. The cold had preserved him well. The knife wound that had sliced across the throat was clearly evident. This death was not an accident.

"Which of them is it?" I asked Tom Balreith.

The keeper stared disbelievingly at the dead man. He shied away. "None of them!" he answered in a thick, choked voice. "This is not possible. This... this is Eric MacLoke!"

Mrs. McBride was home when we trudged along snowy Church Street to her neat painted door. She looked at Holmes and I in surprise. "I thought you were awa' the Flannans," she admitted.

"Mr. Holmes and Dr. Watson have returned," Superintendent Phearson explained. "They made an unfortunate discovery that will require them to remain in town until a Sheriff's Enquiry is complete. I wondered if I could prevail upon you to offer them lodgings. The Board will compensate you, of course."

"Oh. Aye, of course. Come in, will ye? The weather's only going to turn worse."

We re-entered the parlour. Mrs. McBride hastily cleared and string-tied book parcel and straw-stuffed half-filled box of crockery off the table; she was packing to leave. "I wasn't expecting any more company," she apologised.

"You are preparing to remove to your sister's home in Harris," Holmes suggested to her. I wondered what he had observed from the sad widow's meagre carefully-stacked belongings, from the little pile of treasured can-vas-backed books, faded with the years. Again my heart went out to the woman.

"I'm due gone the day after tomorrow. The Board wants this house for one of the new Occasionals until they've cleared some space at Breascleit, do they not, Mr. Phearson?" At last what the Superintendent had said pen-etrated her domestic concerns. "Unfortunate discovery? Sheriff's Enquiry?" She paled. "Georgie...?"

"Not him," I hastened to assure her. "I'm afraid we stumbled across the body of Mr. McLoke."

Mrs. McBride's eyes furrowed. "McLoke? I thought you'd gone to Eilean Mòr?"

"That was where they found him," Phearson revealed. "Although how he got there from his sick-bed, how he could have been stabbed…"

"Stabbed? I dinn'ae understand!" She sat down suddenly. "How could Mr. McLoke be dead? I thought he was improving a little. Wasn't he here to see me only three weeks since?"

Holmes looked up sharply. "McLoke was here? Why?"

The widow realised that there was some urgency and purpose in Holmes' interrogation. She straightened her back and answered him. "George only stayed in Lewis because Eric McLoke fell ill. The Third Keeper hurt his back lifting some crates or the like and was confined to sleeping on a bed of boards. A slipped disc of the spine they called it, Dr. Watson. The NLB needed someone to substitute fast and George had experience as a merchant seaman. I think… well, George would never have applied except it gave him an excuse to stay near me." Mrs. McBride blinked back tears. "George and I were married as soon as he was confirmed in his job. Wishing no ill on Mr. McLoke, but we both hoped that he might retire so that George could be promoted to Third. Even if he stayed ill for long enough, George might get the seniority to be taken on as a full Keeper somewhere else. I would have happily gone with him anywhere. He *promised* to take me away from this dismal place one day."

"But McLoke visited you," Holmes persisted.

"Yes. It would be, let me see, the day before the big storm. The 13th? Wednesday. McLoke limped in to thank me for my kindness in taking him a few pies and loaves during his convalescence. George had met him, you see, when he was introduced to the job. McLoke was unmarried, so the other keeper's spouses and Mr. Wells' daughter would take him food to make sure he was alright. So I thought since I was Georgie's wife now and Georgie was at least an Occasional, that I'd do the same."

"That's very commendable of you, Mrs. McBride," Phearson agreed. He frowned as well, though. "I hadn't realised that McLoke could even get out of bed, let alone make his way from our Breascleit station twelve miles into Stornoway."

"And to Eilean Mòr, evidently," I added.

We had reported our gristly find at the town's tiny police station. Word would be dispatched by the next ferry to Ullapool so that a proper investigation could be set in hand. In the meantime the body had been taken up and laid out in the lighthouse oil store, since Holmes judged that it might suffer from more bad weather if it remained in the open. Captain Harvie had been quick to communicate our discovery to Superintendent Phearson; hence his hasty reappearance.

"But McLoke visited you."

Holmes had added his observations to the initial report. McLoke had been killed by a sharp razor across the neck that had sliced windpipe and jugular. It had been a right-handed cut from behind, probably by surprise. Death had been instant. The body had been moved and concealed soon after. The murderer was about the same height as the keeper, five foot ten. He had probably worn size eleven boots with a nick in the left insole. He weighed around twelve stone eight. He was likely a young man or of early middle years. All of this Holmes had read by tracks and other signs at the scene of McLoke's discovery, by his usual methods.

"How did Mr. McLoke come to be dead... on Big Isle?" Mrs. McBride ventured. What she wanted to ask was 'What does this have to do with my husband?'

Holmes was not to be put off by her waving voice or bewildered grey-eyed gaze. "When McLoke visited you, what did he talk about?"

"He wasn't here long. I gave him a cup of tea. He asked after Georgie. We talked a bit about my husband. I suppose Mr. McLoke was interested in the sort of man who was filling in for him. Perhaps he was worried that George might take his job permanently?"

"Eric McLoke had fifteen years with the Board," Phearson noted. "If he had not recovered we would have pensioned him."

"What did he ask about your husband, Mrs. McBride?" Holmes questioned.

"Well, he was interested in Georgie's sea-faring experience. George ran away to sea when he was thirteen, you know, after his mother passed away. He didn't return to Glasgow until he was twenty-one. And Mr. McLoke was interested in how Georgie and me met, when Georgie was a paying lodger at my sister's husband's house and I was staying there too." She hesitated, scowling at some unpleasant memory.

"You did not like life in Harris," I suspected.

She shook her head. "Nor in Stornoway since father died and we lost the house. Susan, my sister, she married a Hearach man, Jack Gallett, and good luck to her I suppose. I didn't like having to go down to Tarbert and live in their wee dark house with them. I didn't like... well, I did not like it. George McBride, my Georgie, when he came he was the one bright light in that place. He promised to take me away." A tear trickled down her cheek.

Holmes stirred. "Why was McBride visiting Harris?"

Mrs. McBride flushed a little and moved uncomfortably on her chair. "Must I say?"

"Do you want the mystery of the Flannan Light to be solved?" Holmes demanded.

The widow tossed her head defiantly. "Right, then. There was George, back from the sea and a full-grown man now, and he'd come to Harris to see his father, who was serving a life's sentence at Tarbert Penitentiary."

"Dougall McKeith," Holmes suggested.

Mrs. McBride's brows shot up. "How could you know? Georgie had his mother's name, for... well, no shame to George if his father was taken by the police before ever he was able to wed his mother."

"How do you know about this, Holmes?" I murmured to my friend.

"You asked why I came all this way, Watson. It was news of the death on December 15th of the convict McKeith that spurred me here. And now the pattern begins to show. McKeith, McBride, McLoke, missing men on Eilean Mòr, missing box from St Flannan's ruin."

"I don't understand," protested Phearson.

Holmes glanced at the clock on the mantel. "How easily can we hire a carriage to Harris right now?" he asked the Superintendent. "I need urgent conveyance to Tarbert Prison."

The single road that connected the isle of Lewis to its neighbour Harris wound its way through treeless ice-choked landscape that we could hardly see through the heavy snowfall. In summer this would have been a delightful country ride through stunning scenery. By night in blizzard it was a nightmare. Our carriage strained through the storm, slipping and rocking until I despaired for my life.

The thirty-six mile journey rattled us past the shores of Lochs Cnoc a' Choilich, Lathamul, Breugach, Beag na Craoibhe, Leiniscal, Chnoic Dubnhe, and Sanndahat, and then we traced the side of Loch Shobhail for a long time as the wind tried to topple us into it. After that I lost count of the dark chill waters we threaded between; the Outer Hebrides contain almost a third of all freshwater lochs in Scotland. The village of Ballanan marked our half-way point, at which our coachman rested the horses, and then we pushed on into Northern Harris, following the twisting switchback road with Loch Seaforth stretched out below us on our left and the looming peak of Mount Clisham dominating on our right. Our final stretch took us on the storm-wracked coast road to the isthmus link and Tarbert beyond.

"Yon prison's another six miles past this, up towards Loch an Fheor," our coachman told us. His thick scarf was white with ice. "I doubt the road'll be open in this."

I could see why this bleak treeless landscape might be chosen to confine life offenders sentenced to hard labour. Even if some unfortunate convict did break his chains and escape from the gangs who quarried here in this brutal climate, did overcome the perimeter fences and guard dogs to run free across Harris, what then? He faced an inhospitable primitive landscape of rocky slopes and sudden clefts, bounded by a cold and unpredictable sea that only an experienced sailor might cross. For those criminals whose penance had to be severe this was the ideal prison.

"Find us an inn at Tarbert," Holmes instructed the half-frozen driver. "It is not so much the Penitentiary I require as one of its wardens, and his address is in the town."

The sun had set shortly after 4pm and our arrival was not much before eight, so I could not get a very good look at the tiny settlement that was nevertheless the largest on Harris. I got the impression of long rows of small-windowed stone dwellings, some whitewashed, above a tide-lashed harbour wall. A crenulated tower rose above the town but I never found out what it was.

The local pub warmed us with good malt Scotch and helped us on our path. Leaving our coachman to recover by the inn hearth, we set our collars, pulled down our cap-peaks, and pushed through the snow to find Warder Jack Gallett's house. Soon Holmes was hammering on the knocker of one of the terraced houses provided by Her Majesty's Government for the staff at the state penal institution up on the hills.

Gallett was off-shift and at home when we called. He looked upon Holmes' sudden intrusion with a growing discomfort. "What's this about then?" the penitentiary warden demanded.

"Jack, what is it?" a timid voice came from a back room. I caught a glimpse of a pinched pale face that might have been a caricature of Lizzie McBride's, and understood that this must be her sister Susan. Mrs. Gallett's looks were faded now, erased by hard work and hard treatment.

"Get back i' there," her husband roared at her. "Ah'll see tae this."

Before she flinched away I observed the dull bruise around one of her eyes.

I'm sure Holmes did too. Perhaps that is why he was so curt with the warden— although it might just have been Holmes. "This is about the bribes you took, Gallett."

The warden stood dumbfounded in his doorway. Holmes shouldered past him into the house and I followed.

"What d' ye mean?" Gallett managed at last.

Holmes turned back to him impatiently. "Last summer, George McBride came to stay with you as a paying lodger. Who first made that arrangement?"

"I don't know," the warder insisted. "'E paid 'is way."

"Did he? Who funded his stay here?" Holmes demanded. "You can tell me or tell the constabulary when the Sheriff directs his Enquiry to you."

"'E might 'ave 'ad is rent paid from the mainland by Postal Order,"[9] the warder admitted. "At first letters came with 'em in. I didn'ae care so long as the Orders cashed."

"From where were the Postal Orders issued?"

"Glasgow Central Post Office. What does that matter?"

"And then when McBride offered you more money, to convey messages to his incarcerated father?"

"'E never. I wouldn't."

"The police will be able to check your savings book and your spending," Holmes warned.

"It was nae harm to gie' a letter frae a son to his father, nor to hand back a reply!"

I was puzzled. "Couldn't McBride simply have visited his father in gaol?"

"So he could and so he did, Watson," my friend assured me. "But when two men sit at opposite ends of a long table, with whatever orderly is on duty at the time standing watching and listening, then some kinds of conversation are rather stifled."

"I didn'ae mean any harm," Gallett declared fervently. He was beginning to realise that his secret free enterprise had landed him in more trouble than he had expected.

"How often did you exchange notes for McKeith and McBride?" Holmes interrogated.

"Six times. Three from McBride tae his father. Three replies. Over a time of aboot a month. Then McBride got 'is job on the Flannens and moved away tae Lewis and wed Susan's stuck-up perfect little sister and…" He smirked nastily. "And now where is he?"

Sherlock Holmes viewed the man with a cool contempt. "What about McKeith's death? What happened there?"

---

9   In America this kind of promissory note, bought and cashed at Post Offices, would be called a Postal Money Order. These certificates included the name of the person who was entitled to present them for payment but not details of the sender, only of the Post Office and clerk who issued them.

"That's nae down tae me!" Gallett near shouted. "'E was old. 'E'd served twenty-two years hard crack for his crimes and nivver stirred to escape. No-one ever gets away frae Tarbert Penitentiary. It's suicide to try! When he downed MacDawson and made his break for it 'e nivver had a chance."

"McKeith died during an attempted break-out?" I understood.

"Nivver made it past the wire," snorted Gallett. "Fell and broke 'is neck an' good riddance t'him."

"On the 26th of December," Holmes observed. "The day the *Hesperus* returned from Eilean Mòr and news of his son's disappearance was confirmed."

"Maybe," shrugged Gallett, unconcerned.

Holmes had other questions for the unpleasant warder. Had Gallett ever seen McBride with strangers? Had McBride asked questions about the Flannans before he had gone to work there? Had he visited Lewis at all before he had taken a job with the NLB?

At last the detective was satisfied. I was not. "I'm going to treat that bruise on Mrs. Gallett's cheek now," I advised the warden. "I don't doubt but what you gave it her, you nasty ignorant oik. Only a coward and a brute would raise his hand to a woman, let alone his wife. I daresay you're too much a cur to try your fist against me, aren't you? Aren't you?"

Holmes turned his penetrating gaze on the flinching bully. "The evidence we have about your bribe-taking is sufficient to see you dismissed and disgraced, Gallett. My arm is long enough and my gaze sharp enough to know if you wrong your wife or her sister ever again. If you do, expect details of your behaviour to be passed to the appropriate authorities. Expect that I will make your life very unpleasant. I take it even a limited intellect such as yours understands this threat?"

The nightmare conditions of our journey down to Tarbert were eclipsed by the ordeal of our return. Suffice to say that our coachman deserved every shilling of his tip for delivering us whole back to Stornaway.

It was past midnight when Holmes and I made our weary way through the rising blizzard to our digs with Mrs. McBride. I hoped that we would not disturb her too badly with such a late return.

"What are your suspicions, Holmes?" I questioned my friend as we slid up the frozen sea front. "How does McBride having a criminal father relate to the tragedy at Eilean Mòr?"

"There are still links of the chain to be confirmed," Holmes told me.

"I know you prefer to deliver your solutions to me complete and tidy, Holmes, but on this occasion I would appreciate some hint of the work in progress."

"So be it. The crime of which Dougall McKeith was convicted was robbery. On February 7th 1879 a Royal Mail coach was stopped by thieves as it approached its depot in Paisley. The criminals were armed. They stole a satchel containing ninety £100 Bank of Scotland bearer bonds. You wouldn't remember the fuss because at the time you'd gone to India with the 5th Northumberland Fusiliers."

"That was quite a haul," I admitted. "But they were caught."

"Three men were apprehended. The bonds were not recovered. Each felon accused the others of stealing the satchel. The older pair of villains were known offenders. They were sentenced to the rope. The youngest, then twenty-three years old and considered the dupe of his fellows, escaped with a life sentence to Tarbert."

"Holmes, are you theorising that those Bank of Scotland bonds were concealed on Eilean Mòr?"

"One of the reasons that McKeith was sent to Harris is because he originated from the Outer Hebrides. He was born on Benbecula but gravitated to big bad Glasgow looking for work. There he fell in with the unpleasant lads who eventually robbed the mail coach. In the month between the robbery and the arrests it would have been easy for him to return to his home isles and find a quiet spot to bury his ill-gotten gains. It may have been his betrayed fellow robbers from whom he wished to conceal the booty. Of course, he had no way of knowing that his long-deserted desolate isle would become a manned lighthouse station twenty years later."

I snorted. "Imagine McKeith labouring away his life in that bleak prison, knowing that twenty miles to his west his fortune lay hidden under a threshold slab in a ruined chapel. So near and yet so far."

"So it was, if I am correct. And then George McBride turned up, McKeith's lost son, grown to a man. McKeith could never now enjoy the spoils he had looted, but he could pass their location on for his heir's benefit. Perhaps he hoped to make up for all the years he had not been there for the lad."

I followed Holmes' reasoning. "Some private correspondence later, thanks to the detestable Gallett, and McBride was ready to claim his treasure."

"Not quite, Watson. After all, how would McBride reach lonely Eilean Mòr without drawing unwarranted attention? I believe he recruited an accomplice."

"McLoke? A man who hurt his back lifting something! Like a heavy stone slab?"

"Quite possibly. When McLoke failed then an alternative plan had to be tried. McLoke recommended McBride to Phearson as a suitable Occasional. That got McBride onto the island and able to find the chapel and the hiding place. It still didn't help him lift the slab, though. However McKeith had done it, McBride had no assistant to accomplish it."

A nasty doubt assailed me. "What of Mrs. McBride? Surely she would not…"

"You can set your mind at rest, my friend. Lizzie Craig was a complication that McBride had not expected, a girl who burst into his life during his plots and captured his heart. I have no doubt that when he promised to take her away to better places and times he meant every word of it. Indeed, she would be a rich and happy woman if his plans had worked."

"But they did not."

"No. You have probably fixed upon the problem of the Postal Orders, which…"

Holmes fell silent. We had reached the McBride home. The door stood slightly ajar. A little snow drifted onto the woven rug inside the threshold.

Holmes pressed the door back with his walking cane. I stood ready on the step.

The parlour table was knocked over. The crockery box lay on the floor, its broken contents spilled towards the hearth. Mrs. McBride was not in the house.

"A lamp set for us in the window still burns," Holmes calculated. "The fire has not burned down too far. The snow across the doorway suggests less than half an hour's intrusion."

"What has happened to the lady?" I asked, dismayed.

Holmes examined the outer step and road. Already wind-blown flakes were covering the tracks we had made. "Two men, judging by the wet patches in the hallway," he reeled off quickly in that distracted manner he has when his mind is running at its fastest. "They burst in uninvited. See the new chip in the wall-plaster where the door was slammed wide? They did not expect it to be unlocked. They are not local men. Mrs. McBride was in the parlour, waiting our return despite the lateness off the hour, and packing things. She struggled and was knocked down. She tumbled here, between the chairs, where the sewing kit she was holding has fallen. She was seized up again and pinioned. They tore the tablecloth to make bonds and probably to gag her. She was removed from the house in the darkness, and who would venture their noses outside their doors in this foul blizzard to investigate any noise?" He turned to me and cried out. "The harbour!"

I did not hesitate to follow as he rushed from the house and loped away through the tempest.

"You don't know the seas around here, sir. Either you respect 'em or you're drowned."

Captain Harvie was adamant in his refusal to take his vessel out in the worsening gale, until we explained that a woman's life was at peril. Even then he warned Superintendent Phearson, "I cannae be held responsible if we sink the *Hesperus* and all drown!"

"Iphm! I cannot order you to go out," the NLB man admitted, "I can only appeal to you. If Mr. Holmes is right, Mrs. McBride is already out on that terrible sea, in the hands of men who care nothing for her life."

"The Harbour-Master confirms that an unfamiliar steam-boat from Oban left in haste forty minutes ago, despite his storm warnings," I revealed.

Harvie spat an oath and called for MacDonald to stoke the steamer's boiler.

"What's this all about, then?" the *Hesperus*' master demanded as his crew lit the fire-box and made ready for a lethal voyage. "At least tell me why we're all going to die."

"There was a treasure on Eilean Mòr," Holmes summarised. "McBride knew of it and told McLoke. Neither could get to it without help. McBride took his job as Occasional when McLoke was injured. He located the hidden horde but needed a second man to help him to it. Evidently he did not judge any of the other keepers likely to assist him, since the prize was stolen goods."

"NLB keepers are honest men," Phearson boasted. "Usually."

"McBride did not come to the Hebrides alone. He had a sponsor, who paid for his lodging while he visited his father in Tarbert Penitentiary and learned the location of the buried loot. The organised criminals of the

Glasgow underworld have long memories. McBride's return after many years at sea prompted them to approach him with some arrangement for splitting the profit if a long-lost satchel could be retrieved—or so I surmise. The issue location on certain Postal Orders supports the thesis."

"We have steam!" MacDonald called to Captain Harvie.

Hesperus cast off. The wind took the supply packet as soon as she left harbour and tried to kill us. I had thought the chop and turbulence of our daytime voyage to Eilean Mòr to have been rough. It was nothing to the struggles the steamer endured that night. A south-easterly bluster did its best to snatch us up and wreck us across the Minch.[10]

Harvie gritted his teeth and kept *Hesperus'* nose to the gale. Once out of the lee of Lewis and Harris we faced North Atlantic breakers twenty feet high, great waves that crashed across our decks, drenching the gallant little steamer again and again.

"This is utter madness!" Harvie called.

Holmes continued explaining. "On or around the 14th of last month, about the time the great storms began, was when arrangements were made to retrieve the buried goods. Agents must have come from Glasgow to assist, probably to ensure that there was no double-cross. McLoke was roused from his sick bed to act as their guide. That was when he made his visit to Mrs. McBride, to check what she knew of the men who demanded his services. Perhaps McLoke was intending some kind of trick himself. Perhaps he was fearful for his life.

"In any case, some small vessel set out to Eilean Mòr to meet with McBride and dig up the spoils. On a normal evening that would have been quite feasible. McBride might excuse himself for an evening stroll and a smoke, especially if he had made that his habit, and his fellow keepers would think nothing of his absence once his work was done. He could meet McLoke and the Glasgow thugs, remove a heavy stone that had pre-vented earlier access and claim the prize. They'd all be away from Big Isle before morning, back to Stornaway and Mrs. McBride, and then to any-where, richer by nine thousand pounds."

"Unless there was another falling-out amongst thieves," I pointed out.

"Or the worst storm in a century." Holmes added. "Perhaps the sail-or McLoke warned about sea conditions. Perhaps he was overridden by Glasgow career criminals whose brutality exceeded their common sense. Suffice to say they all ended up on Eilean Mòr—though perhaps not as they had imagined it."

10   The turbulent twenty mile wide body of water between the Isle of Lewis and Harris and the eastern seaboard of the mainland's Northwest Highlands of Scotland.

A devastating seventh wave crashed down on *Hesperus*, near dragging us under. MacDonald muttered a blasphemy under his breath.

Holmes was undeterred. "I posit that the criminals were wrecked on Big Isle, unable to escape as they had planned, unable to meet with McBride because he had no excuse to quit the lighthouse while the tempest raged. Indeed, it would have been dangerous for him to try.

"What then were the villains to do? Cast up in high winds on a hostile shore, with no shelter or food? I suggest from what little evidence we have that first they did what they had come for. McLoke knew as well as McBride where the chapel was. They raised the slab and retrieved the satchel containing anonymous bearer bonds."

"The papers that can be exchanged for money?" Phearson checked.

"The same. As good a way of moving anonymous sterling as any devised. We know that a buried box was unearthed; Watson and I saw the hole. We know that two men were required, and the only group in this story likely to do that was whoever accompanied McLoke to the Flannans. And thereafter… well, McLoke was no longer required."

"His death was professional," I recognised. "Practiced."

"Then came the question of survival and escape from the island," Holmes argued. "There was only one source of food."

"The goats and chickens in the lighthouse compound."

"And what goat goes quietly to its end?"

"You believe that our keepers may have heard a disturbance?" Phearson queried. "The two senior men don their wet weather covers and go to investigate…"

"And meet seasoned criminals, armed experienced killers," I concluded. "Easy to murder those poor keepers, abandon their bodies to the furious sea, and then go to the lighthouse for McBride. One overturned chair."

"The lighthouse was the logical place to weather the storm," noted Holmes. "But the criminals were clever enough to disturb little. Some tramped seaweed and a little mud, easily washed away by the assiduous Balreith, but…" Holmes raised an emphasising finger, "I do not think things went well for them thereafter."

Hesperus lurched again. A clatter of pots came from the little mess and a hiss from the water-spattered steambox.

"Why do you think that?" I asked my friend, to distract us all from an imminent appointment with Davy Jones' Locker.

"The abduction of Mrs. McBride. Why bother to seize her unless the villains believe her husband to be alive? And unless he has something that they still want?"

"Easy to murder those poor keepers, abandon their bodies to the furious sea..."

"Somehow McBride turned the tables on the Glaswegians. Somehow he got away, and the bonds with him!"

"He may even have finished one or more of the ruffians, Watson. But not all of them, because one at least remained to be retrieved when the worst of the storms were passed, to report to his boss in Glasgow what had happened. It was probably this man or men who disposed of any of their fallen fellows in the same way they did poor Wells and Farrar."

"Why did McBride not appear when we came to relieve the keepers?" MacDonald demanded.

Holmes lodged his flapped cap tighter on his head.[11] "McBride may not have known they were there. He may have been injured and died of his wounds. Or he might have already found some way off the island. We are too far into the realms of conjecture for my comfort."

I focussed on the important issue. "Suppose new felons were dispatched from Glasgow to hunt McBride and those bonds on that tiny island. That is why they took Mrs. McBride—to force her husband out into the open. They will threaten her life to take his. And if he is not there, or does not respond, they will show her no mercy."

"And that is why we plunge across the Deep at peril of our lives," Holmes summed up. "More killers approach Eilean Mòr. Big Isle has not yet claimed its full measure of blood."

We steamed forward into the teeth of the storm.

There was no chance of landing the *Hesperus* at Big Isle. Even coming close risked the waterlogged vessel more.

"We can try and put the jolly-boat ashore," MacDonald shouted over the ice-flecked wind. Just a short time out of the cabin had rimed his beard white. "Four strong men on the oars, we might just make it."

"I can't spare crew left behind on shore," Harvie objected. "Not in these seas."

"Drop us on land and make your retreat," Holmes advised him. "Superintendent Phearson, you have our sworn testimony in case we do not return?"

---

11   The Canon never mentions Holmes wearing the deerstalker which has become so associated with him in popular imagination. It was Holmes' early illustrator Sydney Paget who decided that Doyle's description of a "flap-eared cap" was likely that popular Victorian hunting hat, the deerstalker. Paget is likewise responsible for Holmes' Inverness cape.

"I have sirs," agreed the inspector. He shook our hands.

"Best do this while there's a relative lull," Captain Harvie insisted, eyeing Holmes and I as if we were lunatics. "Volunteers will try and pull you to shore."

"That's all we can ask," I assured him. I checked the firearm in my coat was well wrapped in oilskin and went astern where the ship's rowing skiff was being lowered into the churning waves.

"I need hardly say that you need not accompany me, Watson," Holmes murmured in my ear.

"And I need hardly say the same to you, Holmes," I replied. "Let us proceed."

It was past four when we made shore, sodden wet and chilled to the bone. I can't record the exact time since the water had stopped my watch. Holmes and I splashed out of the foamed breakers onto a shingle strand and staggered for higher ground before the next big wave tried to suck us back to the sea.

"Good luck!" saluted MacDonald as he turned the jolly-boat away from the wind and began to pull for the *Hesperus*.

Holmes and I scrambled over sharp, ice-slick rocks to gain some safety from the ocean. I daresay that if we had been on the western side of the island we would have been swept away in an instant, lost as those poor murdered keepers to the merciless waves. Instead we managed a desperate scramble to a snowy ridge and dropped to catch our breath.

"This used to be easier, Watson," Holmes huffed. "We are becoming old. It is some twenty years since I confided in Stamford that I sought a fellow tenant to share the cost of new rooms at Baker Street."

"I'm missing those rooms right now," I assured my friend. "And my slippers and the fire and a hot crumpet on Mrs. Hudson's best china. But we must move on. Mrs. McBride needs us."

"Stalwart Watson!" Holmes exclaimed. "Come then. We must trace the shore southward, to where it is closest to the two big rocks they call Làmha Sgheir Bhay and Làmha Sgheir Mhor that protrude from the sea between Eilean Mòr and Eilean Tigh. There, where the Atlantic breakers are most dispersed by the natural outcrops, are cave-like shafts formed as fumaroles during these islands' volcanic origins. If any secret shelter might be found by a man who had spent months exploring this place it is surely there."

"We are risking much on your supposition," I cautioned Holmes.

"Supposition is all we have to save Mrs. McBride now," the detective replied. "There are random guesses and there are calculated estimates made on probabilities, weighing known facts and assessing likelihoods. If we are to ever find George or Lizzie McBride then it will be on the southern edge of Eilean Mòr."

We clambered over the slippery rocks, following the shoreline. On calmer days it would have been easier to use the meagre beach strand. That night it would have meant certain death. Snowfall turned to sleet.

"Why would McBride's criminal sponsors elect to come for him now?" I asked, as much for distraction from our journey as for information. "Why not wait for better weather again?"

"I fear it is our enquiries that have provoked their desperate move, Watson. The name of Sherlock Holmes can stir career criminals to sudden mistakes. When they heard of our arrival, and that we were to lodge with Mrs. McBride, they had to act quickly. The weather chose not to co-operate."

"Holmes! There is something down there, in that cleft by the water!" I pointed to a dark shape below us. Something fluttered in the gale.

We carefully lowered ourselves down the rocks, slipping the last length when the snow under our feet proved to cover sheer black ice. There, tucked in the lee of a weathered boulder, was a grey-faced man in a thick greatcoat. His forlorn scarf was the pennant that had caught my eye.

He raised a revolver when he saw us, but his frostbitten fingers could not pull the trigger.

Holmes knocked the gun aside with his cane. Disarmed, the dying man slumped his head back and released a sob.

I knelt to inspect him. His right leg was bent almost double, folded in an unnatural twist that made clear it was broken. Bloody fragments of his tibia protruded from his flesh. His hip was probably shattered also.

"This damned isle," he muttered, only half-aware of us. "I should ne'er 'ah come back here. Ne'er. It didn'ae kill me last time, like Fitz an' Laurie, but it's got me noo."

"You were here before?" Holmes understood. "Look at me, man! Concentrate. You came here with the keeper McLoke, to meet with McBride? You retrieved the satchel from the chapel ruins?"

The thug nodded, too exhausted and broken to attempt evasion.

"Damned storm. Damned McBride—wouldn't take a bullet t' th' head—b...!"

"You were right, Holmes!" I exclaimed. "The Occasional *did* resist when his supposed partners resorted to murder. Or else they intended to cut him from the deal all along, as they did McLoke."

"We was supposed ter top 'im. He's Dougall McKeith's son. McKeith th' traitor! Why would we ivver let 'im live?"

"You survived when your fellows did not," Holmes declared. "What happened? How did McBride stop you?"

"Him?" The big Glaswegian sneered. "That little twig? He barely stunned Fitz before he rabbited off oot th' lighthouse an' awa'. No, it were this place, this killer island. We was chasin' him along the cliff when the sea just rose up, just came right over th' edge and slapped us doon. And Fitz and Laurie gone! Taken, just like... like that..."

"This man is almost spent," I warned Holmes. I emptied the contents of my hip flash down his throat but I doubted it would revive him for long. Hypothermia on top of critical injuries, blood loss, concussion; he had fallen down the cliff and had been abandoned to die. Nothing I did could save him now.

Holmes was determined to extract as much information as he could from the thug, though. "You survived the storm, holed up in one of the caves. And slaughtered the penned animals from the compound to live on until other colleagues of yours were able to come and see what had happened?"

"Aye," he answered, his voice slurred and faint now. "Th' Big Man hisself came t' seek us and took me off. We couldn'ae get McBride frae his hidey-hole in time 'afore that other ship fired its rocket t' signal to the lighthouse. We didn'ae know how many men was coming, so we set sail and made oorselves scarce. Th' Big Man said to bide our time. If Georgie came out for the rescuers then we'd take him on Lewis. If he didn't, we'd be back wi' bait that'd lure him frae his hole for sure!"

"His wife," I growled.

"And isn't she th' prettiest picture," the enforcer smirked. "But not when we've..."

Whatever terrible boast he was going to make never escaped his lips. He faded from consciousness and we could not revive him.

"Leave him," Holmes commanded ruthlessly. "He is a sign that we are on the right trail. From the dusting of ice and snow on his clothes and the spread of blood on the ground I'd say he has not lain here more than twenty minutes. The crew of *Hesperus* was better at fighting the storm than the sailors who brought 'the Big Man' here. We are catching up."

"Where are they headed, though? The island was searched."

"The safe parts of the island were searched. A search that missed McLoke concealed in a gulley was certainly not thorough enough to check flooded waterline caverns. This felon evidently knew where McBride had retreated but could not get to him. The Big Man knows where to look."

"And McBride has the stolen bonds, else why would the criminals seek him here?"

We followed further along the island's edge, travelling clockwise until we could hear the waves crashing over the big rocks that separated Eilean Mòr from its sister Eilean Tigh. Holmes found a few traces of men's passage, and at one point a woman's shoe print. "Four men, I think. One has better quality boots than the others. One enjoys chewing and spitting Shipmate's Navy Cut tobacco."

After a while all ice-rimed rocks seemed the same. It felt like we were condemned to trudge forever in that freezing wet hell. I wondered if we might end up like the criminal we had abandoned, laying broken under the smothering snow.

A faint orange light flared in the darkness. Holmes and I halted. We had both recognised the inhalation flare of a cheap cigarette.

Holmes gestured for me to stay in place. He circled round and climbed down to the pebbled inlet where the smoker stood sentry. The man had his collar turned against the blizzard and stood well back from the angry wash that rose up this gully every time waves broke beyond its entrance. Holmes approached his blindside and downed him with scientific precision. I came forward to assist in dragging the guard further up the inlet and binding his hands and feet.

We removed the fellow's handgun, a badly-made copy of the American Colt.

Where he'd stood was a low break in the metamorphic rock, eight feet wide but only four feet high, a horizontal rift retreating back a good way into the cliff. Flickering lantern-light illuminated the most distant section and voices echoed up from the depths of the cavern.

"What'll it be, Georgie? D'ye's want tae hear her scream fer ye agin?"

"No. Leave her be. I know ye've got her. But I can't trust that you won't harm her when I've given up these bonds."

"D'ye nae think me a man o' my word, McBride?"

"You turned on McLoke, had your men kill him when he wasn'ae useful any more."

"I'd nivver gi'en my word to McLoke. I'll gie'it to you, Georgie. Here it is. We got yuir pretty wee missus tied up wi' us. She's pretty for now. Niels has some big ideas aboot that, an' plenty else could happen to her. Now you can hide doon there wi that satchel till the supplies you took frae that lighthouse o' yours runs oot. Ye can set yuir lighter to the bonds as ye threaten. But then we're away and lovely Lizzie wi' us, and she won't be dying quick or easy and she'll curse yuir name afore she does. *There's* my word."

Holmes gestured that we should move forward cautiously. We prepared our revolvers and ducked under the shelf, proceeding along the rift on hands and knees.

"I'm scared, Georgie!" came Mrs. McBride's timorous voice. "I thought you were dead. I thought... They're hurting me, Georgie, and I'm *scared!*"

"Y' hear that, McBride. She's scared, and she's right tae be. We're bad, wicked men and cruel wi' it. You know my reputation, or ye would if ye'd spent any time in Glasgow afore ye took my offer to visit yuir old man. He's dead, by the way, tryin' to bust loose tae find youse. And mah patience is done. So before I take my razor to sweet Lizzie's face, will ye come oot and hand over the papers?"

"I... I want your promise," McBride replied, wearily, hopelessly. "You'll not hurt her. You'll take her back to Stornoway and let her go."

"Och aye. I swear it, Georgie. 'Course I do. If'n you crawl oot here now and hand over that bag."

There were three men, crouched because the ceiling wasn't high enough to stand. One of them had Mrs. McBride pinioned on the floor, his boot on her neck. Two men carried rifles and the other had a pistol. The speaker was a big man indeed, a hulking six foot three if he'd been able to walk upright.

Holmes announced our arrival by shooting the man who was treading on the lady. The bullet took the man in his kneecap, spilling him screaming onto the cavern's base.

"Lay down your arms," Holmes advised the criminals coldly. "We have you in our sights."

The Big Man recognised his adversary. "Sherlock Holmes!" he snarled. "Yuir interference has cost me another good man an' forced me to this extreme. But nae more."

We saw then that the Glaswegian gang leader also held a plain soda bottle stuffed with gunpowder and nails, with a very short tow of rag protruding from the neck. It was the kind of improvised grenade that had been popular back in the Crimea half a century ago.[12] The Big Man held it up close to the cigarette at his lips.

Holmes and I paused, stymied. An inch further and the fuse would ignite. We would all die together.

"Yuir sights are no' looking so clear now, are they?" the Big Man sneered.

"There is no way out for you," Holmes warned the criminal. "You are responsible for the murders of Adam Walls, Angus Farrar, and Eric McLoke, and for the kidnap of Lizzie McBride. Whatever twisted sense of criminal's code deludes you to believe you have a right to those Bank of Scotland bonds does not justify those crimes."

"And didn't my own Da swing for stealing them?" the Big Man snarled. "But right an wrong don't count i' the Gorbals,[13] laddie. Only force. And I ha' plenty o' that." He shook the grenade in his hand and grinned viciously.

His screaming henchman passed out, but the other had his rifle turned on us. Our ambush had gone badly.

"Give us the McBrides and we'll go," I offered.

"That doesn'ae work for me," the Big Man countered. "Ah'd hate to disappoint Neils. He's been lookin' forward tae Lizzie for some time."

"Don't… don't give in to them, Mr. Holmes," the trussed woman insisted. "Better we all die here."

Neils moved in to kick her, and that was his mistake. He shifted away from the deeper recess of the tunnel. Mrs. McBride, her head on the ground, had been able to see her husband creeping up. Now George McBride leaped at the Big Man, dashing the bottle from his hand and negating its threat.

Neils turned his rifle on McBride, but when Neils had struck Lizzie with his boot she had wrapped herself around his leg. The thug toppled off balance. I aimed for his arm but my bullet took him in the chest.

---

12   Colonel Hugh Robert Hibbert described its use during the Crimean War (1854-1858) in a letter preserved in the UK's National Archive: "We have a new invention to annoy our friends in their pits. It consists in filling empty soda water bottles full of powder, old twisted nails and any other sharp or cutting thing we can find at the time, sticking a bit of tow in for a fuse then lighting it and throwing it quickly into our neighbours pit where it bursts, to their great annoyance. You may imagine their rage at seeing a soda water bottle come tumbling into a hole full of men with a little fuse burning away as proud as a real shell exploding and burying itself into soft parts of the flesh." *Source:* Letters of Hibbert, Hugh Robert, 1828-1895, Colonel, ref. DHB/57—date: 14 June 1855.

13   Formerly a notorious slum area of Glasgow.

Holmes saw the Big Man's pistol rising. Holmes' shot was right between the eyes.

We dragged the bound guard into the shelter of the rift and laid him beside the thug whose kneecap I had shattered. I had tourniqueted the injured leg but he would not walk again.

Released from his long hiding in the fumarole cave, George McBride refused to release his wife from his grasp for even a moment. He had a bullet-graze on his left shoulder and was feverish from the untreated wound. Half-dead from more than two weeks' terrified concealment in that lightless dead end, not knowing whether the rift was watched by enemies awaiting his escape, battered and injured by his initial encounter at the lighthouse, almost out of his mind with dread, he clung to Lizzie as if she was his lifeline; she undoubtedly was. His wife ignored her bruises and frights to hold fast to the man she had mourned for dead.

Holmes slithered to the fissure's full depth and retrieved the tin box that held the satchel with the stolen bonds. McBride had been bluffing about burning them. He did not have lighter or matches, only the invention of desperation.

"I never realised how bad th' Big Man was," he confessed as we quit the cave for the bitter snowstorm. "When I got back to Glasgow and he approached me with the idea to reclaim my father's hidden wealth it seemed like a grand idea. It was only when his ruffians came for us at the light that I realised how treacherous and dangerous he could be."

"His men murdered the other keepers before they came for you," Holmes noted.

"Aye, but they messed up their go to put me down. I was eight years a sailor. I know a brawl! I decked the one and fled wi' no worse than a flesh wound, but I'd ha' been a goner if the wave hadn't come as we chased along th' tops. But the last of 'em survived to hunt me, and to tell his boss-man. And always the storm, and the waves, and this cursed isle! A scared man can't think straight here, can't plan. They avoided Eilean Mòr in olden times for good reason, sirs. It should be left alone again."

"We arrived by boat," Mrs. McBride reported practically. "It's dragged up on shore somewhere, that way I think. A bigger ship will be coming to meet it in the morning."

"We don't need to find a rowing skiff just now," Holmes assured her. "There is better shelter." He pointed to the lantern that shone up the seventy-five foot tower on the highest part of Eilean Mòr. "That light was built to guide lost travellers to safety. Let it draw us home."

"Home?" George McBride shivered miserably. "Do you think the Big Man's Gorbals friends will let this stand? I'm as dead on shore as I would'a been in that cave. If the police don't take me for trying to retrieve my Da's stolen papers than the bad lads in Glasgow will hunt me down to the ends of the Earth."

"Will they, Holmes?" I worried, eyeing the bedraggled lovers and their forlorn embrace. "Can nothing be done?"

"Here on Eilean Mòr, first of the Seven Hunters, where the little folk dwelled and St Flannan produced his miracles?" Holmes answered me. "Let us see."

The morning after, the weather broke and the *Hesperus* was able to return to check on us and the temporary crew at the Flannan Isles light. Phearson was with them, and four constables of the Sheriff's Office.

To the officers of the law Holmes handed over the battered satchel that contained seven thousand pounds in Bank of Scotland bearer bonds. The missing two thousand was never explained. Only I had seen Holmes count ten of the £100 certificates into the hands of the McBrides, then others to the three keepers, and to Captain Harvie to return privately with the *Hesperus* when the hue had died down and see George and Lizzie quietly on their way.

"A thousand pounds is a fine new start in life far from Lewis, Harris, and Glasgow," I declared to my friend. "Especially if the lighthouse men and the crew of the supply boat keep their silence."

"Call it a finder's fee, doctor. Let some good come from this sorry business."

The island was cruel. Though McBride had hidden wet and chilled in the islet crack for eighteen days, unpredictable tides and winds had conspired to flood it when two captured thugs were stowed in there. Perhaps they had loosed their bonds and sought escape. Perhaps phantasmal Vikings or some great octopus or vicious Kind Ones had come for them.

They were not in the waterlogged cavern when we returned for them, and were never seen again.

Superintendent Phearson's report recorded three keepers missing at Eilean Mòr, lost in terrible weather as they tried to secure equipment on the high cliff.[14] Theories settled around the facts like seagulls on a drowned man and froze into legend.

Holmes and I turned our backs on that lonely fist of rock and returned to London, where warm hearths and Mrs. Hudson's cakes could press from our souls the chill and memory of the sinister failing light of the Flannan Isles.

The End

---

14 Superintendent Muirhead's actual report concludes, "From evidence which I was able to procure I was satisfied that the men had been on duty up till dinner time on Saturday the 15th of December, that they had gone down to secure a box in which the mooring ropes, landing ropes etc. were kept, and which was secured in a crevice in the rock about 110 ft above sea level, and that an extra large sea had rushed up the face of the rock, had gone above them, and coming down with immense force, had swept them completely away."

The full text of the investigation and links to other source documents is available at the LNB's archive site at https://www.nlb.org.uk/HistoricalInformation/FlannanIsles/Report-by-Superintendent/

If Only We Could Consult Sherlock Holmes

Sherlock Holmes is the most famous fictional detective of the Victorian Age; probably of any age. He has become an archetype, inspiring derivatives and parodies because he is so instantly recognisable in manner, skills, appearance, and habit. Holmes has spawned a century of eccentric, irascible, brilliant protagonists from Nero Wolfe to Gregory House, from Hercule Poirot to Doctor Who. Wrap a talking cartoon duck in deerstalker and Inverness cape and he is suddenly a great detective.[15]

Holmes stories exemplify one of the most attractive features of detective fiction, that of deduction, science, and heroism combining to restore justice. The omniscient investigator maintains a world where evil is curtailed and wrongdoing punished. Holmes and Watson encounter malevolent plots and terrible threats to society's wellbeing, but almost always manage to redress the wrong in time to return to the genteel cluttered environs of Baker Street where Billy the page is ready with the newspapers and Mrs. Hudson has their tea. A reality where the sturdy values of our two principles is so secured is an attractive place to live.

Humans have a basic expectation, perhaps hard-wired into us, that "things should make sense". This despite a body of evidence that senseless, terrible, random things happen to us, despite the major gaps in our scientific understandings and the great theological questions of existence. We want the answers, and ideally we want them laid out with proofs. If possible we want to be in on the discovery. Detective fiction in general and Holmes' investigations in particular satisfy that need.

Sherlock Holmes, then, appeared in the natal decades of the detective genre and grew with the writing until he became a vital meme and a pre-eminent icon of the Victorian era. As such there's a natural tendency for modern writers to cross his path with other Victorian fictional icons. Dracula is one of the most popular, but Holmes has also been chronicled encountering the insidious Fu Manchu, Captain Nemo, Wells' Time traveller, Professor Challenger, Sweeney Todd, and many more. He has even

---

15   "Deduce, You Say!" (1954) featured Daffy Duck as Dorlock Holmes and Porky Pig as Watkins hunting the Shropshire Slasher.

teamed-up with modern characters like Batman.[16]

The other popular approach is to point Holmes at some famous actual historical mystery and let him loose to offer an explanation that has eluded us in real life. Sherlock Holmes has tracked down Jack the Ripper on many occasions, including in his definitive biography by W.S. Baring-Gould,[17] wherein the murderer was revealed as Inspector Athelney Jones of Scotland Yard.

Part of the attraction to us in seeing Holmes address real-world mysteries is the imposition on our own chaotic inexplicable world of Holmes' fictional one, where every plot has a denouement and every puzzle can be solved. Even when Professor Moriarty can snatch away victory by causing an "accidental drowning" or James Windibank can walk away unscathed from his plots against grieving Mary Sutherland,[18] there is still a general sense of Holmes and Watson occupying an ordered, just world where decency prevails; a world we cannot help but wish ours more closely resembled. How much better would life be if Sherlock Holmes were around to stop every serial killer and thwart every terrorist outrage?

So enticing is the opportunity to pit Victoriana's great fictional detective against its great real-life bogeyman that many other opportunities have been neglected. I took the opportunity to rectify that in some small way in "Spring-Heeled Jack", my story for *Sherlock Holmes: Consulting Detective* volume 7, where Holmes was loosed on the trail of the seemingly supernatural monster who may well have contributed to popular culture naming his more visceral and better provenanced namesake, the Ripper.

Even after that I felt there was still space for another historical anomaly

---

16   *Detective Comics* vol 1 #572, March 1987. Dr. Watson and Professor Moriarty appear only in flashback but the elderly Holmes is still alive in Batman's contemporary era. Holmes' earlier guest appearance with Superman in *Action Comics* vol 1 #283, December 1961, must probably be discounted since he was only a mind-projection caused by Superman's exposure to red kryptonite.

17   *Sherlock Holmes*, W.S. Baring-Gould, 1962, ISBN-10: 0586042601, ISBN-13: 978-0586042601, and now also available in kindle and e-book editions; highly recommended as essential reading for Holmes aficionados.

18   Jack Douglas was "lost overboard" from the steamer *Palmyra* en route to South Africa after being supposedly delivered from his enemies by Sherlock Holmes. Unfortunately James Moriarty had other ideas and an extensive network of agents (*The Valley of Fear*). Miss Sutherland consulted Holmes about the disappearance of her fiancé Hosmer Angel and Holmes felt it best to conceal from her the truth that Angel was secretly her step-father Windibank successfully seeking to break her heart to prevent her marrying anyone and taking her income with her ("A Case of Identity", *The Adventures of Sherlock Holmes*, 1891).

to receive Holmes' attention. Holmes was a little young to investigate the abandoned *Mary Celeste* in 1872 but he was at his full powers in 1892 when Dr. Thomas Neil Cream, the top-hatted Lambeth Poisoner, claimed at least seven victims with strychnine. In 1910 Dr. Hawley Harvey Crippen became the first murderer to be caught with the aid of wireless telegraphy, seven years after Holmes had retired to bee-keeping but still before "His Final Bow". But right in the middle of Holmes' glory days came the puzzle of what had happened to three keepers at the storm-wrecked and isolated Flannan Light.[19]

It's a case that has occupied me before. My non-fiction essay volume *Where Stories Dwell*[20] includes a chapter on the affair—which was useful as a source of easy research materials when I came to preparing a fictionalised account. The anomalies of Eilean Mòr have become a staple of unsolved mystery lists, attributed to psychopathic keepers, to wreckers, to pirates, to sea monsters, to fairies, and to aliens. The story has inspired the Genesis song *The Mystery of Flannan Isle Lighthouse*, Peter Maxwell Davies' opera *The Lighthouse*, and the *Doctor Who* story "Horror of Fang Rock."

Once I imagined Holmes and Watson there on that bleak windswept isle examining the abandoned lighthouse by the ruined chapel to a forgotten saint I knew there was a story to tell.

Much of the Canon features Holmes and Watson in urban settings, almost always London and its environs, in a civilised society where a hansom cab is always within call and a police whistle brings aid and support. Occasionally, however, Doyle sends his protagonists further afield, into the countryside where mysteries are older and sometimes darker. Sometimes Holmes and Watson must face the Grimpen Mire.

The only Canon story that sends Holmes abroad is the one that almost kills him, his flight to the falls at Reichenbach.

This other kind of Holmes story, in which our heroes adventure "beyond the pale", often offers a more physical experience for the detective and his amanuensis. For example, in "The Adventure of the Solitary Cyclist"[21] Holmes indulges in fisticuffs in the village bar. In *The Hound*

---

19   I noted as much in my article "Sherlock Holmes vs Jack the Ripper" for *Sherlock Holmes, Consulting Detective* volume 7. Yes, now even my essays are developing continuity.

20   "Whatever Happened on Eilean Mòr?" *Where Stories Dwell*, I.A. Watson 2014, Pro Se Press, ISBN-10: 1500666173, ISBN-13: 9781500666170

21   From *The Return of Sherlock Holmes*, 1903

of the Baskervilles he is hunted across Dartmoor. Danger is often more sustained, not confined to the story's climax, and sometimes a measure of the peril comes from the environment itself.

It was to be Holmes addressing a mystery that fascinated and baffled the Victorian world, battling the elements and his adversaries far from his usual haunts and advantages, then. That seemed like a proper place to put the detective in peril and a satisfying way to offer a different kind of Holmes episode that might still stand beside his other cases with frost-whitened head held high.

I've done ten stories for nine volumes of Consulting Detective now. I think for volume ten I will really have to find a way to celebrate the anniversary properly.

I.A. WATSON's criminal career had been tragically curtailed by his literary duties. He has been kept honest by producing short stories for *Sherlock Holmes: Consulting Detective* volumes 1-8, most of which have been nominated for Best Pulp Short Story in their time, and one of which has won the award.He has most recently produced the novel *Holmes and Houdini.* For Airship 27 he has contributed to the anthologies *Sinbad: the New Voyages* 1 and 3, *Zeppelin Tales, The Amazing Adventures of Harry Houdini,* and four *Robin Hood* novels, *King of Sherwood, Arrow of Justice, Freedom's Outlaw,* and *Forbidden Legend.*

To avoid recidivism, and since Airship 27 insists on publishing material from authors other than him, he has also authored for other publishers the novels *Labours of Hercules, Sir Mumphrey Wilton and the Lost City of Mystery, The Transdimensional Transport Co., Vinnie de Soth, Jobbing Occultist, Blackthorn: Spires of Mars,* the novella *Richard Knight: Race With Death,* the story collection *Women of Myth,* and many anthology contributions.

A non-fiction collection of I.A Watson's essays, *Where Stories Dwell,* is due in Summer 2014. This includes chapters on Spring-Heeled Jack and the Flannen Isles Lighthouse Mystery.

A full list of his publications and hidden clues to his many criminal plots may be found at http://www.chillwater.org.uk/writing/iawatson-home.htm—but you'll never catch him alive!

Sherlock Holmes

in

"The Adventure of the Three-Strand Garotte"

By
Fred Adams Jr.

When my friend Sherlock Holmes is worrying at some puzzle or another, afternoons spent in his company are often little different than those spent alone, but sooner or later, he always "comes up for air," as I put it. Sometimes it occurs when he's reached a solution, sometimes when a boulder has landed in his stream of thought and he needs a sounding board for his dilemma, and sometimes, when the stillness of the afternoon is interrupted. Today was one of the third type.

I was reading the *Times* and Holmes sat chin in hand staring at a group of calculations scrawled on a piece of foolscap when Mrs. Hudson knocked at the door. Holmes's head snapped up and he was about to deliver an imprecation over the disruption of his thoughts when he heard her voice from the hallway.

"Excuse me, Mister Holmes, one of your boys is here to see you." Mrs. Hudson never said so outright, but I believe she disapproved of Holmes's use of his "Baker Street Irregulars" in investigations, fearing that he thrust them into unnecessary peril from time to time, despite the argument that the compensation they received helped feed the hungry mouths of their siblings. She overcompensated at times by treating them more fondly than she might have otherwise.

I opened the door and beside Mrs. Hudson I saw the towheaded Charlie Wiggins. He was a quick lad of eleven years and had served Holmes well for some time. They met when he almost succeeded in picking Holmes's pocket one afternoon. Rather than whistling for a bluecoat, Holmes offered the lad a place in the Irregulars, believing that such talent and enterprise would better serve the right side of society than the wrong.

Mrs. Hudson ushered the boy into the room, a protective hand on his shoulder as if he were one of her own. The boy stood in short coat and knickers, turning his cap in his hand. "Go ahead, Charlie," said Mrs. Hudson. She looked expectantly at Holmes and he sat unmoving. "Tell Mister Holmes why you're here," she said.

Holmes turned his eyes to her. "Thank you, Mrs. Hudson, you may go."

She hesitated a moment then backed out of the room closing the door behind her. Holmes picked up his pipe from the table by his chair and began to fill it with tobacco. "So, Wiggins, what is it you have to say?"

Mister Holmes, sir." Charlie spoke in full cockney, dropping every H and pronouncing long A as if it were "eye." "I need some help, sir. Well, truth be told, it's me uncle Henry and his mate. They're in a pretty tight crack, sir, and I'm thinking that you may be the only person can help them out of it."

Holmes and I exchanged a glance. Holmes struck a match on the sole of his shoe. "Do you have a coin in your pocket, Wiggins?" Holmes said, around the stem of his pipe.

The boy looked down and scuffed at the floor with his toe. "Uh, no, sir, sorry to say I do not."

"Watson, lend the lad a shilling, would you please."

I long ago learned that no matter how odd a directive from Holmes may seem, it was the course of true wisdom to follow it. I fished in my waistcoat pocket and pulled out a shilling which I handed to Charlie.

The boy looked at the coin, puzzlement on his face.

"Give it to me," Holmes said, extending his palm. Charlie dropped the coin into Holmes's hand and Holmes crossed to his writing desk. He dipped a pen in the well, scratched a few words on a sheet of paper and handed to Wiggins. "Now Mister Wiggins," said Holmes, "you have paid a retainer for my services and whatever you tell me about this matter is bound in the strictest professional confidence."

"Does that include the rozzers, sir?"

My eyebrow raised but Holmes's did not. "Indeed, young sir, it does. Not a word you tell me will find its way to Scotland Yard."

Charlie hesitated a moment, looking in my direction. "Begging your pardon, Mister Holmes, but that does include Himself as well?" He jerked his head toward me.

"You may trust Doctor Watson as implicitly as you trust me. Now, tell me, Wiggins, what is this all about?"

"The coppers come 'round the last two days looking for my uncle Henry Wiggins and his pal Seth Canty. They think they've done somebody in, more than one maybe, but I know they couldn't be guilty."

"And of the two, which is blind and which has lost a leg?"

The boy's mouth fell open and then mine did as well when Charlie said, "How did you know that, Mister Holmes?"

"Because of what the newspapers are calling the 'Monday Murders.' Watson give me yesterday's *Times*, would you?"

I handed him the paper and after some shuffling of pages, Holmes read aloud:

In a bizarre case, Scotland Yard is seeking a pair of murderers in the strangulation deaths of two men a week apart, Hamish Murchison of Cheapside and Walter Murtaugh of Whitechapel. Both victims of the Monday Murders were found with a braided three-strand garotte tied around their throats. An anonymous source in the Yard revealed that two distinct sets of footprints were found at both murder scenes, leading them to the conclusion of two killers. The first set indicated a one-legged man using a crutch, and the second a normal pair of different size closely parallel to the first man's tracks.

Holmes folded the paper and set it in his lap. "That is an odd choice of words, 'parallel.' The Yard is seeking a pair of men; one a one-legged man who walks with a crutch and who else would walk in tandem with him but a blind man, a hand on his shoulder?"

"My Uncle Henry walks with a crutch in his right oxter, and his friend Seth Canty lost his sight in the Queen's Service in Afghanistan, the same fight as where Uncle Henry lost his leg."

Holmes drew at his pipe and let out a slow cloud of smoke. "So, Mister Wiggins, how is it that your uncle and his friend came to the attention of Scotland Yard?"

"No disrespect intended, sir, but I believe they'd be the better to tell you themselves."

"Very well," said Holmes. "How may we arrange for them to meet with us?" He looked in my direction. "I do expect Doctor Watson will also be present." I nodded my affirmation.

"No offense, Mister Holmes, but being that it's not safe for them to be seen about the city, they'd rather not come here. Tonight, sir, at eight o'clock at Hansen's Wharf at the edge of Chinatown. They'll be there, if that suits you."

"I know the place," said Holmes. "I'm sure we will have little difficulty identifying them, but will they know us?"

"Indeed they shall, Mister Holmes. We watched you and the Doctor come and go three times yesterday from a covert up the street."

I chuckled to myself. Perhaps Mrs. Hudson believed Wiggins to be as innocent as a newborn lamb, but I could see he possessed the guile of a fox despite his tender age.

"Very good," said Holmes. "Please tell the gentlemen that Doctor Watson and I shall meet them at the appointed time and place."

"Thank you, Mister Holmes. Thank you." The boy's gratitude was genuine.

"Watson," said Holmes over his shoulder, "please show the lad out."

I opened the door to the hallway and found Mrs. Hudson standing on the landing holding a glass of milk in one hand and a plate of gingerbread in the other. "Oh, Doctor Watson, I thought perhaps Charlie might be hungry as growing boys will be. I brought these for him."

"Thank you, Mrs. Hudson," I said. "Our business with young Wiggins here is concluded. He was just leaving."

"Well, perhaps he can come downstairs to the kitchen for a bite before he leaves." She gave Wiggins a beaming smile and with a matronly arm across his shoulder, escorted him down the stairs.

I recounted the incident to Holmes and said, "Good that Mrs. Hudson is our landlady; otherwise I'd wager she'd lose her purse to that young scamp."

"Redemption, Watson; redemption and rehabilitation. I sincerely believe that working on the right hand of the law has weaned our young friend from its left. However, that feral cunning bred of the streets runs a strong current in him yet."

"And what was that business with the shilling all about?"

"My reasons were manifold; the first, pride. Charlie Wiggins is a very independent lad. I did not wish to insult him by forcing him to take charity."

"But I gave him the coin."

"No, Watson, you lent him the coin. The fact that his pockets were empty when he arrived suggests to me that he is no longer picking those of others. I would wager a hundred times as much that he will repay you and take great offense should you refuse it.

"Further, I wanted to establish a legitimate ground for keeping his confidence should the Yard come calling. As I have been retained, I cannot divulge any information against my client's interest to the police. After all, Watson, what would become of the Irregulars if we were enlisted by the Yard in this case and simply handed Wiggins's uncle over? How can we trust them if they can't trust us?"

"Indeed. I should think some fellow's head is in the noose at Scotland Yard for giving those details to the newspapers."

"Perhaps," said Holmes. "However, Lestrade occasionally exhibits a bit of cleverness. It is possible that he intentionally let that information out to shake the bushes. People talk, especially if they think a reward is in the offing. That may be what led the Yard to Wiggins and Canty as suspects."

"Sensible enough," I said. "What do you make of the situation?"

Holmes gazed out the window to the street below. "I make nothing of it yet. I need facts and we will have them tonight. In the meantime, we should determine whether Messrs. Murchison and Murtaugh served the Crown, and if so, where that might have been."

Holmes's pipe had gone cold. He rooted in the bowl with a matchstick. "Unless I am mistaken, Watson, more connects those two dead men than a three-braid thong."

Holmes was, as usual, correct. An examination of The National Registry revealed that Murchison was a hatter and Murtaugh a millwright. Both served in the second Afghanistan campaign in the 2nd Battalion Loyal Lancashire Regiment, as did Henry Wiggins and Seth Canty.

"There, Watson," Holmes said, "is the first strand of the cord that binds these men each to each."

Our cab rolled through the early evening, street lamps glowing like balls of smoldering wool through the fog. We had left Baker Street some time before and were winding now through the fringes of Limehouse.

"Do you suppose Scotland Yard has made that connection?"

"Very likely. Though they lack ingenuity at times, they do have a plodding way of reaching conclusions. I would suppose that is the reason why Lestrade has not yet come to us about this matter. He believes that he and his men have a true fix on the culprits."

"Just as well," I said. "If Lestrade had come to you first, you couldn't very well have taken young Charlie's cause, could you? After all, the Old Bailey is full of men who claim they are wrongly accused."

"Had Lestrade come first, I would be resting on the horns of a difficult dilemma, Watson." Despite his outward lack of sentimentality, Holmes held a deep sense of loyalty to those in his employ. "As it is, we're walking on a slippery fence helping these men at all."

"The Monday Murders," I mused. "The newspapers love to hang a monicker on crimes and criminals."

"Especially one so alliterative; it sells the rags, Watson. They'd use blood for ink if they could."

"And what if Canty and Wiggins are indeed the Monday Murderers?"

"If we determine their guilt beyond question, then we have no choice but to see justice done. However, while I do not wish evil to befall anyone,

I would say that since today is a Monday, if the Monday Murderers strike while Wiggins and Canty are in our company, they may easily be cleared of suspicion."

He rapped on the ceiling of the compartment with his stick. "This is close enough. We should walk from here to be safe."

"Safe?" I peered through the mist at our shadowy surroundings. "This is a likely neighborhood to have our throats cut."

"Not to worry, old fellow," Holmes said. "I have my stick and I trust you have your revolver."

I nodded and patted my right coat pocket.

"I should say we can give a proper accounting of ourselves." Holmes spoke to the cabbie. "Here is a crown," he said, handing him the coin. I will have another for you if you return to this corner in one hour."

"Indeed, sir," he said. "And thank you." He flicked his whip and the cab disappeared into the mist.

"Well, Watson," Holmes said, "Let us learn what Mister Wiggins and his blind friend have to say." We set off at a brisk pace down a brick street that wound between blocks of canneries and warehouses. I felt unseen eyes on us peering from dark doorways and shadowed alleys, but no one ventured forth to interrupt our passage.

Hansen's Wharf was a ramshackle clump of pilings capped with rotting planks and a shanty at its end that must have held its office in more prosperous times. I fancied that I could feel the whole mass rise and fall with each swell that lapped at its foundations.

We walked to the center of the wharf and waited. Holmes took out his pipe. By the time he had it going, a voice I recognized as Charlie's hissed from the shadows, "Into the shack, sirs."

"Come along, Watson. I believe our friends have arrived."

The door to the shanty barely hung on rusted hinges, and once we stepped inside and pulled it shut behind us, we were in complete darkness.

Someone scratched a match and held it to a coal oil lantern. In a moment the shanty was dimly lit with a harsh brassy glow. "Good evening, gentlemen." The speaker was a short lean fellow in a shabby mackinaw, leaning on a pole crutch with a peg handle and a padded yoke under his armpit. Behind him stood a once taller man in a dark threadbare suit and a derby hat. I say once taller because he had become stooped from years of walking with a hand on the shorter man's shoulder. His eyes were hidden behind dark lenses that wrapped around the sides of his face and hooked over his ears.

"Mister Wiggins, I presume," Holmes said.

"The same," the short man replied. He jerked his head over his shoulder. "This here's my friend Seth Canty." Wiggins spoke with the same Cockney dialect as young Charlie. "The lad said you'd help us."

"If I can," said Holmes," but first, please tell me how you came to be in this predicament."

"That I will," said Wiggins. "Quite a tale it is." And he proceeded to tell it.

"It was November of 1878. Lieutenant-General Sam Browne had just led us on a campaign to take Ali Masjid, which we did with no casualties to speak of. Me and Seth were corporals in the Loyal Lancashire Regiment."

"As were Hamish Murchison and Walter Murtaugh," said Holmes.

"Yes, sir. You know that already. Young Charlie said you was a sharp one. We were sent to fight in the second Afghan campaign. I understand, Doctor that you was in that bloody hell hole for a time as well."

"Yes, and have an injured leg to show for it."

"Then you know, sir, what it meant to go there and fight there, never knowing from one day to the next if you'd ever see home again."

I nodded. "Yes, please go on."

"Well, Seth and me, we was 'volunteered,' if you get my meaning, to spy out the territory for old Sam so's he could move on Kabul. Eight of us there was and Sergeant Daniel Cuthbert leading that sortie, including Murtaugh and Murchison and a chap named Oliver Langdon."

My face gave me away. "So, Doctor, the name is known to you, is it?"

"Yes. It was associated with a scandal that cost some people their stripes. Something about leaving wounded behind."

"Specifically Oliver Langdon, Doctor, but he weren't the only one."

Canty spoke up. "We all knew the odds against us." Where Wiggins's voice had a sharp nasal quality to it, Canty's was a rich baritone like a country vicar or a member of Parliament. "But 'orders is orders,' as they say, so we marched straight into the breach. We followed the Kabul River toward the city, keeping an eye cocked for outposts and villages where Old Sam might find resistance.

"We'd been two nights out and following a trail a bit inland from the cliffs overlooking the river. The moon was new and there was only the faintest starlight to see by. Johnny Watts was at the front of the file. I was straight behind him when all of a sudden he fell backward against me and I found he didn't have a head. They swarmed on us like wolves."

"It was like they come out of the very rocks," said Wiggins. "I couldn't count them in the dark, but I reckoned there were plenty more of them than here were of us. Sergeant Cuthbert saw right away the fix we was in and he ordered us to fall back."

"That's when one of the wogs caught me across the face with some kind of flail or a whip," said Canty. "They make them with shards of bone tied at the end of the strands. That's what did this to me." Canty took off his dark glasses and in the brassy glow of the lamp, his ruined eyelids looked ghastly. "It hurt like nothing I ever knew, but I had to keep fighting or die. They couldn't see in the dark any better than I, so I just kept swinging my saber."

Wiggins broke in, caught up in the story. "That's when I grabbed Seth and said, 'Scarper, mate,' and he says, 'Can't. They got my eyes.' So I says, 'Take my arm,' and we ran, me firing my pistol over my shoulder to hold them off. I know I got one of them for sure, 'cause I seen his ugly face up close in the flash and heard him scream.

"But it was a mistake, you see. The muzzle flash gave them a target, and one of the unholy bastards got off a lucky shot. A ball from some old flint-lock, I suppose, hit me in the knee, and I went down. Then Seth grabbed me up. He was my legs and I was his eyes."

Holmes said, "And how does Oliver Langdon fit into the picture?"

"I was coming to that, sir," Wiggins said, pausing to light the stub of a cigar. "We ran into a copse of trees and things got quiet. They couldn't see us in the dark and were waiting for us to make a noise. By the sound, I knew we was close to the river. Then I heard a voice cry out, 'Don't leave me!' I knew that voice; it was Oliver Langdon. 'Don't leave me!' he cried again, but whoever was carting him ran off to save his own hide."

"And you don't know who that was?" Holmes said.

"No, sir. In the dark I couldn't tell. The animals heard him and they were coming. We had no choice but to run for it."

"We got to the edge of the cliff, and I could hear the river rushing below," said Canty. "Charybdis and Scylla, it was. Do we jump for the river and likely bust up on the rocks or drown, or do we stand and fight, a blind man and a cripple against a gang of those bearded devils? That's when we heard a god-awful scream and knew the wogs had found Oliver."

"That made up our minds for us," said Wiggins. "We learned early on what the Afghanis do to prisoners." He looked at me. "You know, Doctor; you seen it ain't you?"

"Yes," I said. "They stake a man down and the women have at him with knives."

"They do indeed," said Wiggins, emotion choking his voice. "Castrate a man they would, and then prop his jaw open with a stick and take turns squatting over his face and pissing in his mouth 'til he drowns in it." He shuddered. "Then they'd leave the corpse for us to find. Who can blame us for the choice we made?"

"Certainly no one," said Holmes, "and since you are here now, I can see that you survived the leap. What happened then?"

Canty replied, "We swam for it as best we could. We were found down-river by another regiment and returned to our own."

"And the others," said Holmes. "What of them?"

"Sergeant Cuthbert returned alive and well, as did Murtaugh and Murchison. Edwin Dobbs and Peter Gibbon turned up a week later pretty badly hurt from the fight. Johnny Watts was dead, as I told you, and of course Oliver was lost."

"Watson, you said there was a scandal over this incident." He turned to the veterans. "What was its outcome?"

Wiggins snorted. "Oh, for certain, Mister Holmes there was an official inquiry." He put a sneering emphasis on the last word. "It was dark, and nobody saw nothing, to be sure, but whoever left poor Oliver to those animals bloody well knew who he was. All swore they didn't do it, no one fessed up, and in the end it was never settled.

"They busted old Cuthbert down to corporal since he was in charge of the mission, although I heard he got his stripes back later on, and they reprimanded Murtaugh and Murchison, put them back to private, they did. Me and Seth and Dobbs and Gibbon weren't blamed because they figured we give as good as we got. Seth and me was mustered out with a pension and we had a long, painful trip home to London where we've been together ever since."

"And how do you occupy yourselves?"

Wiggins looked at the floor. "It shames me to say so, Mister Holmes, but we beg."

Holmes was silent for a moment. "And you never heard of the Langdon matter again?"

"No, Mister Holmes," said Canty. "But just a few months ago, Henry and I were passing a shop in Knightsbridge when I heard a familiar voice.

You know, sir when a man loses his sight, his ears grow keener to make up for it."

"Indeed," said Holmes. "And whose voice did you recognize?"

"Sergeant Daniel Cuthbert's. He was dressing down some haberdasher about a hat. I said to Henry. 'Look sharp behind us. Is that old Cuthbert?'"

"I turned, and by the saints, it was him. All tricked out in a fancy suit and looking prosperous, and still had those big grey mutton chops growing into his dot and dash. I called to him, and he give me a startled look and turned and hurried straight away. Hobbling on a peg with Seth in tow, I had no chance to catch him, but we found him later."

"A few inquiries got us his address in Knightsbridge," Canty said. "We thought we'd look him up for old times' sake and maybe put the touch on him for a few bob."

Wiggins went on. "We went to his place, a good walk it was from Soho; took us a half day. We rung his bell, and his house keeper come to the door. A big imposing woman she was, bosoms the size of my head, and a homely face like the prow of a locomotive. She was wearing a big old fashioned skirt, she was, and she must have an arse to match her chest, her bustle was so broad.

"'Who are you and what do you want?' she says, eyeballing us as if we was dogs in her flowerbed . I tell her, 'I'm Henry Wiggins and this here's Seth Canty. We served in Afghanistan with Sergeant Cuthbert; are you Missus Cuthbert?' She says, 'I am not. I am Mrs. Hawkins, Mister Cuthbert's housekeeper. Himself is not at home, and I'd venture to say he'll want nothing to do with such riff-raff as yourselves. Be gone and don't come back, or I'll call a constable on you.' And she slammed the door in our faces."

"And that voice of hers," said Canty. Harsh for a woman and it sounded for all the world as if she hated us like the Antichrist."

"I looked back once," Wiggins said, "and I seen that nasty face of hers glaring out a window with the curtains pulled back. I pity the man what married her."

"And did you ever see Sergeant Cuthbert again?" Holmes asked.

"No, sir we ain't," said Wiggins. "We figured one try at him was enough as we didn't want trouble with the law, but we got it anyway. A week later Murchison was murdered and then Murtaugh. Soon after that the Yard came looking for the two of us. We was nowhere near Cheapside nor Whitechapel, but can't prove it. Each of us is the other's alibi, and we're both suspects. Now I ain't saying me and Seth have always been lily-white, but we sure ain't..."

A sharp whistle interrupted Wiggins. I heard shouts and feet pounding on the planks of the pier.

"Go!" Said Wiggins to Canty, and like some magic trick, a trap opened in the floor. In a blink both were gone just as the door of the shanty wrenched open and we found ourselves staring into the startled countenance of Inspector Lestrade.

"Holmes," he snarled, "What the deuce are you doing here?"

"I would venture to say the same as yourself, Inspector, pursuing the cause of justice."

"Don't you be cheeky with me, Holmes."

At that moment, a uniform came in red in the face and breathing heavily. "No sign of them, sir, and the boy got away too."

"If I catch that rascal, I'll give him a sound thrashing, interfering in police business, warning them like that." He turned to us. "Where are they, Holmes?"

"Whom do you mean?"

"You know damned well who I mean! The blind man and the cripple, Canty and Wiggins. Don't tell me they weren't here." He pointed to the two sets of prints in the dust, one with two feet and another with a foot and crutch. "Where are they?"

"I am afraid they left, just before you arrived. How did you happen to come here?"

Lestrade glared at us. "You're not the only one figures things out, Holmes. We have our eyes about. We got word the two were in this neighborhood, but not together; the cripple was on his own and the blind man had a young boy leading him about who brought him to this wharf. What's your hand in this, Holmes?"

"I am pursuing the interests of a client who has retained me to look into the deaths of Hamish Murchison and Walter Murtaugh."

"You'd best tell me what you know about all this, Holmes and tell me this minute."

Holmes made a show of packing his pipe before he spoke, which made Lestrade fume with impatience. "Never let it be said that I impede a police investigation, Inspector. Since you are pursuing Messrs. Wiggins and Canty, you appear to be following the same line of inquiry as my own. Three things I would suggest, Lestrade: first, determine the whereabouts and condition of two other men who served in the Loyal Lancashire Regiment in Afghanistan, Edwin Dobbs and Peter Gibbon; second, throw a protective net about one Daniel Cuthbert of Knightsbridge, for he may be in mortal peril; third, determine what relatives if any survive the late

Corporal Oliver Langdon of the Loyal Lancashire. There is no more that I can tell you."

Lestrade looked about to explode. "Where are Wiggins and Canty holed up? Tell me, damn your eyes!"

"I do not know, Inspector, nor does Watson. If you are quite through with us, we have a cab waiting."

For a moment Lestrade seemed teetering between having us cuffed and shooting us outright, but his better judgment prevailed and he let us go. Our cab was waiting at the appointed place. Holmes gave the driver another coin and said, "Drive about for a few moments."

"We're not going back to Baker Street, Holmes?"

"No, Watson, I want another look at that shanty once Lestrade and his men have left it. I hope that in their customary clumsiness they have not impeded my investigation."

"What do you mean, Holmes?"

"Evidence, Watson, evidence that may expediently clear Wiggins and Canty, if I am correct." Holmes relit his pipe and disappeared into labyrinths of thought.

The shanty was dark when we returned and no guard was posted outside. Holmes tried the door and stepped in. The shanty was empty. Holmes struck a match and lit the lamp. He held it high away from his eyes and peered at the floor.

"I say, Holmes, what are you looking for?"

"Those, Watson." He pointed to the footprints in the dust. "Wiggins stood here, evidenced by the round of his crutch, and Canty stood here, just behind him. Hold the lantern, would you."

I took the lamp and held it while Holmes produced a tape measure from a pocket in his cloak. He measured the length and breadth of Canty's tracks and jotted the results in his notebook. He then measured the print of Wiggins's left shoe and the diameter of the crutch tip. "It is a pity both men are down on their luck. Their shoes are so worn that there is little to distinguish them, but their sizes may be a help. Come Watson, we have much to do."

"And what must we do now, Holmes?" I said.

"We must do precisely what we told Lestrade to do, save protecting Cuthbert. Tell me, Watson, does Canty and Wiggins's story about the Langdon affair ring true to you?"

"It is consistent with official accounts that I know of. The story has become something of a cautionary tale among soldiers in the region."

Holmes nodded. "I believe their account as well. It is a pity that we were interrupted before they could finish their tale. We must locate them, Watson, before Lestrade does. There may be more they can tell us, and if he locks them up, Lestrade will allow us no access to them."

We climbed into the cab. Holmes rapped the roof with his stick and called, "Baker Street," to the driver, and that brought an end to the evening's adventure.

Holmes left the next morning before I had risen, and in the midst of my breakfast, he came bustling in. "Pour me some of that coffee, would you, Watson," he said, shouldering off his cloak and hanging it on the tree in the corner.

"And where have you been so early?" I said, reaching for the carafe.

"Prospecting, my dear fellow," he said, "I was mining the records."

"And what nuggets did you find?"

"First, that Edwin Dobbs resides today in Bromley, Kent where he is a cobbler. Second, his fellow member of the Loyal Lancashire Regiment Peter Gibbon works as a groom at a stable in Brighton. Third, that Oliver Langdon was born in Nettleton, Lincolnshire and he had a younger brother named Timothy."

"And his location?"

"In Heaven, Hell, or Limbo, Watson. According to parish records, the boy died when he was two years old."

"And where does that lead us?"

"To Victoria Station to catch the 10:05 train for Bromley, Kent."

I was soon dressed and in a railway car waiting for the train to depart.

"What if this Dobbs fellow is not in Bromley?" I said. "We'll have made the trip for nothing."

"Oh, he will be there, Watson. I cabled the police station early this morning and told them his life was in peril. I suspect they will see that he remains in the city until we arrive."

"How did you have the authority to order them about?"

"Simple, my dear fellow. I told them I was Inspector Lestrade."

"Really, Holmes," I snorted. "And what if they cable Scotland Yard to confirm the order?"

"I expect and I hope that they do, Watson. It will put Lestrade on the track toward removing Wiggins and Canty from suspicion. In fact," he

"We must locate them, Watson, before Lestrade does."

said, looking out the window, "I believe I see him coming down the platform now."

In minutes, Lestrade was storming down the aisle of our coach with two of his subordinates in tow. "Holmes!" he roared, turning heads the length of the car. "I should have known you were behind all this."

"Behind what, Inspector?" Holmes said with a guileless smile.

"This." Lestrade pulled a telegram from his pocket and thrust it in front of Holmes's nose."

"Oh dear," Holmes said. "This is unfortunate." He turned to me. "The telegram is from Chief Whitehead of the Bromley, Kent Constabulary. He writes that Edwin Dobbs was found dead in his shop by an officer sent to enquire as to his welfare."

"Now, Holmes, you'll not get off this train until you tell me the story—in detail."

"I will share what I know, Lestrade, but instead of confining us to the train, I would respectfully suggest that you allow us to accompany you to the scene of this crime and pool our resources. After all, we both desire the same end, the guilty punished and the innocent exonerated."

Lestrade let out an exasperated huff. "Very well, Holmes, you may come along, and you too, Doctor. But first, you will tell me all you know about this matter."

As the train rumbled to Bromley, Holmes gave a concise summary of what we had learned in the case but adamantly refused to reveal the name of his client, to Lestrade's annoyance.

"And what about this other fellow, Gibbon?"

"I would hope he is safe. I sent a similar telegram to the constabulary at Brighton. The killers couldn't have gotten there as well in so short a time. No trains leave Bromley Station in that direction before half-ten."

When our train pulled in, three uniformed officers were waiting on the platform. As we alighted, the senior officer, a sergeant, approached us. "Is one of you gents Inspector Lestrade?" He rhymed it with "parade."

"I'm Lestrade," the Inspector said emphasizing the second syllable and correcting the pronunciation.

"Sergeant Hopper," the officer said with a salute. "These are my men Cosset and Smalley. We're to take you to the murder, sir. Are all of you together?"

Lestrade hesitated a moment then said, "Yes. Please take us there at once."

Dobbs's shop was on a crooked little byway a few blocks from the station. Outside its door, the small crowd that had gathered was kept back by another uniformed constable. "I say, Holmes," I quipped, "nothing like word of a murder to gather the morbidly curious, eh?"

"Either that, Watson, or they simply came for their shoes."

Hopper shouldered the crowd aside and led the five of us into the cramped shop. It was little more than a counter dividing the room with ceiling high shadowboxes on the wall behind it, most stuffed with pairs of shoes and boots. The room smelled of leather, saddle soap, bootblack, and death.

"Back here, Inspector," said Hopper, leading us around the counter to the back of the shop. Behind it, Dobbs's corpse was sprawled on the floor beside his workbench, his upturned face almost black. His tongue lolled out and his eyes bulged.

"Has anyone disturbed anything, Sergeant?" said Holmes.

"Here, now, I'll ask the questions, Holmes," Lestrade snapped.

"Holmes?" said Hopper, eyebrows rising. "Sherlock Holmes?"

"I am he."

"Well if that don't beat all, a Yard Inspector *and* Sherlock Holmes in my case. No, sir," Hopper said, ignoring Lestrade. "We've been careful not to muck things up. It's all as we found it."

Holmes crouched beside Dobbs's corpse and peered at his throat. A three-strand leather garotte like a short whip was knotted around it. "Inspector, is this weapon comparable to those found on the other murdered men?"

Lestrade stooped beside Holmes. "Yes, they seem to be the same, a braided leather thong."

"Watson, how long would you say that Dobbs has been dead?"

After a cursory examination, I said, "I would judge no more than a few hours."

Holmes turned to Potter. "I saw no sign on the door. What time did Dobbs ordinarily open his shop?"

"Like most of the tradespeople he was always open early. Surely no later than half seven, sir."

"So he was likely killed this morning soon after he arrived."

"Was anything stolen?" Lestrade asked Potter.

"Not that we can tell, Inspector." Potter nodded toward one of his men. "Follansbee here found money in the till, and Dobbs's purse was still in his pocket with a few bob in it; his watch as well."

"So, robbery was not the motive." Lestrade tugged at the end of his moustache. "Did you find other evidence?"

"Indeed we did, Inspector, queer footprints out back in the alley."

"Show us," Lestrade said.

Behind the shop was a rickety lean-to and a dustbin. "Right there beside the shed," said Follansbee "in that patch of mud." He pointed to a small dark patch below a rain gutter. "Sharp they are."

In the mud we found two sets of prints, a pair of boots and a left boot of a different size alongside the divot left by a crutch-pole. The prints were as consistently close to each other as if they'd been stamped by a die.

"There, Holmes," said Lestrade. "Canty and Wiggins for sure. Am I right?"

"Not necessarily," Holmes said, drawing the tape measure from his pocket. "Before we hang the two of them, let us gauge the size of these prints." Holmes bent over them for a moment taking one measurement then another. He frowned.

"Well?" I said.

"They are the same sizes as the tracks I measured last night."

"And after they escaped last night, they would have had time to catch the last train out of London," Lestrade said. "Potter, what time does the last train from London roll through here?"

"That would be the mail train, Inspector. It comes just after eleven. There's a few passengers on it any given night, but not many. Most of the coaches are empty."

"Well, Lestrade," said Holmes, "a cripple and a blind man traveling together would surely be remembered. Potter, who in this town might have been on that train last night?"

"I can't say offhand about passengers, Mister Holmes, but Sam Tate the conductor should be on the line today. We can bring him 'round when the train pulls in. Should be within the hour."

"Very good, Sergeant." Holmes pulled a railway timetable from his pocket and thumbed through it. "It appears that there have been only two trains leaving Bromley this morning, but the killers could have escaped by other means."

"You persist in calling them 'the killers,' Lestrade snorted. "Call them who they are, Wiggins and Canty."

"I will not do that without proper evidence of their guilt."

"You have your evidence right there," Lestrade said, pointing at the tracks.

"Circumstantial evidence at best, Lestrade."

"Answer me this, Holmes, do you know for a fact where Wiggins and Canty were this morning or that they aren't still right here hiding out?"

"I will answer that after you tell me why in an otherwise dry alley a killer trying to escape detection would walk through a patch of mud." He turned to me. "Come, Watson, I need your assistance inside."

Holmes stood for a moment studying the shadowbox wall of shoes. "What do you see, Watson?"

"I see shoes, Holmes." Dozens of soles, chalk marked with names and fees nested in the compartments.

"But look closely, old fellow. What is out of place?"

"I can't see anything out of place."

"Nor did the constables, nor did Lestrade. Look there, Watson." He pointed to one of the compartments. "And there." In both, the soles were turned inward, the tops of the boots protruding from the openings. Holmes pulled out a pair of the boots and held them out for me to examine. The chalk marks were obliterated from the soles and traces of mud nestled between the sole and the welt.

He pulled out the other reversed pair. "As I thought," he said. The right boot was clean and still had Dobbs's chalk marks. The left boot held the same trace of mud as the first pair. "I will venture to say that the mud on these boots matches that outside. These are not the same boots that Canty and Wiggins wore last night, Watson. Look at this heel."

He pointed to one of the pair of boots. "You see the faded trademark, the star in the circle. It matches the track we just saw. Canty and Wiggins's boots were so worn as to be featureless. Someone came here, Killed Dobbs and put on customers' boots to purposely make those tracks in the alley."

"Yet they are Canty and Wiggins's proper sizes, Holmes."

"True. Watson, I believe we are witnessing a diabolically clever plot designed to unrightfully send Wiggins and Canty to the gallows. In the vernacular, they are being 'fitted up'."

"But why, Holmes?"

"Why, indeed, Watson. When we find our killer's motive, we will find our killer."

Tate the conductor said that he took tickets from only eight passengers on the last train from London, six from men and two from women, none of them blind nor missing a limb. Holmes and I left Lestrade in Bromley and returned on the next train to London. He spent the entire trip puffing at his pipe and gazing out the coach window at nothing in particular. I knew better than to interrupt his deliberations.

Once again Holmes was gone when I woke. There had been no word from Canty and Wiggins nor from young Charlie, and that was likely sensible on their part. I had no doubt Lestrade was watching our lodgings from every corner.

I was almost through the *Times* when Mrs. Hudson came to the door. When I opened it, I could see she was visibly upset. "Doctor Watson, there are tradesmen below and they want to bring things up here that I…"

"Please allow me to deal with them, Mrs. Hudson," I said. I stepped out onto the landing and looked downstairs to see two workmen struggling to wrestle a mortar trough through the front door. "Here now," I called down. "Where do you think you're going with that?"

One of the two men pulled a slip of paper from his beneath his cap and read aloud, "Mister Sherlock Holmes, 221B Baker Street. Is that you guv'nor?"

"Assuredly not. I am his associate Doctor John Watson, and I know nothing of all this."

"It is quite all right, Watson," came a voice from just outside the door. "I ordered these items be brought here." Holmes stepped through the doorway carrying a large parcel wrapped in brown paper under one arm. He said to the men, "I am Sherlock Holmes. You men are in the right place. Just bring that trough up the stairs." He turned to two men in coveralls who followed him carrying heavy burlap bags over their shoulders. "You men come along too."

As he reached the top of the stairs, I said, "What the devil's going on, Holmes. What's in those sacks?"

"Earth, Watson, soil if you will." The workmen shouldered past us and set the bags on the parlor carpet.

"Oh my heavens," said Mrs. Hudson. "You're bringing sacks of dirt into my house?"

"No cause for alarm, Mrs. Hudson." Holmes smiled benignly. "That's why I had a trough delivered, to hold the soil all in one place. If you would be so kind as to show these men to the pump, I need a few buckets of water."

Mrs. Hudson was too rattled by it all to protest. She turned on her heel and started for the back stairway. "Follow her, gentlemen." He waved with a hand and the two bag men clumped down the stairs behind her.

"What are you going to do with all that, Holmes?"

"Footprints, old fellow; I am going to study footprints, and you are going to help me."

Within fifteen minutes, the carters were gone and Holmes was pouring a bucket of water over the dirt he'd dumped from the burlap bags into the trough. "Be a good fellow, Watson and use that paddle to stir the mix for me while I add more water. I want to get the consistency right."

"What consistency, Holmes?"

"I want this trough of mud to be the exact consistency of that which we found in the alley behind Edwin Dobbs's shop yesterday."

"Well, wouldn't any mud puddle do the job for you?"

"Perhaps, but I need privacy, Watson. I can't risk someone seeing what I am about to do and perhaps alerting the killer."

"You say 'killer'? Only one? I thought there were two."

"As does Lestrade, but now I am not so certain, my friend. I hope to determine by this experiment whether or not we may be dealing with one man not two." Holmes cut the twine from the parcel he carried in earlier and pulled away the paper.

It was a limb. To be more accurate, it was a prosthetic leg.

"I went to Lathrop and James this morning and I was in luck. They had this artificial limb on hand, made for a customer who died before he could take delivery. A little alteration on the straps and it fit well enough for my purposes."

Holmes held the contrivance against his right hip. "Help me buckle the harness, Watson, and put a shoe on this foot. We'll see whether my idea has merit." With a bit of adjustment, Holmes soon stood on a tripod.

"I need a crutch. Rinse the mud from the paddle and give it to me, would you." Holmes put the blade of the paddle in his armpit and stepped over the side of the trough. He walked its length, leaving a set of prints behind.

He eyed them critically. "They seem to have a similar configuration to the prints we saw, but they aren't quite right. The false limb leaves a much shallower impression than the other two."

"Of course it does, Holmes," I said. Your full weight isn't on that leg as it is on the others. There is bound to be a disparity."

"Let us try again." Holmes raked over the prints to leave a fresh surface. He stepped through the trough, this time leaning slightly forward to shift the distribution of his weight. The result disappointed him equally. Well into the afternoon we repeated the experiment, Holmes repositioning the prosthetic leg and even shifting it to his left hip for a time. He went so far as to pack the inside of the hollow leg with mud from the trough to more closely approximate the weight of a real one. His frustration was evident.

"Blast it all, Watson, no matter how I try, I cannot duplicate those tracks."

"You may try all you like, but it's still unnatural. It is an interesting theory, Holmes, but as hollow as that limb. A fake leg is a fake leg. And you can't expect a man to grow a third one now, can you?"

Holmes froze as if thunderstruck. Then he scrambled to undo the straps and buckles of the prosthetic leg. "Get your coat, Watson. Hurry, and bring your revolver."

"Where are we going, Holmes?"

"To save a man's life, Watson, perhaps more than one."

We opened the front door to leave and found Lestrade poised to knock. "Holmes," he said.

Visibly annoyed at the delay, Holmes said, "What is it, Lestrade?"

"I wanted to tell you myself," he said with a smug grin. "We rounded up your friends Wiggins and Canty. They're in custody as we speak."

"Did you have a carriage, Lestrade?" Holmes said.

"Uh, yes. I do."

"Good. That will save us the trouble of finding one. Come with us, Inspector, and if I am right, Wiggins and Canty will be free men before midnight."

If Lestrade were not with us, Holmes may have confided his suspicions to me, but despite Lestrade's harangues, Holmes kept his counsel. "Damn it, Holmes. Tell me where we're going and what you think you're going to accomplish."

"If I am correct, Inspector, we shall all know soon enough. If I am not, I shall look less foolish for not telling you in advance."

The carriage arrived at Sergeant Cuthbert's front door as the last of the street lamps were being lit. Holmes rapped at the door with his stick, and in a moment, a woman whom I recognized from Wiggins's description as Mrs. Hawkins opened the door. She glared at us. "Who are you and what do you want?"

"My name is Sherlock Holmes, and I am here to see Sergeant Cuthbert."

"Himself does not receive visitors at this hour," Mrs. Hawkins said and began to close the door.

Lestrade put his foot in it and said, "My good woman, I am Inspector Lestrade of Scotland Yard, and you will open that door and tell Sergeant Cuthbert that we are here."

"Mrs. Hawkins, what's the commotion?" A voice came from the hallway and over the woman's shoulder I saw a tall man with grey mutton chops, Sergeant Cuthbert.

"I am Inspector Lestrade from Scotland Yard."

"Let them in, Mrs. Hawkins," said Cuthbert.

She reluctantly stepped aside and as we entered, I noticed the accuracy of Wiggins's description. Mrs. Hawkins was a big-busted woman, clad in an old fashioned dress with voluminous skirts and petticoats and a bustle the size of an armchair. Her grey hair was pulled up in a tight bun held by a tortoise shell comb. Canty's appraisal of her attitude was accurate as well. She fairly radiated animosity.

Cuthbert gestured toward a doorway to his right. "Won't you gentlemen come into the parlor?" He turned to Mrs. Hawkins. "Please bring tea for us." She snorted and strode toward the kitchen.

Cuthbert led us into the parlor, a room more masculine than feminine, attesting to his bachelorhood. He waved toward a settee. "Please, sit down. Are these men also from the Yard, Inspector?"

Lestrade shook his head. "No, sir, this is Mister Sherlock Holmes, and the other fellow," he nodded in my direction, "is his associate Doctor Watson."

If Cuthbert were surprised or impressed, he didn't let it show. He simply nodded. "I suppose you're here about the murders of Murchison and Murtaugh."

"Indeed we are," Lestrade said. "And of Edwin Dobbs."

Cuthbert's eyebrows rose in surprise. "Dobbs as well? When did that happen?"

"This morning in Bromley Kent. I have no doubt you can see the connection among the three."

"Yes. A few of your fellows came earlier today to offer me protection, but I declined." He pulled back his vest to reveal the pearl handle of a small revolver. "If someone comes for me, I'll handle him."

"That may no longer be necessary," said Lestrade. "We have two men from your old unit, Henry Wiggins and Seth Canty in custody."

"Poor chaps," said Cuthbert. "They saw me on the street, or I should say Wiggins saw me, and I snubbed them. I felt badly for that afterward and I've looked for them since to help them out if I can, but I haven't seen them again. You believe they are the killers?"

"I have every reason to believe so, yes," said Lestrade.

At that moment, Mrs. Hawkins entered with the tea tray and as she crossed the room in front of us, Holmes thrust his stick under her skirt and between her feet, sending her sprawling headlong and the tea service crashing on the hearth.

"Holmes, what the deuce are you doing?" shouted Lestrade, but he couldn't see what I saw. Beneath Mrs. Hawkins's skirt, amid the flounces and petticoats, I saw not two feet but three.

Holmes dove from the settee onto Mrs. Hawkins's back as she pulled the comb from her hair and slashed at his face with its sharpened tines. "It's a man. Not a woman!" Holmes cried as he wrenched his opponent's arm behind his back. "Help me, Watson!"

The figure on the floor twisted its head to and fro, teeth snapping, snarling like a trapped beast. We wrestled him to his feet and as Lestrade and I held the erstwhile woman by the arms, Holmes seized the front of the dress by its placket and tore it from the thick padding of a false bosom. Another yank at the dress and it came away completely, revealing a third leg.

Cuthbert stared open-mouthed as Holmes said, "Sergeant Cuthbert, please allow me to introduce you to Timothy Langdon." He picked up the silver teapot and sniffed at the spout. He thrust a spoon into it and drew it out with a green residue. "And if I am not mistaken, this is not sugar in the bottom of the pot. Our friend intended death for us all."

Langdon shrieked and although Lestrade and I had a good hold on him, he broke free and hurled himself at Cuthbert, knocking him to the floor. In a second, his hands were on the sergeant's throat and all three of us were hard put to pry him loose in his fury. Then a gunshot ended the struggle.

Langdon slumped sideways to the floor clutching his chest. Cuthbert lay wide eyed clutching his smoking pistol. I tore away Langdon's undershirt to stanch the wound, and found tattooed on his chest an odd symbol. A triskele, three bent human legs projecting from a central point to form a triangle, the same symbol found on the flag of the Isle of Man.

Cuthbert's bullet had passed through one of the triskele's feet and into Langdon's lung. I made a compress of the shirt and held it against the hole, but to little avail. I could see that Langdon's death was coming swiftly.

"Bastards," he wheezed. "I'll see you all in hell." His head lolled to the side and he was gone.

A search of Timothy Langdon's quarters produced shoes of a size to match Canty's feet and a left boot of a proper size for Wiggins as well as a pole crutch jointed to fold in two for concealment. A third item: a pair of braided three-strand leather garottes.

"Like the triskele, three strands; one for each of his legs, a signature to his crimes," Holmes said. "One garotte for Gibbon and one for you, Sergeant Cuthbert," Holmes said. "Then the execution of Wiggins and Canty for the murders would make his revenge for his brother's abandonment complete."

"But how did you guess it, Holmes?" Lestrade said.

"I do not guess, Lestrade, I deduce. My conclusion sprang from two things that Watson said. First: a man can't grow another leg. But what if he were born with an extra one? And second: my attempts to recreate similar footprints to those found at the sites of the murders failed because it was 'unnatural.' But for a person who had three legs his entire life, walking and balance would be no difficulty, and his body weight would be evenly distributed.

"Timothy Langdon's tombstone notwithstanding, I submit to you that he did not die at the age of two but rather was raised as a girl by adoptive parents, his deformity concealed under skirts and dresses. Oliver Langdon was his only living relative and a protective older brother. When Oliver was left to die at the hands of the Afghanis, Timothy swore vengeance on those he believed to be responsible, the members of the scouting party under your command, Cuthbert."

"Dear God," Cuthbert gasped. "For more than a year he's been living under my roof, cooking my food, plotting while I slept. He could have killed me at his leisure."

"True," said Holmes. "He was biding his time, patiently scheming when Wiggins and Canty's visit crystallized the plan. They were the last two men of the party he had not yet located, and when he saw them, he realized how he could have his revenge and escape unpunished. I have no doubt that he followed them after they left and studied their odd tracks to duplicate them with his own feet."

"He may well have succeeded," said Cuthbert with a shudder.

"Indeed. Langdon wished to kill Gibbon and yourself before their arrest but Inspector Lestrade's arrest of Canty and Wiggins spoiled the plan. Lestrade, in what form did you receive the tip that put you onto Canty and Wiggins?"

"It was an anonymous note sent to the Yard."

"I would submit to you that if you compare the writing of that note with a sample of Timothy Langdon's, you will find a match. From the moment he saw Wiggins and Canty, he knew exactly how he would proceed."

"But we stopped him, Holmes," Lestrade protested. "We alerted

Cuthbert and Gibbon and he couldn't have murdered either of them."

"Not this week, nor perhaps even this month," Holmes said. "Langdon's vision of vengeance was long-sighted. Imagine allowing Wiggins and Canty to hang and then to strangle Gibbon six months or even a year later and perhaps Cuthbert as well, leaving the same garotte and footprints, making fools of us all. Then Langdon would escape in his female disguise while we all sought a pair of killers. But he tripped over his own feet, if you will pardon the expression, by setting the Yard on them too soon."

"But why Monday Murders, Holmes?" I said. "What significance does Monday have in this business?"

"Sergeant?" said Holmes. "Can you answer that question?"

"I can't say as I can," said Cuthbert. "It had nothing to do with the incident. We lost Langdon on a Thursday."

"Inspector?"

"Damned if I know, Holmes, but I suppose you'll tell us?"

"Simple, really. Monday was the killer's day off, making him free to move about. And now, Lestrade, I believe it is your duty to release Wiggins and Canty posthaste with full apologies. Come, Watson." So saying, Holmes strode through Cuthbert's front door into the night.

Three days later, a messenger delivered a cylindrical parcel. Holmes stared at it for some time before he finally cut the twine and removed the wrapping. From a cardboard tube, he produced a rolled poster. As he opened it, I saw "Fedderer's Circus" at the top in playbill script. Near the bottom under the title "Sideshow of Wonders" between Betty the Bearded Lady and The India Rubber Man was the name Tap-Dancing Three-Legged Timothy.

"There, Watson is an end to the mystery of Timothy Langdon's whereabouts lo these many years."

"He turned his liability into an asset," I said.

"In more ways than one, I fear."

"One thing still puzzles me, Holmes."

"What would that be?"

"Why Timothy Langdon used shoes from Dobbs's shop."

"Expedience, my friend. He was able to travel lightly and unobtrusively as a woman carrying nothing more than a handbag. Knowing Dobbs was a cobbler, Langdon figured rightly that there would be shoes on hand to fit his purpose. And it is well that he did; otherwise we may have been much slower to see the true picture.

There was a knock at the door. I opened it to find Charlie Wiggins. "May I come in, sir?"

"Come in, lad," I said.

He stood for a moment turning his cap in his hand. "I come to thank you, Mister Holmes, and you, Doctor for helping my Uncle and his friend."

"You are quite welcome, Mister Wiggins. I trust they both are doing well."

"Indeed they are, sir. Mister Cuthbert says he will help them set up a business that will allow them to live decently and they won't have to beg on the streets no more."

"Excellent," Holmes said.

"And, Doctor," Charlie said, "This is for you." He handed me a shilling. "I thank you, sir, and this is for you as well." He placed a small envelope in my palm. Charlie bowed to us both. "Now if you'll excuse me." He turned and left, closing the door behind him.

"Quite the young gentleman, isn't he, Watson?"

"I suspect he's been under Mrs. Hudson's tutelage." I opened the envelope to find a gold regimental fob I'd lost from my watch chain many months before.

"What is it, Watson?"

"Evidence that your estimation of young Charlie's rehabilitative state is absolutely accurate."

The End

A Tale of Veterans

The first book I ever checked out of the Uniontown (Pennsylvania) Public Library was a collection of Sherlock Holmes stories by Sir Arthur Conan Doyle. I was six years old and was immediately hooked.

Consequently, I had to take a deep breath and think a while before writing a Sherlock Holmes story, partly because of my reverence for the original stories and partly because I wondered whether I could do the characters and the body of stories justice. I took the plunge and the result is "The Adventure of the Three-Strand Garotte."

In his attention to Holmes and Watson, I believe Doyle overlooked a rich vein of plot to be found among the Baker Street irregulars. Each of these boys could be a story unto himself. So I began the "what-if?" chain of reasoning. What if one of the Irregulars came to Holmes for help? How would Holmes react, particularly if it might put him at odds with the authorities? I believed that Holmes, being the honorable man that he is, would side with one of his operatives over Lestrade and the Yard.

I also give Mrs. Hudson a little extra attention by showing a fondness in her for the Irregulars. I can't imagine that the kindly woman she is she would ignore the boys and not be concerned with their welfare.

The plot took many twists and turns and revisions before it ended as you see it here. As is the case with most of my stories, I have an ending in mind as well as a beginning and work from both ends to the middle. Sometimes it is like building a bridge from opposing banks; sometimes things don't exactly jibe with each other, but when it works, it is the magic of writing fiction.

The story of the second Afghan campaign was inspired by Rudyard Kipling's haunting lines:

When you're wounded and left on Afghanistan's plains,
And the women come out to cut up what remains,
Jest roll to your rifle and blow out your brains
An' go to your Gawd like a soldier.

The plight of Wiggins and Canty as disabled veterans was inspired by friends and relatives of mine who have come back from a number of wars to lives that were less than they deserved.

I hope "The Adventure of the Three Strand Garotte" touches a nerve in everyone who reads it. In many ways it has relevance to our world and the way America is going today.

Sherlock Holmes

in

"The Betrayal"

By
Erik Franklin

*B*efore you read this tale, I must preface the adventure by saying that this story represents possibly the darkest chapter between Holmes and myself. Though I have been decidedly cross with my friend on many occasions (as any sane person would be apt to do with Holmes), I had never outright opposed him... until this case entered our lives. As always, I have related the events as they have happened, though Holmes has his opinion that my perception of events was skewed by my emotional state at the time. Nevertheless, I had previously sought special permission from Holmes before I had any more of our adventures published (which I can assure you there are still a great many). It was to my great surprise when I received a letter from Holmes asking me to publish this specific adventure. Though his reasons are entirely his own, I never wished for this story to be revealed. I reluctantly followed his request accordingly and now present you with this case from many years past.

*T*his tale began much like many of our other investigations: at our flat in Baker Street. Having finished reading the morning paper, and already growing weary of hearing Holmes scratch mercilessly on his long suffering violin, I decided to challenge my friend with a little hypothetical conundrum that I had been toying with for some time. Though it seemed like an amusing diversion at that moment, I had little idea of how pivotal this conversation would become in the days to follow.

"As interesting as your theory is, old fellow, it is simply impossible." Holmes stated as he raised his eyebrow and nestled the violin against the crook of his neck. I had interrupted him with a notion of something that could be virtually impossible to solve: the motiveless murder.

"But think Holmes," I protested "most criminals, no matter how clever, cannot help but reveal some psychology through their crimes. You would never anticipate that Professor Moriarty would accost a man in an alleyway merely to rob the poor fellow. Moriarty has far too great a criminal mind for such a menial crime! His psychological makeup would not allow it."

"That is true... and if Moriarty were to commit such a crime, I would expect that the offense in question would be but a small part in a larger enterprise." Holmes said. By the expression on his face, I judged that he was hypothetically pondering what Moriarity's endgame would be if such an event was to take place.

"Yes, but as I was saying Holmes, we know all of that because of Morarity's psychological temperament. Now, say a man or woman murders another person randomly. Scotland Yard will be unable to catch the murderer because when they do their usual investigation—you know this well, Holmes, who were the victims friends, acquaintances, enemies and the like—they will find nothing of consequence!" I said defiantly. I watched Holmes' eyebrows narrow as he tapped the bow of his violin against the strings gently, as he was in the habit of doing whenever he was deep in thought.

"And this is assuming, of course, however impossibly, that there is no direct physical evidence or witnesses linking the murderer to the victim?" Holmes asked.

"For argument's sake, yes. I think it would be the perfect murder." I said, feeling triumphant. Holmes seemed genuinely stumped, and I enjoyed watching his face contort ever so slightly while trying to solve my challenge. A few moments later, to my great dismay, Holmes began to play his violin again as a tiny smile formed at the corners of his mouth.

"It was a very interesting concept, old fellow, but it is entirely impossible."

"How so?" I said, feeling annoyed.

"For the very reason, my dear Watson, that there simply cannot be a motiveless murder. Crime cannot be committed without motive." Holmes was content to let the matter drop at that, as the notes of his violin began to permeate the air. I, however, was far from done with this discussion.

"Listen here, Holmes," I began, "let us say that I grab my revolver, walk out the door, and shoot the first person that I see right between the eyes! What is my motivation? I do not know the person, so have no grudge against them or a reason to kill them! I would never be suspected!"

Holmes, with his usual coolness, turned to me with a smile. He stopped playing to say, "Watson, assuming that we ignore the fact that the bullet in the man or woman's head would match the same caliber as your revolver, and that you live in extremely close proximity to the crime scene, and that you would have shot the poor soul in broad daylight with witnesses lining the street...you would be caught red handed...and your motive is quite obvious."

"But as I have explained, Holmes, I did not know the victim! I had nothing to gain by his or her death. What motivation could I have?" I protested, flabbergasted.

"Quite simple, I'm afraid. Your desire to prove that there could be a random, motiveless murder *is* your motivation. It is quite elementary, my dear Watson."

I paused for a moment, as I often find myself doing when Holmes presents me with a bafflingly simple and obvious solution to a complex problem. My face must have revealed my disappointment, for Holmes allowed himself to express a brief moment of compassion on my behalf.

"That is not to say that it would *not* be an interesting problem..." Holmes said, softening the blow, "...but thankfully evidence and scientific observation speaks more to a jury than the random conjecture regarding the state of the human mind."

"What you refer to as conjecture does indeed have a basis in fact, Holmes." I chided him. At that moment, there was knock at the door and I rose to answer it.

"It's Inspector Lestrade, no doubt," Holmes said as he played on. I had ceased to be amazed by this particular feat of deduction some time ago, for Lestrade's heavy footfalls and belligerent, brutish knock was distinctive enough even for me to recognize by now. I opened the door and was greeted by the drooping, frustrated face of Inspector Lestrade. We exchanged casual greetings, but I knew that the Inspector was not here for a social call. Holmes set his violin aside and motioned for Lestrade to sit down.

"Good morning, Inspector Lestrade. Please take a seat."

"Yes, good morning. Well, here's the thick of it, Holmes..." Lestrade began. He was always a bit reluctant to bring Holmes in on a case. Lestrade feared that his dependency on Holmes would damage his reputation as a competent detective. However, Holmes and I are the souls of discretion itself, with Holmes insisting that Lestrade and Scotland Yard receive the credit for cases that have been solved by Holmes and yours truly (an arrangement I have never agreed to, which is why I pen the true accounts of our adventures). Nevertheless, I could not help but feel Lestrade's unease with this arrangement "...there's been a murder, a gruesome one at that, and I think you'll find this one interesting."

"Really? How so?" Holmes inquired as he placed his pipe in his mouth while searching for a match.

"Well, you might find it a curiosity to note that the victim was already dead!" Lestrade said, eager to see our reaction. For my part, I looked to Holmes with what I imagined to be an expression of mild confusion.

Holmes' brow lowered and his eyes narrowed. Overall, he was not given to flamboyant displays of emotion.

"Already dead? I'm afraid that you'll need to clarify, Lestrade." Holmes said as smoke rose from his pipe and began circling around his head.

"Well, the thing is, Holmes, the victim was a woman see, working as a waitress at the Bradley Inn..."

"That's not too far from here..." Holmes noted "... I did not mean to interrupt, please continue."

"Well, as I said, she was going about her job, working her tables and the like, when she goes outside to fetch something. One of the patrons is observed following her out the door, where he proceeds to stab her in the back and then flee the scene!" Lestrade explained.

Holmes' expression had not changed, though I certainly felt repulsed by the chilling tale. Shifting in his seat, Holmes took his pipe out of his mouth and pointed it at Lestrade as he talked.

"This case sounds intriguing...you had mentioned that she was "already dead"?"

"Ah yes, that is the queer thing, Holmes. You see when the coroner made his report, granted the cause of death was not difficult to determine, he discovered that the name of the woman, Alice Maybell, belonged to someone else...who had died at the age of four. According to her employer, the manager at the Bradley Inn, she gave him the very same information that was on the dead girl's birth certificate." Lestrade said, watching for Holmes' reaction. My friend, for his part, shifted an eyebrow...which I interpreted as a sign of growing interest in the murder.

"An alias... interesting..." another puff on his pipe. "I suppose that no one was able to catch a glimpse of the assailant's face, correct?"

"Yes, you're right about that Holmes. Apparently the man wore an overcoat with the collar popped up and um..." Lestrade broke off as he pulled a notebook from his pocket and flipped to the appropriate page "... see here, according to the waitress, he ordered a black coffee and nothing else. When we got to the scene, we noticed that it didn't look like he drank much of it, or even touched it for that matter."

"Popped up collar to conceal his identity, did not touch his coffee...a woman with an alias...all of this strongly suggests premeditation. Did Alice Maybell happen to converse with her murderer?" Holmes asked. This last question convinced me that Holmes would take the case. Perhaps it was the mystery within the murder that intrigued him. My friend stood up and began to pace the room as Lestrade followed him with his eyes.

"No, he only talked with the other waitress there, Tilly Fawkes. We questioned her earlier. Simple Yorkshire girl, she remembered that the man ordered black coffee. She was quite shaken up, I must say," Lestrade said, scratching an itch on the back of his neck.

"Black coffee...a simple order that even the most inept waitress would correctly remember. No sugar or cream to ask about or bring to the table... an easy dismissal on our clever murderer's part. Poor Tilly would never have had time or the inclination to catch sight of his face." Holmes said as he threw his coat over his arm and reached for his hat. His pace accelerated, and he turned to me with an eager, yet impatient expression. "Come Watson, get your hat and coat. You have a body to examine, for the game is afoot!"

"But it's already been examined," Lestrade protested as he rose from his chair to follow us. "I can give you the coroner's report!"

"It has not been examined by Watson though," Holmes said, giving me an affectionate tap on the arm. Expressions of humanity and warmth from Holmes are, as you should know by now, a rarity, so when one comes along you hold onto it for dear life.

Stepping into the morgue, one is always greeted by the odor of decay, chemicals and a perpetual chill that creeps along your skin. During my time as a medic in the British army, I had become accustomed to dealing with gruesome sights and horrific sensations, so the morgue had little effect on me. Holmes was his usual self, interested in the case at hand, not letting his external environment affect his internal judgment.

The body of Alice Maybell was laid on the table, her face frozen in a state of shock and horror. I felt a deep swell of pity for her, knowing that the last thing she felt was her assassin stabbing her mercilessly in the back. Still, I had to put my feelings aside and begin my examination. Though Holmes, no doubt through his remarkable powers of observation, could likely make a similar diagnosis to my own, I appreciated it greatly that he differed to me in matters such as this.

"The victim...Alice Maybell...supposedly..." I added, remembering that this was an alias. "By my estimation, the victim is approximately in her late thirties to mid forties...a liberal application of facial makeup has had the unfortunate side effect of seemingly advancing her age rather than detracting from it." I observed as I saw that she made a great deal of effort to conceal any wrinkles or blemishes.

"Yet another attempt at a disguise, however subtle," Holmes stated. "Perhaps, now that you have examined her face, we can remove the make-up and reveal the true woman underneath?"

"Certainly, Holmes," I said.

I did so with the utmost care not to bruise or damage the skin. I was so completely absorbed in my task of removing the layers of cheap makeup that I failed to properly look at the woman's face until I had completely stripped the skin clean of caked-on powder. When I finally looked at her, I let out an audible cry.

"Great Scott, Holmes!" My voice echoed inside the small, tiled room. Holmes looked with great interest and alarm, first at me, then at the corpse.

"What is it, Watson?"

"Holmes, I know this woman! We were assigned to the same Army hospital when I was serving in the war I had spoken with her on many occasions..." I said, shuddering. Of course she was older now, and her hair was dyed black (it was blonde during the war). I had recognized her by a collection of small beauty marks located below her right eye... previously concealed by the makeup.

"Yes, and what is her name?" Holmes said urgently.

"It...it was still Alice...I believe. Our acquaintance did not continue be-yond the hospital." I was struggling to remember.

"So we can assume that she was living under a different name for a number of years...right, well continue, Watson. I need to know more."

I then had the thoroughly unpleasant task of examining the knife wounds inflicted on this poor woman. They were deep and deliberate. "Judging by the bruising around the wounds, the killer drove the blade in with great force. The multiple stabs to the front and back tell me that the killer likely approached her from behind to deliver the first attack, and then spun her around to finish her off. The killer took an awful risk by turning her around. What if Alice survived? She would be able to identify him."

"He wanted to see her eyes as she died...to him, it was a risk worth tak-ing," Holmes said in a muted tone as he studied her terrified expression. Then he looked back at me, "Watson, what kind of knife would you say inflicted wounds such as these?"

I leaned in and examined them. "I would say a narrow blade, almost like that of a rapier with a tip designed to penetrate flesh by means of a stabbing motion. Though the edge of some of these wounds suggest that this blade has been sharpened as well."

"But not a rapier obviously...a military knife. Possibly a disgruntled soldier who decided to use his keepsake from the war as an instrument of murder. We know that Alice has a military background as a nurse, thanks to you. Perhaps she made enemies in the war." Holmes said with his customary rapidity. He was as sure as ever of his conclusions.

After learning all that we could from Alice Maybell's corpse, we left the morgue and made our way to the Bradley Inn.

The Bradley Inn was a charming, Tudor-style building located on an otherwise modern London street. The hand-painted sign above the door swung gently in the breeze, as Holmes and I made our presence known to the policemen who were posted outside the door. In fact, one of them was arguing with an older woman who was growing more unreasonable by the moment. She was a short, plump woman with strong arms and a hardened face.

"But the murder took place out there! Not in here!" she bellowed. "Do you know how much business I am losing because of you coppers hanging around here, scaring off the customers? There ought to be a law, I tell you!"

"I understand your predicament, but Inspector Lestrade has already explained to you the importance of preserving a crime scene..." but the poor officer was promptly interrupted.

"Some louse that Inspector was! All the murderer did what sit over there! I bet that this whole thing is a waste of time, and even if Sherlock Holmes himself was here he could not find a bleeding reason to close down my business for a whole day!"

"That remains to be seen, my good woman. I am Sherlock Holmes, and you are the proprietor of the Bradley Inn?" Holmes said with a gracious smile and an extended hand. I knew these gestures were for a deliberate effect, hoping to disarm the woman and allow Holmes to proceed with his investigation in relative peace.

"Yeah, I'm Judith, and I hope you're worth the wait." Judith said, though her voice had dropped from belligerent shouting to more controlled, yet still bitter, tones.

"I promise you, Judith, that as soon as I finish my examination of the table where the killer sat, the police will allow you to resume your service," Holmes said as he stepped past her and into the dining room of the Bradley Inn.

"If you work as fast as The Strand says, then I suppose I can manage to feed *a few* customers before closing." Judith crossed her thick arms, before turning to me with an obvious look of contempt. "And who's he?"

"I am Doctor John Watson—the one who writes the articles in The Strand about Sherlock Holmes," I extended my hand with what I am sure was one of the most insincere smiles I have ever offered anyone. She looked at my hand like it was diseased and refused to shake it.

The dining room of the Bradley Inn was delightfully quaint, mirroring the outside facade. As soon as the table was pointed out to Holmes, he went over and began his thorough observation. The table and chair were by the window, crammed next to another table and chair, and thus the space could only be occupied by one person. Since I felt it more important for Holmes to be there, I decided to question Judith, knowing that my friend would be listening.

"If you don't mind me saying, you do not seem to be very upset by Alice Maybell's death. Any particular reason why?" I enquired as delicately as possible, fearing that Judith would once again transform into a loud and disagreeable creature. To my great relief she just sighed.

"I knew that woman was trouble—just had a sense about her, like. She was qualified for the job and I needed somebody fast. I couldn't *not* hire her just because I didn't like the feeling I got from her. I always had a feeling that trouble would catch up with her in the end." Judith said as a look of sadness and fatigue crept across her hardened face.

"I see. How long did she work here?"

"About a year or so. Customers seemed to like her, and they would ask for her."

"Did you know if the killer asked for her by name?"

"No—but now that you mention it, something strange did happen. When you said *asking for her*, it reminded me of something that's been going on for the last few months." Judith put a finger to her mouth, her eyes suddenly focused with intense concentration. I saw that Holmes' ears had perked up, though he was intent on examining what looked to be minute fibers on the carpet.

"Well, the thing is, quite a few gentlemen had asked for her in the last three or so months. It was never the same gentleman, mind you. I mean, nothing unusual if a regular was asking for a waitress, but these were not regular customers. And let me tell you that I remember every repeat customer that comes into my establishment! Good for business it is! But it's been bothering me—why would they ask for Alice if they never been here before?"

"And you said it was never the same man?"

"No. The thing is see, these men started coming after she was gone for a month or two. She found out that her mother was sick and Alice needed time off to care for her like. I would be short a waitress sure, but I'm not totally heartless see? I gave her the time off." Judith said, and this was evidently a monumental decision for her. I gave what I hoped she took to be an approving nod, then I heard Holmes' footsteps approach us. He leaned in close to me so as not to be overheard by Judith.

"I have a picture of this man, Watson, but we're not done here." Holmes then turned to Judith, "Thank you, Judith, you have been most helpful, and if I may impose once more, I need to speak with Miss Fawkes. I understand that she served the murderer black coffee?"

"That she did, Mr. Holmes. Tilly's in the back room. She is very upset about what happened to Alice, they were friends, you know. I'll go and fetch her."

When Judith left the room, I asked Holmes "What did you find, Holmes?"

"To begin with, I examined the rug beneath the table. The man left prints from the soles of his boots. Heavy shoes, meant for a laborer, traces of mortar and dirt suggest a bricklayer. Wool fibers of the cheapest variety from his jacket hanging on the back of the chair indicate a man of limited means, and considering the sheer number of fibers, it is evident that the coat is falling apart with age. He must have either purchased it sometime ago or got it second-hand. His coffee had barely been touched, but when he did grab the cup, he left traces of dirt, again supporting the fact that he came from a work site. A slight spill from the coffee onto the saucer suggests that he was a rough man, not accustomed to appreciating the finer things in life. He was right handed, but appeared to be clumsy, as if holding the cup were difficult for him..."

"From the placement of his cup and saucer?" I ventured.

"Correct, but that is not the only bit of evidence to support this claim. I found several strands of ginger hair clinging to the tablecloth. I deduce that this man has a nervous habit of running his left hand through his hair, and no doubt he would be feeling anxiety, his mind focused on committing murder. Furthermore, we know that he is a military man not only from the blade he used, but because of his posture. Though his collar was popped up and no doubt he tilted his head down, the firmness of his feet on the floor and the depressions on the cushion of the chair tell me that he is used to sitting bolt upright, similar to you, Watson." Holmes continued.

Just then, Judith returned with Tilly Fawkes following behind her. Tilly's head was tilted downwards, her shoulders stooped. When she looked up at us, it was obvious that she had been crying for some time. A waifish, meek girl in her early twenties, Tilly slowly sat down in the chair I pulled out for her.

"Miss Fawkes, my name is Sherlock Holmes, and this is my friend, Doctor John Watson. We are assisting Inspector Lestrade with the investigation. I have a few questions for you." Holmes spoke gently to her.

"I told the Inspector all that I could remember..." Tilly said.

"Well, I'd like to hear it for myself, Miss Fawkes. You say that this man ordered black coffee, correct?"

"Yes, yes he did."

"And you did not see his face?"

"No...just a bit of red hair sticking out of his cap, but that's all."

"Do you remember exactly what the man said?"

"All he said was *black coffee*"..."

"Did you notice anything peculiar about his speech?"

Tilly thought for a moment, before her eyes widened. "Yes, yes I did as a matter of fact! He had a bit of an accent! Scottish, I think...but I don't know for sure..."

"Excellent. Did anything unusual occur when you returned with the coffee? Anything that would cause you to spill it?"

"No, sir. He did that himself—you see, he had this horrible scar on his hand. It looked like a zig-zag and his middle finger was missing. It made me shudder..." Tilly began to cry anew.

"Oh Mr. Holmes! Why didn't I think of this when the Inspector talked to me?"

Holmes took Tilly's hand in his. "Miss Fawkes, you had just seen the body of your friend and thus were in a state of shock. You have helped us immeasurably." Letting go of her hand, Holmes turned to me, and his face dropped when he saw my expression.

I felt that my world had abruptly stopped. I stood there in a stupor for some time, for I vaguely recall Holmes shaking me as he spoke with concern in his voice.

"Watson! Watson what is wrong with you?"

"I—think I know this man, Holmes. He is my friend, and he is no mur-

"Did anything unusual occur when you returned with the coffee?"

derer! It's impossible!" I declared. There had to be some terrible mistake.

"Who is he?" Holmes pressed.

"His name is Nicholas Bateson."

To explain my shock at this revelation, I must take you back to a distant time, to my past: the Battle of Maiwand to be precise, where I had received the wounds that had discharged me from service. It took place during the Second Anglo-Afghan War, and though it is officially known as a battle, in my opinion it should have been more accurately titled "The Slaughter of Maiwand". The casualties were mostly English, many of them friends. I later discovered that the Afghans too felt a bitter disappointment in the outcome of the battle, they had sacrificed far too much in order to gain a minor foothold.

Considering this, I was lucky to have been shot only twice, one bullet to the leg and one to the shoulder. I had mentioned both separately in previous stories, and am remiss that this has caused some confusion amongst my readers. Moments before the bullets penetrated my body, I was attending to a man with shrapnel embedded in his arm and hand. He had already lost a finger, and I was determined to save the rest of the mangled appendage. Thankfully, the majority of the metal was still protruding, and I carefully extracted it—as carefully as one can under fire.

"Just hold still, I'll have you patched up in a moment!" I assured the man. I looked at him to see if he had acknowledged me, and saw that he was nodding his head while he extended his injured arm with great difficulty. He had a thin, slightly pointed face with intelligent looking, sky blue eyes and short-cropped orange hair. To keep him mentally occupied during the procedure, I decided to engage him in some trivial banter.

"So, what is your name?" I said as I began to extract the shrapnel piece by piece from his forearm.

"Sergeant Nicholas Bateson." he said, straining the words through gritted teeth.

"You can call me John, John H. Watson." I said as I delicately plucked the largest bit of shrapnel from his wound. I moved to the smaller pieces, which I knew would cause him considerably less pain when removed.

"Distinguished name, isn't it? What does the "H" stand for?" Nicholas asked, breathing heavily and doing his best not to yell out.

"If we survive this, I will tell you." I said, trying to add brevity to the proceedings. I happen to dislike the middle name that my parents had foisted upon me, and I would take any opportunity I could to avoid revealing it. Recalling these events, I find it somewhat bewildering that I could have even cared about such an insignificant matter in the middle of combat.

While I worked on his arm, Nicholas kept an eye out for the enemy. He inspected his rifle with his free hand and cursed aloud. "I'm out, do you have any ammunition?" he asked.

"I am afraid not, chap. Just my kit."

Suddenly, I heard the sound of men yelling behind me and saw Nicholas' eyes go wide with fear. I wheeled around to see an Afghani soldier raise his Jezali rifle, pointing it at us! I felt myself leap in front of Nicholas to protect him. The Afghani's Jezali blazed with a thunderous roar and I felt an indescribable pain sear through my shoulder! This was followed, seconds later, by another similar sensation of agony coursing through my leg. Though it was the most excruciating physical pain I have ever felt, I did not succumb to shock, and thus was able to witness the events that followed.

As I was hurled to the ground by the force of the bullets piercing my flesh, I looked up to see Nicholas grab his knife with his uninjured hand and hurl it with great force at the Afghani soldier. The blade pierced the Afghani's heart and the man dropped to the ground, dead. In that instant, I realized that if I was able to recover from my wounds, then Nicholas Bateson would be my savior. He looked over me, examining the bullet holes. However, without medical knowledge there was little he could do for me.

"Help me patch you up! Talk me through it!" he pleaded.

"Too dangerous here—take me back!" I exclaimed while the battle reached a fever pitch.

"Some bloody medic you are!" Nicholas quipped. "Here I am with my arm blown to bits and I end up saving *your* life!" he said as he hoisted me onto his shoulder (I was considerably lighter back then).

"I'll put the shrapnel back in your bloody arm if you like!" I shot back at him. Though our attempts at banter may seem unusual to the reader, it was all we could do to keep calm and endure the slaughter that followed. Soon after, our forces were defeated in a battle that, as I stated earlier, was deemed "pointless" and "unnecessary" by the generals and military historians of the world.

Though my wounds have continually plagued me throughout my life, I had taken something positive away from that horrible war: a friendship with Nicholas Bateson. Soon after I was brought to the field hospital by

Nicholas, I contracted enteric fever and was later sent back to England following my recovery. Because of the poor state of health I was in, it was deemed that I could no longer fulfill my duties as a medic, and I was promptly dismissed. I will confess to being in poor spirits at the time, and the only pleasant moments came from the correspondence between Nicholas and myself. He had continued to fight and was able to stay for the duration of the Second Anglo-Afghan War, before returning to England.

Though readers may get the distinct impression that Holmes is my one friend on this earth, I must respectfully point out that I had kept in touch with Nicholas since we met years ago. We exchanged letters and met a few times a year for a game of cards and an evening out. Life had not been as kind to Nicholas as it had been to me, though. He still kept his rough-and-tumble manner, but I got the distinct feeling that he was never quite able to settle into an occupation. He had worked at various jobs over the years from carpenter to dockworker, then a factory worker, and lately, as of our last meeting, a bricklayer.

I related all of this to Holmes, who nodded with keen interest. After I had finished my tale, he told one of the police officers to report on my suspicions to Lestrade and get him to search every construction site for Nicholas Bateson. As for the two of us, we took a hansom cab to Nicholas' home, or at least the last address posted on a letter that he wrote to me. Glancing at Holmes, I could see his remarkable mind running at its full, feverish pace yet again.

"It is rather curious that you should be both acquainted with the victim and good friends with the murderer, don't you think, old fellow?" Holmes asked me, the tone of his voice betrayed a man clearly shifting puzzle pieces around in his head.

"A frightening coincidence I should think..." I said, and I saw Holmes' mouth open again, and I decided to talk over him, knowing what was about to come out "...and yes, I remember well what you and your brother say about coincidence..."

Holmes shut his mouth and gave a small shrug. Clearing his throat, he decided to change the subject. "Merely apprehending the murderer will not bring closure to this case, old fellow. There is still the mystery of who Alice Maybell actually was. As we had established earlier today, there is no such thing as a motiveless murder."

"I say, Holmes, do you think that she could have been a..." I began to theorize, but Sherlock held up his hand to stop me.

"Watson, remember what I told you about the dangers of speculation. It can take you down the wrong path rather swiftly, just look at poor Lestrade. Furthermore, we also need to solve the mystery of those questionable men who were asking after her for several months."

"That's right, Holmes! I'm afraid I quite forgot about them after I remembered old Nicholas." I said, not with a small degree of embarrassment. I was afraid that Holmes would give some comment as to my emotions interfering with our investigation. It was with some relief that I saw Holmes let my forgetfulness pass with a slight crook of his head.

"Understandable, dear fellow. Lastly, since Alice Maybell is a pseudonym, we can also assume that she is lying about having a sick mother. Where was she actually going? Once we make a search of Nicholas Bateson's place, I suggest that we move on to Alice's flat." Holmes said plainly, organizing the rest of our day for us.

"Right, Holmes." I replied. The truth was that I started to feel my stomach grow queasy when I looked out the window and saw that we were drawing closer to Nicholas's home. We had ended up in a rough section of the city, and I for one, was not familiar with it. Holmes strode out of the cab with his usual confidence, paying the fare and tipping the driver, who looked anxious to leave the vicinity as quickly as he could.

A feeling of pity overcame me as I looked around at the slum that my friend was calling his home. The area was dark and dreary, each surface seemingly covered in a layer of grit and grime. I could have sworn that I saw some of the infamous Baker Street irregulars scampering about, although Holmes made no notice of them as he headed down the street. A large, bald man reached an arm out to block our progress, and I noticed that he had a particularly sinister expression on his face as he grinned at us.

Holmes, of course, happened to be an expert in the European fighting art of Bartitsu, and while I cannot claim to be an expert, I will say that I know how to handle myself in close-quarters. The man slowly moved his arm down, and I somehow knew that Holmes was able to deduce everything about him from his ill-fitting grey wool coat to his worn out shoes.

"You don't look like you belong here." The man said maintaining that same, ignorant grin.

"Indeed, but nevertheless we need to be here, and perhaps you can help us. I wonder..." Holmes started in a business-like fashion.

"Yeah, I can help you. My name's Big Hugh, by the way. As I was saying it's downright dangerous around these parts, 'specially for a couple of rich dandies like you lot. Somebody might try to jump 'yah. I can make sure that don't happen to the likes of you." Big Hugh said, folding his arms and leaning back assuredly, confident that he was frightening us.

"And by that you mean, if we do not pay you, then you will attempt to pummel us and rob us yourself." Holmes said coolly, shifting his body, readying to counter any attack that the large man could attempt. I saw Big Hugh grow visibly confused for a moment, and then he finally realized that Holmes had anticipated his "business strategy".

"Well, uh... yeah something like that." Big Hugh said, whatever zeal he had put into his "sales pitch" had vanished.

"If you do so desire a physical confrontation lest I pay, may I first request that you remove your coat? It is a vital piece of evidence in an investigation I am conducting." Holmes said, pointing to the grey coat. Big Hugh looked at the coat, then at Holmes, with an expression that suggested he was emotionally attached to the garment.

"Not this coat! I was just given this coat as a gift! And let me tell you it gets bloody chilly around here at night."

I saw Holmes' eyes dart down to Big Hugh's hands. Holmes later told me that he noticed no signs of bruising on Big Hugh's knuckles, nor any recent cuts or scrapes on the inside of his hands. Holmes deduced that Big Hugh did not steal the coat. In this instance at least, Big Hugh was an honest man. Knowing this, Holmes pressed forward with another question.

"And the man that gave you this coat; is his name by any chance Nicholas Bateson?"

"The Sergeant? Well, sure, that's what we call him around these parts. He's a good man!" Big Hugh said the pride of their friendship showing on his face.

"Yes indeed, we are on our way to see him." Holmes replied.

"Hang on a minute!" Big Hugh said, with hostility and suspicion. "You said you was on an investigation! What are you investigating a good man like the Sergeant for?"

"I am a friend of his," I chimed in. I thought that mentioning the fact that Nicholas Bateson was the suspect in a murder would exacerbate an already tense situation. I was careful though, not to tell a lie, so my wording was creative. "You see, Nicholas, the Sergeant, saved my life in the war, and I helped patch him up during a battle. It has been a long while since we've seen each other, and I have no clue as to where he lives. I followed the address from the last letter he sent me..."

Big Hugh nodded. "Just like the Sergeant to be saving a man's life when he's supposed to be takin' 'em. Then you know he's a good man, too. I reckon I could show you the way, I know he's home now. Be pleased as pie to see you, I imagine."

We followed Big Hugh, and I could see that Holmes was pleased with me. Arriving at a squalid, tired looking apartment building, Big Hugh indicated the first floor with his thumb. "There he is. A man like him deserves better."

"Yes, indeed he does." I said as I opened the door for Holmes to walk through.

It was a depressing sight to say the least, and I felt ashamed that I lived in such ignorance as to the true state of affairs of a man whom I called "friend." Nicholas had always looked presentable at our luncheons, and it occurred to me that it must have taken him a great deal of effort to keep up appearances. I knocked on the door of his apartment.

"Yes? Be with you in a minute!" I heard Nicholas say. A sink was running, then became silent. A moment later the door opened, and he was taken by surprise upon seeing Holmes and me. "John! What on earth are you doing here? I say, what a pleasant surprise! Come in, come in!"

I noticed that he sounded nervous. Perhaps he was embarrassed by the untidy state of his flat, or it could have been that he was guilty of what Holmes suspected and was in the act of concealing or destroying evidence. In any case, he looked at Sherlock Holmes and his jaw dropped.

"Then—then you must be Sherlock Holmes! Ever since John told me that he became a writer, I haven't missed a single one of your adventures! It is an honor, sir!' John said, forcing Holmes into a hearty and vigorous handshake. "So... what brings you here? It's uh... unexpected, obviously."

"I..." I started to speak, but Holmes cut me off, perhaps thinking that my attachment to Nicholas would hinder the investigation.

"Mr. Bateson, I am here on an investigation, and have a couple of questions for you." Holmes said directly.

"Investigation? Into what?" Nicholas asked, his body becoming tense. He shot a glance at me, as if I would provide some kind of clarity.

"Did you know an Alice Maybell?"

"Well, yes. She was a nurse in the army, you remember her, John! I would see her from time to time at the Bradley Inn, where she works. She'd always take something off my bill, she is a good sort."

"Did you go there this morning?" Holmes asked.

"Yes I did, why? Did something happen there?"

As Nicholas was speaking, Sherlock looked over at some water droplets on the counter, and then moved over to see the trail end at a spot behind a stack of dirty plates. He gently reached his hand over and removed a military-issued knife. I saw Nicholas's face drop, and then he quickly put on a nervous smile.

"Well, that must make me look suspicious of something!" he said with a false laugh. I was in agony; my friend could not have looked more guilty if he had tried. "I was, believe it or not, giving the place a good tidying up when you called. You would be surprised to know how useful those knives are in the kitchen."

"Indeed... by the way, are you planning on purchasing a new coat?" Holmes asked.

"What? No...why?" Nicholas asked blankly.

"Because a man by the name of Big Hugh said that you gave your old one to him." Holmes said plainly.

"Well, it was getting old, and yes, now that you mention it, I have saved up enough money to get a new one. I thought I'd give the old one to Big Hugh, on account of him complaining about the cold." Suddenly, Nicholas rounded on me and started to grow angry. "Listen, what's all this about? You come here out of the blue and start asking random questions? Tell me what all of this is about right now!" he ordered, slamming his fist on the counter.

"You see it's..." I began, but Holmes interrupted me yet again.

"Quite simply, you were seen at the Bradley Inn this morning wearing that coat..." Holmes looked to the apartment door, and saw a pair of worn, heavy duty work-boots pushed against the wall "...and wearing those boots. Tilly Fawkes was your waitress. You ordered a black coffee..." Holmes trailed off, as if challenging Nicholas to contradict him.

"Yes, yes, it's all like you said. Then I left. I followed Alice outside and asked her a question, that's all. Then we said our goodbyes and I went home. I gave Big Hugh my coat, talked a little bit with him, then I started housekeeping." Nicholas explained, and I wanted to believe him. He spoke with such honesty and sincerity that I was almost contented to leave and offer an apology. Holmes, however, was not finished.

"What question did you ask her?"

"I—I asked her if she wanted to go to the theater with me tonight. It's a shabby little theater, but I have a friend who gave me two tickets and—You still haven't told me what this is all about!" Nicholas snapped.

"Nicholas—" Holmes said, "you're lying to us. You went outside, but

"You still haven't told me what this is all about!"

you did not ask Alice Maybell a question. Instead you stabbed her in the back and turned her to face you. You wanted to see her terrified eyes as you delivered the final blow!"

"What?" Nicholas yelled, and he turned to me. His eyes were pleading, desperate, and filled with rage and betrayal. "John, why are you doing this to me? I thought we were friends!"

"We are..." I said meekly.

"You know who Alice Maybell truly is. I suggest you tell us now and save everyone the trouble of a needlessly long investigation." Holmes said. I rarely knew my friend to become agitated when asking questions, the majority of the time he treated crime as an intellectual problem, not an emotional one. His method of questioning has always been one of cold, calculated delivery, designed to calm whoever he was questioning.

It had the exact opposite effect. Nicholas gave a yell and charged at Holmes! However, Holmes was ready and intercepted Nicholas's attempted tackle. I ran over as the two struggled, trying to separate my friends, but I only made the situation worse. As I shoved Nicholas off of Holmes, I used far too much force, and sent him crashing into a kitchen cabinet! I watched as Nicholas slumped over, unconscious. After I helped Holmes up, I rushed over to Nicholas and examined him and could see that he might possibly have a concussion...or worse.

"Holmes, get help!" I shouted at Holmes, who was off like a flash.

After admitting Nicholas to the hospital, Holmes insisted that I accompany him on his investigation of Alice Maybell's flat. I had wanted to stay with Nicholas, feeling responsible for his condition, but Holmes would not hear a word of it.

"I understand your sentiment," Holmes commented, "but the fact is that you could be of better use to me than sitting by your friend's bedside. He is in good hands, Watson." I reluctantly agreed and left the hospital, after giving the medical staff my professional opinion and instructions.

The search of Alice Maybell's flat turned up nothing immediately useful to our investigation. Holmes had discovered an address book, but no mention of another Maybell family member could be found.

"Just as I suspected... the sick mother was obviously a ruse." Holmes declared.

During his search, Holmes spent a great deal of time examining her shoes.

"Did you find something, Holmes?" I asked eagerly.

"Possibly. These are not the shoes of a waitress, or any other job that requires one to be on their feet. These look more suited for secretarial work, and they show signs of being worn recently."

"Well, I suppose it is possible that she went out from time to time." I suggested, playing my usual devil's advocate role. Holmes shook his head with a low murmur.

"These are too plain to be considered fashionable. These are practical and business-like—which brings me to the matter of Alice Maybell's occupation. Why is she a waitress, when she could find better paying employment as a nurse?"

"Perhaps she lost her stomach for the work, it can happen you know." I remarked.

"True—although I wonder—her lack of personal effects suggest a meager income, and I doubt that Judith is a generous employer. Alice could scarcely afford to take that much of a leave of absence—unless she was being supplemented by someone else or needed a job where she could leave without making much of an impact. An absent nurse would cause quite a stir, but not a waitress."

Indeed, Alice's flat was a very impersonal space. Holmes took it as a sign that she was used to moving around, and did not have time for personal effects or decoration.

We spent a cold evening at Baker Street, even though the room was warmed comfortably by the welcoming fireplace. I was having a difficult time speaking to Holmes, for not only had he summoned an ambulance, but also Inspector Lestrade. He told Lestrade that we had found our man. Nicholas had taken a horrendous blow to the back of the head, and it would be a considerable time before he awoke, and I could not feel any more guilty about the situation. I knew that all of the facts were stacked against Nicholas, and, upon reflection, I might have felt the same way as Holmes. The truth is, however, that I knew Nicholas and Holmes did not.

"But you know nothing of the man!" I protested.

"I know everything I need to convince a jury to hang him. I have facts, evidence. An innocent man would not attempt to flee." Holmes countered crossly.

"He might attempt to flee if he knew he was being framed! I know certain facts too, Holmes, and I know for a fact that Nicholas Bateson is not a murderer!"

"Why? Because he saved your life? That is not evidence, Watson, that is an emotional response of sentiment and gratitude on your part. People can be easily bought. Big Hugh said that Nicholas Bateson was a great man because he gave him an old coat. You assume that he is innocent, but remember how often I have demonstrated to our friend, Inspector Lestrade, that he cannot twist facts to fit a theory—I do not want you to make the same mistake old fellow." Holmes said firmly, and, I felt, dismissively.

"Be that as it may, you are forgetting that Nicholas is a man of honor!" I stated with the utmost conviction, feeling my blood begin to boil. The fact that Holmes was nonplussed by my emotional state made me even more furious.

"May I remind you, my dear Watson, that when you first encountered the man, you watched him kill an enemy soldier with a knife in a similar manner to which Alice Maybell was murdered. If you want to discuss psychology, then Nicholas Bateson has obviously demonstrated the capacity to kill."

"It was war, Holmes!" I snapped back. "You've never been at war! You may think, because of your superior intellect, that you are able to grasp everything, but there are certain things that you cannot fully understand!"

"Such as?" Holmes said, interested in hearing what I had to say. It was almost as if he was enjoying our discussion, as if it were a pleasant debate that amused him.

"Holmes...a person's character is revealed under pressure, and Nicholas did what he had to in order to save my life! I doubt that he wanted to kill that man, he simply *had* to! Keep in mind that he did not have to kill Alice Maybell!"

"So, he would kill because he had to. Watson, what if he felt that he *had* to kill Alice Maybell?" Holmes suggested eagerly.

"Holmes! My god, man! He had no reason to kill her! He asked her to the theater! It would be a motiveless murder which you yourself said was an impossibility!" I yelled at Holmes, and found myself waving my finger at him.

"Perhaps you do not know Nicholas Bateson as well as you claim. After all, you had no idea of the conditions that he was living in." Holmes said dismissively, "The look on your face told me a great deal, dear fellow, of your recent relationship with him."

Enraged, I found myself unable to speak. I said nothing to Holmes as I stormed out of the room. I heard Holmes call after me with a note of alarm in his voice, but I could not pretend to care. In truth, I did not know where I was going, all I knew is that I had to get away from Holmes and

clear my head. I needed to distance myself, and then, perhaps, I could begin working to clear the name of Nicholas Bateson. I owed him that much.

I found myself walking towards Nicholas's flat again. Though Holmes,
Inspector Lestrade, and myself had made a comprehensive search of the
flat, I was hoping against hope that there was something that we had
missed. When I reached the neighborhood, I came across Big Hugh once
again. He looked at me, but with an expression of concern draped across
his face.

"Ay', I saw a bunch of bobbies and docs around the Sergeant's place after
you and your friend left. Is he all right?"

"He's in the hospital now, bad concussion. He will recover, though it
make take some time..." I paused, and then a thought occurred to me
"Listen to me, Hugh. Nicholas—um—that is, the Sergeant—is in trouble,
major trouble. He's the prime suspect in a murder case."

"*Murder!*" Big Hugh repeated, his jaw agape. "He could never do a thing
like that, not on your life!"

"I know it, but the police do not, and neither, I am afraid, does my
friend, Sherlock Holmes. Maybe you can help me." As soon as I said these
words, I struggled to invent some way for Big Hugh to be of assistance, for
I had no idea where to begin. Looking back on these events, I wondered
that perhaps this is the same way that Holmes felt about me! But I digress,
because I quickly came up with a solution. "You said you know the area
well. Nicholas mentioned that he was going to the theater tonight. Do you
know which one he was referring to exactly?"

"I do indeed! And furthermore..." Big Hugh reached a grimy, thick hand
into his pant pocket and removed two yellow, threadbare tickets printed
on cheap stock. "...before those ruddy bobbies took my coat as evidence, I
managed to sneak these out of my pocket! The Sergeant must have forgotten that they were in his pocket when he gave the coat to me. I swear I was
gonna give 'em back, then the bobbies showed up and, well—"

I studied the tickets and noticed that on the back of one ticket there
was a woman's handwriting. "Meet me backstage" it said, and my curiosity
was immediately piqued. If Nicholas was already taking Alice to the show,
why would he be meeting another woman? Of course, I did not wish to
think ill of my friend and I did not want to assume that he was involved in
some sordid affair. Nevertheless, if I was to clear his name, I had to follow

this clue through to the bitter end.

"I guess that I will be going to the theater tonight! Lead the way, Big Hugh." I said, and the large man nodded, guiding me through the dark, grim alleys of the slum. I can say that I was truly thankful to have such a brute of a man as my escort, for no sooner had we begun our trek to the theater when I was accosted by a dark figure who thrust a cup in my face.

"Alms sir!" he pleaded, though his tone was decidedly aggressive. "Help a fellow traveler fill his empty stomach?"

"You'll be eatin' without any teeth if you don't take your 'ands off him, you wretch!" Big Hugh said, grabbing the beggar by the collar. Instantly, the beggar shrunk back and held up his hands as if to indicate that he meant no harm.

After that little display of force, the journey went smoothly.

I arrived at the theater, "The Grand Empire Theater", and that name could not have been more ill-fitting for the disheveled, crumbling, neglected building that stood before me. It was on its last legs so to speak, and there were only a few patrons outside waiting for the show to begin. The poster announced that abridged version of Shakespeare's "Richard III" was to premiere tonight. Big Hugh and I parted ways; no doubt he was not interested in seeing the bard performed. Upon presenting a ticket, I was handed a program, a sheet of paper that was cheaply printed out, and glanced over the actors' names listed. Several women were in the cast, and any one of them could have written the message on the back of Nicholas's ticket. I would have to investigate the matter and interview the actors before the stage curtain was drawn.

Heading backstage, I was stopped by an usher, but I presented my ticket to him, and he nodded with a knowing and rather wolfish smile. Evidently he assumed that I was there for an illicit liaison. I was a bit offended, but did not have time to address the matter. Nevertheless, I was thankful not to have to explain the real reason I was there, and I quickly began looking around backstage. The actor's changing room was separated only by a torn, moth-eaten curtain that was hastily strung across the center of the room, and I waded through a sea of cheap, dusty costumes and second-hand props. I stopped one of the actors who was a tall, handsome fellow, and I showed him the ticket. I asked him if he knew who had written the message.

His reaction was curious, for he seemed taken aback by the handwriting, but then quickly masked his emotions. "Oh, you'd be looking for Gertrude then," he said, before placing a hand against his mouth and shouting, "Gertie! Gentleman here to see you!"

A few moments after that, I saw an attractive woman who looked to be in her late thirties emerge from the woman's dressing area. She was heavily made up, and looked to be playing a character much older than her actual age. She wore a coarse, grey wig which was draped over her head and had penciled in dark lines on her skin to accentuate wrinkles. Her face was expectant at first, ready with an eager smile—and it dropped as soon as she realized that I was not Nicholas Bateson

"Who are you?" she asked, not bothering with tact or decorum.

"I am a friend of Nicholas Bateson—he asked me to meet you." I lied, thinking that if I had revealed too much, I would have caused her concern I would not have been able to discover any secrets that she might have held about my friend.

"Why would he do a thing like that?" Gertrude said, and it was clear that deceiving her would be more difficult than I had anticipated. I fumbled for an excuse.

"Perhaps he thought that I would enjoy the show and he suggested that we should meet. I am not exactly sure myself why I am here. He just told me that you two were old friends." I ventured, hoping that my guess was correct.

"I wouldn't say way back, but we are pretty close—platonic like, if you get my drift." she said, her tough exterior starting to fade. "Where is he?"

"Oh um—he is in the lavatory and will meet you shortly," I lied again. I felt my insides heat up and a cold sweat coming on. Holmes was a master at keeping his emotions in check, he could lie with the best of them. I, on the other hand, could not. Nicholas could only believably remain in the lavatory for a few minutes before she got suspicious, and I had to find out what I could. So far, I was failing.

"Listen, before he gets here, I'm rather concerned for Nicholas. He seems to be acting strangely as of late, saying that he has made an enemy of someone."

"Does he now?" she said, suddenly looking greatly interested in what I had to say. I felt that I had to press further, however I had to proceed delicately. Gertrude then asked, "Did he say anything about them?"

"Just that he was concerned for another friend of his. Alice—I think her name was. I am concerned for him; he is not acting like himself." I said feigning ignorance. The look on Gertrude's face change back to a cold, hard stare. This time, instead of merely being annoyed at my presence, it was if she despised my being there.

A door opened behind me and I jumped. I saw that it was that handsome actor from our earlier conversation, and Gertrude snapped at him tersely.

"Where the 'ell have you been, Ethan!" Gertrude shouted at him.

"Just in the loo, if you don't mind!" Ethan said, annoyed at being interrogated. I could feel everything within me sink; my deception was revealed by Gertrude's next question.

"Anyone in there with you?" she asked, hands planted firmly on her hips.

"No, why? Why are you interrogating me about this?" Ethan asked, exasperated.

"It's not you I'm interrogating, it's him," she said, nodding her head at me. "He knows about Nicholas and Alice." My back was to Ethan, and I heard him quickly reach into his coat pocket and then felt a small pistol swiftly being pressed against my back. I went to raise my hands but he leaned towards me and quietly growled into my ear.

"Don't raise them here, you idiot! Too many witnesses."

"We have ten minutes before the curtain rises. Take him to the storage room, nobody's using that. Find out what we need to know." Gertrude ordered, and I felt Ethan push the pistol even further into my back, ushering me towards another door at the opposite end of the room.

"I'll scream." I challenged, but I soon saw that this was an empty threat. The room was alive with activity. The actors performing their loud and flamboyant vocal exercises and this would surely drown out my cries for help. If I tried to run, I would risk putting the innocent actor's lives in danger. I judged it best to follow their demands. It was then that I realized I was quite alone, and I wished Holmes were with me. He could surely outwit these two ruffians and have the whole case solved just by looking at Gertrude's hands or some other trivial observation—I could not.

I was taken to a dark, cramped storage area adjacent to the room we came from. It was dim, with the only light source coming from a large window located near the ceiling. It illuminated the space just enough to reveal that the room was cluttered and packed to the brim with old props and costumes, a veritable maze of the theater's history. While Ethan held the pistol to my back, Gertrude entered the room and propped up a chair. She grabbed some rope from a nearby box. I soon found myself bound to the chair, with Gertrude and Ethan looking at me fiercely.

"Find out who he is and what happened to Nicholas! I'm on in a few minutes, so you'll have to do most of the work." She ordered, clearly the brains behind their sinister operation.

"Right. How should we kill him? It's not like the audience won't hear the noise of a gunshot!" Ethan demanded, clearly he was itching at the chance to eliminate me, considering me a loose thread to their plan.

Gertrude replied, "The battle scene ought to cover it up nicely. You'll be on stage then, Ethan, and I'll do the job. It'll give you plenty of time to find out what we need from him—this one doesn't look like he'll talk so easily." Gertrude made her way towards the door.

"I say, isn't it a bit dangerous keeping me here? Someone is liable to wander in at any moment." I was doing my best to think on my feet. The truth is, I was attempting to emulate Holmes' penchant for escaping perilous situations and terrible danger. I had noticed that in my chronicling of my friend's adventures that he was generally able to question the villain's logic and have them subliminally alter their plans to allow for his escape.

"No, no one comes in here anymore. Get started, Ethan!" Gertrude said as she closed the door. To my dismay, it was obvious that I had yet to master my friend's methods. Ethan turned to me, pistol at the ready. Before he got a chance to speak, I blurted out the first thing I could think of.

"Why did you kill Alice Maybell?" I heard myself say. Ethan recoiled, however subtly, not expecting that. Though I am not the expert at reading people that Holmes is, I felt that I had an answer: they had killed Alice and Nicholas was going to be next! By sending Nicholas to the hospital, I had inadvertently rescued him from the trap that the two had set.

"I ask the questions here!" Ethan snarled as he got ready to strike me with the butt of his pistol.

"If you do that, you risk rendering me unconscious, then how will you get your information?" I snapped, feeling a small rush of adrenaline coursing through my body. I began to recall certain feelings I had during the war, a mixture of sheer terror and the unmistakable, if utterly unfathomable excitement of danger. Then my mind drifted back to Nicholas as Ethan lowered the pistol, a look of contempt on his face.

"Fine. Then let's start with who you are. Keep in mind that I have been trained to detect deception, so don't think you can lie to me." Ethan threatened as he sat down on a crate across from me.

"From your phrasing you sound as if you are a spy of some kind..." I said.

"Answer my question. Who are you?" Nicholas asked and by the ex-

"Why did you kill Alice Maybell?"

pression on his face, I could tell that if I delayed any longer, it would have severe consequences for me.

"I am—a friend of Nicholas Bateson. He sent me here." I wondered if my half-truth could fool him. Indeed, the quest to save Nicholas had inadvertently sent me to this theatre, so I suppose that there was some truth in it. For whatever reason, Ethan seemed to buy it.

"What's your name!" Ethan growled.

"John...I was Nicholas's friend during the war."

"Why did he send you here?"

This was going to be a lie. I quickly remembered that Holmes had previously written a mimeograph (arguably his most popular) on the common characteristics and symptoms of liars. In order to pass under Ethan's intense scrutiny, I had to maintain a natural amount of eye contact, keep my voice even and plain, avoid stammering or stuttering, looking to the right, and then I had to say something that was within the realm of possibilities. However, I had been at the end of a gun barrel during the war, and having already faced that, I felt confident that I could survive this encounter, though God knows how I was going to escape. Thinking quickly, I decided to try to avoid answering him once more.

"Before I answer, I want to know why you killed Alice Maybell!" I demanded, trying to buy some time. "She was a perfectly innocent woman!" I thought that would bait him.

"Perfectly innocent..." Ethan said with disdain, falling for my trap. "We make a mistake and that devil of a woman persecutes us for the rest of our lives!" he yelled, breaking his calm demeanor. I could not risk him becoming enraged, for he could still impulsively shoot me. I played it safe for a moment.

"Nicholas told me that he would not be able to go to the show, but that it would be a shame if the tickets went to waste. He said you were friends of his."

"We sent the tickets all right, and pretended to be his friends sure—" Ethan scoffed "—he was probably on to us, and knew that he was sending you into the lion's den."

"I really have no idea what is going on," I confessed.

"I'm really sorry, old man, but you've seen too much and unfortunately for you, I let a little too much slip for you to live." Ethan sighed, though it was quite a theatrical one. I doubt that he was much of an actor.

"But Gertrude said for you to kill me during the battle scene! And if I know my Shakespeare, which I do, it's the climax of the play." I protested, grasping at any hope of prolonging my life.

"Doesn't mean I have to listen to you." Ethan stuffed a paint-stained rag into my mouth. He then exited the room, probably preparing himself for his stage entrance. I was left stranded and utterly unable to free myself. Gertrude was quite the expert on binding, it seemed.

Outside I could hear a hansom cab on the cobblestone street. It moved slowly, as if the driver was looking for passengers. Then I heard a voice that I recognized call out.

"Alms for the poor!" It was that beggar from earlier.

"Walk on!" I heard the cab driver shout at him.

"Whazzat you say!" I heard the beggar yell, whereupon a scuffle took place. I rolled my eyes and sighed. In a matter of moments I would meet my end in a dingy, dark storage room of a lackluster theatre, and some of the last sounds that I would hear were of two ruffians brawling. I thought of home, of Baker Street, and of Holmes. The last thing I did was storm out on him, and if I had known that my impulsive decision would have lead to this—I found myself wishing that I could have known to say goodbye.

"Police! Police!" the cab driver yelled, interrupting my thoughts. Evidently the beggar had got the better of him. I heard the sound of footsteps running away from the area. Moments later, I saw the beggar peek into the window, and I guessed that he was looking for a hiding place from the police. I moved around and made as much noise as I could, but I was unsure if he could hear my muffled screams. The beggar examined the room through the window, and then took off like a flash. There went my savior—

However, in my attempts to get the beggar's attention, I had loosened some of the joints on the chair. It was a rickety, old chair that had probably been used in many productions. Though I could not undo the ropes around me, I *could* break the chair. It was with tremendous effort and struggle that I eventually caused it to collapse, and was able to slip out of the ropes. As I got to my feet, I looked around, knowing that Gertrude would be arriving at any second.

Suddenly I heard someone outside the door! I looked for an improvised weapon, but it was too late. A streak of light cut through the floor and widened, revealing the silhouette of Gertrude standing in the doorway. We both froze, neither of us anticipating seeing each other like this. My first thought was to escape, but she was blocking my path. I grabbed the closest object to me, a prop candlestick, and hurled it at her. Despite being weighed down in a medieval gown, Gertrude still displayed great agility as she dodged my attack. The prop broke apart against the wall, and I rushed towards her. My attempt to tackle her was brought to a halt by Gertrude suddenly drawing a pistol on me. It was the same as Ethan's, so I assumed that he had given it to her.

"Please—reconsider this—" I said, instinctively putting my hands in the air.

"It's too late..." she aimed the pistol at my head.

I closed my eyes and heard the gunshot—but, by some miracle, I was still alive and unharmed! I opened my eyes to see Gertrude grappling with a tall man in a black suit, both vying for control of the pistol. The man wore an expression of fury on his face, and it took me a moment before I realized—

"Holmes!" I bellowed.

Gertrude was able to escape from Holmes momentarily and, seeing that she was trapped between us, she balled up her fist and struck me with quite a blow. The intense pain in my side suggested that Gertrude was no stranger to fighting. She was about to attack me once again, but Holmes grabbed hold of her and, using a bartitsu move, had Gertrude knocked to the ground in the blink of an eye. As the dust settled, I rolled Gertrude over, checked her pulse and looked into her eyes.

"She is alive, though you rendered her unconscious." I said to Holmes.

"Capital. Now, Watson, do you have any idea where the man is?" Holmes inquired as he assisted me in getting to my feet. Gertrude's blow had caused me tremendous pain, and I was grateful for the help, but I was determined to remain upright.

"Either onstage or backstage, I suppose."

"I had the police seal the exits, and I am afraid that we'll have to interrupt a rather turgid performance in order to catch him." Holmes said as we raced out of the room and towards the stage.

"How did you know where to find me, Holmes?" I asked, once again amazed at my friend's brilliance.

"All in good time, Watson, all in good time. First we need to apprehend the man. You will be able to identify him, and as soon as you spot him..." Holmes started as we stormed through the actor's changing room, though it was now vacant.

"Yes, Holmes, but how will we keep the actors safe?"

"We will improvise; at least there is not much of an audience."

Holmes and I walked onto the stage from the side, where an assistant director attempted to stop us, but Holmes dismissed him by saying that we were from the police. The stage was indeed unremarkable, with the dim, weak stage lights flickering from time to time. We had entered the production during the battle scene of Richard III, and the costumes looked cheap and threadbare. I saw Ethan and pointed him out immediately.

"Stop that man!" I yelled.

Ethan's eyes widened as he spotted Holmes and me. The other actors looked around, confused, some annoyed that we had interrupted their performance, but they were all too stunned to stop him. Holmes made his way towards Ethan, who, thinking quickly, held his sword up in desperation.

"My dear fellow, if you do attempt to kill me, at least dignify the attempt by not using a stage sword."

Ethan looked down at his weapon, and it was all the time that Holmes needed. He closed the distance rapidly, bringing his hand down on Ethan's wrist with a swift downward motion. The prop sword clattered to the ground as Ethan yelled out in pain. He attempted to punch Holmes, but like an expert pugilist, my friend slipped under Ethan's fist and struck him with his elbow, straight to his head. Ethan fell to the ground.

"Watson, keep an eye on the woman! You there," Holmes pointed to one of the actors "watch this man while I alert the police."

We found ourselves in Inspector Lestrade's office. I was worse for wear, Lestrade looked tired, but Holmes looked exuberant and refreshed, excited to tell us mere mortals the truth to the whole affair.

"To start with, the four main players in this case all had one commonality which clearly stood out: transient employment. As actors, Gertrude and Ethan could travel to wherever there was a theater and use that as their cover. Nicholas was able to work as a laborer virtually anywhere, and Alice could find temporary employment at any establishment, ranging from waitress to nurse if need be. The reason for this was elementary: all four were undercover agents, though they were working at cross purposes, with Alice and Nicholas on one side, Gertrude and Ethan on the other." Holmes said as he paced about. I saw Inspector Lestrade scoot forward to the edge of his seat, eager to hear more.

"That's all well and good Holmes, but let's start at the beginning of this whole bloomin' thing! That way I can get all the facts straight." Lestrade said.

"To start at the very beginning of this case, I'm afraid that we have to go to the Second Anglo-Afghan War, more specifically to the Battle of

Maiwand. You may recall, and of course I know that you already know this, old friend—" Holmes said, giving me a pat on the shoulder "—that the battle was an absolute disaster for the English. While many can find blame with military strategy or resources, there was another factor involved: counter-intelligence and double agents." Holmes expounded.

"And by that you mean, Gertrude and Ethan?" I asked, to which Holmes nodded. He took a moment to light his pipe before he continued.

"Yes, but British Intelligence was not too far behind them. The British knew that there was a leak somewhere, yet they did not want to alert the unknown double-agents and have them escape detection. Therefore, they recruited several agents of their own and sent them into the field to investigate."

"And that would be Nicholas and Alice?" Lestrade asked.

"Amongst several others I imagine, though by the time the war ended, I have no doubt that Nicholas and Alice had discovered who the spies were, so we can infer they were the only ones that knew." Holmes had a thoughtful expression stretched across his face as he blew a smoke ring and watched it gently vanish. "Gertrude must have been in the medical field for she knew precisely where to strike Watson to render him helpless."

"Yes, and quite expertly done—" I admitted feeling the effects of her punch to my ribs.

"Sorry, old fellow. I can only imagine that she would gather information from the wounded soldiers she treated, by weakening their resolve with various medicines at her disposal. Ethan was most likely a soldier near the front, along with Nicholas, where he would be able to sneak away and report his findings to his superiors." Holmes explained as he paced about the small room, pointing in the air with his pipe to illustrate certain facts.

"All right, all right! So who killed Alice Maybell then?" Lestrade asked, his impatience getting the better of him.

"Though I refer to Alice and Nicholas for convenience-sake, I must point out that Alice Maybell was not her real name, nor is Nicholas Bateson his real name respectively." Holmes clarified.

"Then who are they?" I asked, wishing to know the true name of the man I'd been calling my friend for many years.

"Alice's real name is immaterial, to be blunt," Holmes said "but Nicholas Bateson's true identity is Percival Andrews. For the sake of national security, we shall keep this to ourselves. Now, about the mater of Alice Maybell's murder—it was Gertrude who wielded the knife."

"What? A woman did that?" Lestrade said, aghast. "The witnesses described a man who looked just like Nicholas Bateson, not to mention that a woman is not likely to commit a murder in that fashion—poison is more their weapon of choice, in my experience."

"In my experience with women, they have stabbed, shot, poisoned, and invented many curious ways of murdering," I chimed in, feeling the need to jump into the conversation. Amongst these two, I think I held the higher opinion of the fairer sex.

"Indeed Watson," Holmes intoned, and from his expression I could see clearly that he was reflecting on his complicated relationship with Irene Adler (or "The Woman" as he preferred to call her). "Nevertheless, Gertrude did stab Alice Maybell to death, wearing a disguise that mimicked the distinctive wardrobe and hair color of Nicholas Bateson. The hair was obviously a wig, and the wardrobe and necessary makeup were procured from the theater where they were engaged."

"Hang on a minute!" Lestrade interrupted, thinking he had found a contradiction in Holmes' explanation. It has forever amused me to no end when Lestrade did this, and I think Holmes enjoyed the opportunity to demonstrate how complete his thought process was. "What about the witnesses who saw Nicholas Bateson ram the knife into her?"

"They saw a person with a threadbare coat and with red hair stab a woman. You see, Gertrude and Ethan had planned to murder both of them, but thought that it would be too risky to leave two corpses behind. One of them, and I have a feeling it was Gertrude, decided it was better to frame Nicholas instead. It would be impossible for Nicholas to tell his side of the story to the police without breaking his cover, which was why he chose to attack me instead of talk." Holmes expounded. "You see, Lestrade, Nicholas did follow after Alice. After working closely together for many years, the two had determined that Gertrude and Ethan were indeed the double-agents they were after. They were confirming their plans to rendezvous at the theater and apprehend the two."

Holmes cleared his throat and continued. "Nicholas had befriended Gertrude and Ethan earlier, I would estimate when they started rehearsals for Richard III. Researching Nicholas's background, I found that he was employed at a construction site located close to the theater. Obviously he made some pretense of becoming friends with Gertrude, for several of the men at the site recall seeing them conversing. No doubt both parties pretended that they were unaware of the ruse. The ticket was a trap, one to which dear Watson stumbled—but back to the murder of Alice Maybell. Gertrude, waiting in a nearby alley, watched as Nicholas and Alice spoke, she then waited for him to walk away, and then committed the foul deed."

"Any explanation as to why all those men were asking for Alice at the inn?" I chimed in.

"Yes. That was Ethan, in various disguises. It would have seemed suspicious if the same strange man kept asking for Alice. As for Gertrude, military records show that she and Alice had worked together in the same medical tent during the Second Anglo-Afghan War. Therefore, no matter how expertly the stage makeup was applied, Alice would have recognized Gertrude. As it happened, Alice was on a mission abroad for three months, leaving Nicholas to pursue the two here. They would have killed both of them sooner if Alice was not abroad." Holmes said.

"And killing Perc—excuse me—Nicholas would have confirmed Alice's suspicions." I ventured.

"Precisely, Watson. Being professional agents, Nicholas and Alice would have been in constant contact. His sudden silence would confirm their guilt." Holmes nodded approvingly.

Lestrade stood up, shaking his head. "We've been at this for hours and I still don't know what's going on exactly, but it sounds to me like we've freed an innocent man and put two traitors behind bars. Correct?"

"Elementary, Inspector Lestrade!" Holmes said to him before turning to me. "Nicholas is being released soon, Watson, if you want to speak with him, you should hurry." I did very much.

Outside of Scotland Yard, I caught up with my friend Nicholas. I found the entire situation to be awkward and uncomfortable. His injuries aside, Nicholas appeared tired, in pain, and he wore a weary smile. For a moment we did not speak, then I broke the silence.

"I'm sorry..." I said, indicating the bandage on the back of his head. Nicholas laughed.

"I always said that you were a lousy doctor—" Nicholas said with a tired smile "—but a good friend. Thank you, John."

"You're welcome—It was nothing really." I felt compelled to say. We were silent again, but I was determined to keep talking. "So—you're an agent then?" I asked, for want of something more intelligent to say. Nicholas laughed and looked around.

"Yes, well, I was. I swore that I would retire after this assignment, and I think I'll stand by my words. Not sure what I'm going to do now, but I think I'll be happy once I put the past behind me."

"That sounds like a grand idea—" I said before one more thought occurred to me "So do I keep calling you Nicholas? You did say you were going to retire?"

"I like the name Nicholas, it suits me," he said with a shrug. "Tell you what, since we are talking about names, and now that you know my real name—tell me what the "H" in John H. Watson stands for. You never did get around to that."

I paused before answering, "I will be seeing you—Nicholas." I said walking away from him. I suppose that I liked the idea of some mystery between us—

Holmes looked uneasily at me as I read the evening post. I had not spoken a word to him since Nicholas was released from jail, and my silence was clearly bothering him. Though I had calmed somewhat, I was still angry at Holmes for accusing Nicholas of murder. Clearly, Holmes did not value my opinion as much as he claimed.

"You know, Watson, you are entirely responsible for your friend, Nicholas's, release," Holmes said, watching me like a hawk for a reaction.

"Am I now? I was about to get myself killed if you had not shown up," I countered.

"Be that as it may," Holmes said, never one for false praise, "it was your instinct about Nicholas Bateson that set you on the right course. In fact, I suspect that you were instrumental in catching the traitors, because they were ready to flee the country."

"You did the catching, Holmes." I said glumly.

"Watson, perhaps your best trait is your loyalty to your friends— I should know." Holmes said as he slowly crossed the room to his desk. "Though you did not heed my advice and ignored facts to support a theory, you did manage to find the truth instinctually. For you, Watson, a man's character is evidence enough, and though it may not be rooted in science, there appears to be something to it after all."

"A simple deduction, Holmes," I said, starting to warm to my friend once more. "We had already established that there could not be a motiveless murder, and Nicholas had absolutely no reason to kill Alice Maybell. Therefore, he could not be the killer, despite whatever evidence there was."

"I agree with you, Watson and unfortunately my timing could not have been worse for these—" Holmes said as he produced two tickets from the desk drawer, "I bought these tickets some time ago for the Royal production of Shakespeare's Richard III for tomorrow. However, I doubt that you are in the mood to go—" my friend said, looking nervously at me.

I smiled in spite of myself, for Holmes never could stand seeing me upset (particularly at him) for long. Knowing that he was trying to do his best to win back my affections and loyalty, I would feel downright guilty had I not accepted.

"It sounds delightful, Holmes—only I do not wish to meet with any of the actors, you understand."

Holmes smiled and clapped me on the shoulder.

"It's settled dear fellow; we're going to make an evening of it tomorrow!"

"Throw in dinner and I'd say that we're in for a fine time." I added, pressing my luck.

"Watson, I was begging for alms but a few days ago—what makes you think I can afford dinner?" Holmes retorted. I looked upon him incredulously. My friend and I shared a laugh for the first time since this case began. "You see Watson, I had to trail you without being spotted, and since you've never been able to detect one of my disguises, I knew you would not give me away. I'm afraid that I was forced to attack that poor cab driver in the hope that he would summon the police. That taken care of, I then had enough time to save your life. It was simple, really."

I rolled my eyes as I sipped my tea.

The End

Accepting the Challenge

Sherlock Holmes can easily be considered one of the greatest and most enduring fictional characters ever created. His stories are still thrilling today, and the entertainment industry keeps reinventing him over and over again to attract new audiences. However, and this is most important, the character never changes. Holmes is still brilliant and cold, Watson human and impulsive. To get the opportunity to add to Holmes' near endless library of stories was frightening, to say the least. I could never top Sir Arthur Conan Doyle, that is impossible.

Instead, I did what I generally attempt to do when approaching a well-established franchise or character: I look for the unexplored. Now, I doubt that I am the first writer to explore Watson's military past, but when I was researching what little was revealed in Doyle's stories, I then proceeded to read up on the Second Anglo-Afghan War. The more I read about the war, I suddenly realized that my antagonists could be spies, and suddenly the entire story (well, most of it) seemed to fall into place.

Ron had accurately told me, when I pitched him the story, that it would be very difficult for me to have Watson find something that Holmes missed. How right he was! Both were men of action, but I had a feeling that Watson would be more drawn to psychology (considering that he is a writer) than Holmes would be. Though I put this legendary duo at odds with one another, it was interesting to see how Holmes and Watson would reconnect (and it took me awhile to figure out the climax of the story as well)!

Though I tried to draw primarily from Doyle's works, I could not resist putting in a touch of my favorite Holmes film series: the Basil Rathbone series. I enjoyed that portrayal of Lestrade the most, and hope that readers can hear the actor, Dennis Hoey, saying his lines in the story. I also patterned Holmes slightly on Rathbone, because, for me, he is the definitive Holmes. However, I saw my Watson as Ian Hart, because, though I enjoy Nigel Bruce, I felt that he was a truer Watson to Doyle's material. Whenever I write, I always picture my dream movie cast reading the parts aloud, and if the dialogue sounds natural to them, I feel I then have it.

The theater and greenroom experience was taken from my own background in high school theater. It was pleasant to relive those memories and sensations while I wrote, though thankfully we were not holding hostages in the storage room (—I think). Speaking of school, I would like to dedicate this story to Mr. McCarthy, my 8th grade English teacher, for he was the one who gave me my first Sherlock Holmes story to read: "The Adventure of the Speckled Band". Thank you, Mr. McCarthy!

ERIK FRANKLIN - is a writer/actor/filmmaker based in Seattle. Recently graduating with honors from the Art Institute of Seattle in film production, he is the co-President of Franklin-Husser Entertainment LLC. He is working on two upcoming feature films for his company: A dinosaur action film "Revenge of the Lost" and the martial arts comedy "3 Morons Fighting Ninja". You can give the company page a "Like" at: https://www.facebook.com/pages/Franklin-Husser-Entertainment-LLC/290795021042906.

Drawn to pulp fiction through his love of history, literature, and Americana, he is grateful for Airship 27 Productions giving him the opportunity to write his first story. He looks forward to writing more adventures!

Sherlock Holmes

in

"The Adventure of the Picked Pocket"

By
Fred Adams Jr.

On any given afternoon, Sherlock Holmes may be found engaged in anything from comparing the textures of clay from eight different regions to reading the Malleus Maleficarum in its original Latin, so it was no surprise when I returned from lunch at my club to find him standing on his head, heels against the wall of our study and his elbows and head forming a tripod.

"Holmes," I said, "What the devil is this about?"

"Research, Watson. I am attempting to determine how long I can remain conscious while I am in an inverted position."

"Well, I'm certain that will come in handy if you're ever hung by your heels."

"Watson, one never knows when he might be in a spot in which…"

A knock at the door interrupted his rationale. I opened it to find Mrs. Hudson on the landing. "Doctor Watson, there's a gentleman here to see Mister Holmes." She whispered, "I asked his name and he just said, 'Smith.' No Christian name, no card, just Smith."

Holmes jackknifed his feet to the floor and righted himself. "Please send him up, Mrs. Hudson."

Because of our pursuit of unusual matters, we were frequently visited by unusual people, and a visitor who identified himself simply as Smith was no more out of the ordinary than Holmes standing on his head. He was shouldering into his smoking jacket as the mysterious Mister Smith passed through the doorway.

Smith looked to be in his forties. He was a tall man, I would judge six feet even, and he weighed about thirteen stone. He was lean rather than thin, and seemed fit. He wore a tweed chesterfield coat and a bowler which he removed and held with both hands in front him as if it were a shield. His chestnut hair was thick and dark as was the drooping moustache that framed his mouth.

"I am Sherlock Holmes. This is my associate Doctor Watson. You are Mister Smith?"

"Smith will do for the moment." He turned his hat by its brim between his thumbs and fingers. His speech was good but had a forced precision to it, like a street urchin educated in public school.

I offered him a chair and the three of us sat by the hearth. Smith didn't take off his coat.

"Tell me, Mister Smith," said Holmes, "when did you give up boxing?"

Smith's head twitched and he stared at Holmes. "What?"

"Your hands." Holmes pointed at them with the stem of his pipe. "Your knuckles are scarred, and the third finger of your left hand has a bulge that must make getting your wedding ring on and off rather difficult. That suggests a finger broken and healed badly. None of the scars is fresh, so you haven't used your fists for some time. I would also say that you were quite good in the ring, judging by the fact that your brow is scarred as well but by no means as severely as your hands.

"You are a boxer and a formidable fellow, yet you are no longer in the ring. You are not a policeman, otherwise you would have identified yourself as such immediately. Your clothing leads me to think that you are one of two things, a professional thug for some criminal figure or a bodyguard to someone of importance. Your manner of speech and comportment suggest the latter."

"Your reputation is well deserved, Mister Holmes. I am the latter, although 'bodyguard' is perhaps a sterner term than I'd use."

"And your employer…"

"Has nothing to do with this."

"I see." Holmes reached forward and rattled the grate with the poker. "How may we be of service?"

"It's an old story, Mister Holmes," Smith said, leaning forward in his chair. "I've done something foolish, as most men will at one time or another."

"This foolish thing you have done, does it involve a woman?"

Smith nodded. "Yes it does. And she blackmailed me."

"You speak in the past tense," Holmes said. "If the blackmail has ended, why is it still a bother?"

"That's the rub. It is over, but I fear it may begin anew."

"Please explain," Holmes said, sitting back in his chair.

"As you noted, Mister Holmes, I am married and I have a family. A year or so ago, I became smitten with a younger woman and made the mistake of having an affair with her. I realized my error and broke it off six months after it began, but she wouldn't have it. She threatened to go to the newspapers with the story and they'd print it gladly, my employer being who he is. It would have cost me my family and my job as well."

"Surely no reputable newspaper would print such a story based on hearsay," Holmes said.

"More than just hearsay, sir. She had proof. A letter."

"A *billet-doux*?"

"Yes, sir. I was a fool to write it, but she begged me for it. Said she wanted it to read when we were apart. I realize now what she wanted it for was leverage against me. I got a note from her last week saying she'd give it to me for a thousand pounds and say no more about it."

"And she still has the letter."

"No, she gave it to me this morning. I went to her flat, I gave her the money, and she handed it over as nice as you please in a pretty little perfumed envelope."

"Then why is it still a problem?"

"Because it was stolen from me this afternoon." His face darkened with anger. "I was in Victoria Station. I had just stepped off the train and was crossing the platform when a fellow collided with me. He was very apologetic and bowed and scraped, I thought because of my size compared to his. He tipped his hat and disappeared into the crowd."

"And when did you discover the letter was missing?" Holmes said around the stem of his pipe.

"A few minutes later when I stopped by a stall to buy some cigars. I reached for my wallet and found it was gone and the letter with it. I must get it back. If the thief realizes what he has, the whole business will begin again, and I can't raise another thousand pounds."

Holmes said nothing.

"Well," said Smith, "when can you begin to help me get it back?"

"The minute you begin telling us the truth." Homes eyed Smith sharply.

Smith leaped to his feet. "Whattaya talking about?" The sudden burst of anger scuttled his precise demeanor and the ruffian underneath emerged. His fists clenched.

"If you want our help, sit down and behave properly, and tell us the identity of your employer, the man who really had the affair and wrote the letter. Without the truth, there is little I can do to help you."

Smith seemed for a moment to teeter between doing as Holmes said and stalking out the door. "What makes you think my boss wrote the letter and not me?"

"First, with due respect, based on your clothing, you do not look to be able to raise a thousand pounds on a few days' notice. Second, you said that the lady in question gave you a pretty little envelope, yet you made no mention of verifying the contents. Third, if you were so concerned with the proof the letter contained, you would have destroyed it on the spot; burned it in her fireplace or simply put a match to it outside her door.

"No, sir, you acted as the agent of the true author, who sent you on this errand, provided the ransom, and instructed you to not read the letter. Now it has been stolen from you, and you are desperate to get it back safe before your employer learns what has happened to it. Correct me if I am mistaken."

Smith sank into the chair. "You're right on all counts," he said, wringing his hands with agitation. I had no other way to turn but to come to you. I can't go to the police. I can't tell you who my employer is. If I did you'd see why I can't."

"Understand, Mister Smith, or whatever your real name may be, that all matters undertaken by Doctor Watson and myself are absolutely confidential and handled with the utmost discretion. However, we will set those details aside for the moment. Tell us about the pickpocket. What was his appearance?"

"He was a little fellow with spectacles and a thick moustache like the hands of a clock at eight and four. He wore a sort of floppy felt hat and a long coat, almost to his shins, as if it were too big for him. And I recall he wore gloves with no fingertips."

"Besides the spectacles and moustache, which may have been false to conceal his identity, what else do you remember about his face?"

"His chin was long and pointed, as if it belonged to somebody else."

Holmes said, "You used the word 'little' to describe the thief. Stand for me, please."

Smith stood, a puzzled look on his face.

"Now place the edge of your hand palm down on your body where you would judge his height to be." Smith followed the instruction and placed his hand an inch below his chin. "That would make him five feet five inches or a bit shorter. Now, which pocket held your wallet and the envelope?"

Smith opened his coat to reveal an inside breast pocket. "They were both right here. The pocket was buttoned up."

"Please describe the envelope."

"About four inches by three." Smith framed the size with his large, rough hands. "Cream-colored, it was."

"And was it sealed?"

"Yes. It was sealed with a blob of red wax."

"No signet or other imprint on the wax?"

"The seal had a horse's head with a horn sticking out between the eyes."

"A unicorn." Holmes leaned back in his chair and puffed at his pipe for a moment before he spoke. "I will look into the matter, Mister Smith, but without all of the facts, I am hampered in my efforts. Perhaps you might consult your employer and ask his permission to speak freely."

Smith looked at the floor then back at us again. "Very well. He'll find out I've failed him sooner or later, and mayhap it's best he hears it from me first."

"And how may we contact you?"

"I'll return later this evening after I've discussed it with him. If he agrees, then I'll tell you everything."

"As you wish," Holmes said. "In the interim, we will make some enquiries. Watson, please show the gentleman out."

I returned from the door to find Holmes still sitting by the hearth staring into the fire.

"What a mess that fellow has gotten himself into," I said. "Rather like trying to pull a man out of a quickmire and falling in with him. He has given us precious little to work with."

"Indeed. He hoped for an easy solution to a complex problem. I have little doubt that he will return tonight with full information. So, Watson, which do you think, Commons or Lords?"

"What?"

"Do you think his employer is from the House of Commons or the House of Lords? Although he is well spoken unless he forgets himself, Mister Smith is not dressed suitably to accompany a wealthy businessman. Underworld figures would have little need for articulate speech, but a politician might as a matter of image."

"And I suppose you have an opinion on the matter."

"I believe our Mister Smith is the personal bodyguard of a member of Commons. We may eliminate those who are not family men, but further speculation would serve little purpose at this point. Instead, let us focus on the thief. The question we must answer at this point, Watson, is whether he acted on his own or is perhaps in league with the blackmailer."

"You mean steal back the letter to blackmail him again?"

"Possibly, or simply to hold it as insurance against reprisal, since the blackmailer is intimately known by the victim. Among the pickpockets in London, who has the skill and best fits best the *modus operandi* and physical description our Mister Smith provided?"

"The Little Dipper?"

"Very good Watson. We should speak with Oliver Norwood."

Oliver Norwood, given the moniker "The Little Dipper" by London's clannish underworld, was one of the most artful pickpockets alive. Holmes had employed him on one occasion to pluck a dainty address book from a notorious madam's handbag at the opera and return it again before she realized it was missing. The word "little" referred to Norwood's diminutive stature. His forte was slipping through crowds in railway stations, markets, bookstalls, and other places to ply his trade on preoccupied people.

"And where might we find him?" I said.

"I do not know. Get your coat, Watson," he said rising from his chair. "Perhaps the Vicar can help."

In the East End, Robert Townes, known to the criminal element as The Vicar of Thieves operated the Saint Dismas Mission. Townes, the convicted leader of a gang of burglars found religion in prison and once released, opened the Mission to help other unfortunates. Saint Dismas Mission, named after "The Penitent Thief" crucified with the Christ provided what the ex-convicts called "cot and hot" to men recently paroled with an eye to preventing them from returning to their criminal ways and helping them rejoin society. Many jaded souls, however, doubted the Vicar's altruism and suspected the Mission also served as a harbor and a clearinghouse for felonious talent.

We arrived at the tumbledown building, a former beer hall with a cross painted crudely over the door. Holmes pushed it inward and we found thirty or so men eating their evening meal at long tables. They were a coarse lot, many still clad in the grey coats given to prisoners on their release, and many more in shabby threadbare castoffs found in some rag bin. The smell of pork and cabbage mixed with the odor of unwashed bodies wafted from the dimly lit common room.

A burly giant with a bald head and a huge red spade of a beard blocked our path. He held a cudgel as thick as my forearm across the doorway like Little John at the log bridge with Robin Hood. "State yer business," he snarled.

Beyond him I could see the men at the tables raise their heads from their plates and stare at us. Their rough conversation and laughter ceased abruptly.

Holmes said quietly, "I am Sherlock Holmes and I come to speak with the Vicar."

"Is that so?" said the giant. "And what business might a fancy bloke like you have with him?"

"I am sure he will tell you if he thinks it your concern," Holmes said coolly.

The giant snarled and raised his cudgel. He might have bashed in

Holmes's head if a sharp voice from behind had not said, "Brom! Stand away. Let those men pass."

Robert Townes, The Vicar of Thieves was a tall spare man, whose thick grey hair fell to the clerical collar of his shabby black coat. His face was seamed with age and harsh experience but his dark eyes were as alive as a ferret's. He placed a hand on Brom's shoulder and with a gentle motion thrust the beastly fellow aside as if he were made of paper. I had no doubt that at a different signal from the Vicar, Brom would have remorselessly beaten us both to a pulp.

Holmes said, "I am…"

"I know who you are," the Vicar said, "you and your friend Doctor Watson. What brings the great detective to Saint Dismas?"

"A matter that should be best discussed privately, Vicar."

After pondering the request for a moment, he nodded his head. "Very well, come with me, gentlemen." He turned to the men at the tables. "These men are guests." I understood the statement to mean that we were not to be molested. He led us to the back of the common room past a simple altar with a crucifix and chalice. I felt all eyes follow us and marked emotions ranging from suspicion to fear to outright hatred. I wondered how many of these men we had helped put behind bars and what they might do should the Vicar rescind his protection.

Townes's office was a windowless little room that shared the odor of the rest of the place. In it were a cluttered desk and two chairs. "I haven't an extra seat, and if I did, there's no place to put it anyway. He pulled his chair from behind the desk and set it before me. "Please sit, gentlemen. I don't mind standing." As he shut the door, I saw Brom take a position just outside, cudgel in hand.

The Vicar leaned back on his desk and looked down his long nose at us as if he were studying some rare insect. "I must say that you have pluck if not good sense coming here, considering that many of my flock would take pleasure in killing you."

Holmes smiled. "Sometimes, in the pursuit of justice, prudence must be set aside."

"Why is it that you have come to me, Mister Holmes?"

"I need an intermediary, Vicar. I must contact Oliver Norwood, the Little Dipper. Being that he flees from the sight of law enforcement or anyone associated with it, I hoped that you might be able to locate him."

"And why would I do such a thing?"

"For his good as well as that of your flock. Holmes set a Sovereign on the desk. "I am prepared to contribute to Saint Dismas in exchange for the service."

The Vicar stared at Holmes, not the coin. Holmes set another Sovereign on the first, then another. A fourth satisfied the cleric, and he spoke.

"You say for his good, Mister Holmes. Please explain."

"I believe the Little Dipper has picked the wrong pocket and unknowingly involved himself in something very dangerous. If I can reach him and retrieve my client's property, I can guarantee that the Yard will not become involved. Should my client ply the considerable resources at his disposal and find him first, I cannot guarantee the Dipper's life nor his liberty."

The Vicar chuckled. "So this is a matter to be kept quiet." He stared once again at the stack of coins then back to Holmes, who placed another on the pile. "He is not among us, Mister Holmes. I do not know Oliver's whereabouts, but I 'd venture to say that he's on the circuit."

"The circuit?" I said.

"A network of hotels, rooming houses, and lodgings that house and conceal the criminal element," Holmes explained. "To avoid capture, men move from one place to the other every so many days."

"On the circuit, Oliver could be in any of a score of places, so I can't say he is in this place or that. However, I will make enquiries."

Holmes nodded. "I thank you, Vicar. And should you find him?"

"I will send word round, Mister Holmes. I know that your word is good, so I will take your gold and play fair with you in return." He scooped up the coins from his desk and dropped them into his pocket, sealing the deal. He then opened the door and we rose from our chairs.

"I would invite you to stay for services. Prayer is a balm for the soul, but I fear your presence would agitate my flock. I suggest that neither of you ever shows his face here again. My curiosity is the only reason I permitted you to enter the Mission. Brom will see you to the door. Beyond that point, I can't guarantee…" he cocked his head to the side. "What was your phrase?" He smiled wickedly. "Ah, yes; your life nor your liberty."

Holmes nodded. "I expected no less." As we followed Brom through the common room, the men at the tables glared at us in silence. At the doorway, the brute shoved us out into the street with his cudgel and slammed the door to behind us.

In the cab on our way back to Baker Street I said, "I've never seen anything like that place, Holmes. I hope you take his advice and never go back there again."

"If I do, Watson," Holmes chuckled, "it will be as I have done twice before."

"You've been there before?"

"In disguise, old fellow, but I felt that this occasion demanded the direct approach. It seems I was correct."

"We might have been killed."

"Watson, we might be killed any day of our lives. When did that ever stop us?"

"Mister Smith" returned to our lodgings that evening shortly before nine o'clock. He looked like a man who had been shown the gates of Hell and offered one final chance to redeem himself. Whereas he looked gruff and imposing in the afternoon, he now looked tired and defeated.

Holmes rose from his chair and said, "Well, sir, have you come to enlighten us, or are we to continue groping in the dark?"

"I'm given a free hand to manage things," Smith said, "and although I can't reveal my employer's name, I can give you the name and address of the tramp that caused all of this. I was also told to give this to you." He handed a small leather purse to Holmes. Holmes hefted the drawstring bag in his hand and I heard the coins in it jingle.

"The woman's name is Annie Sweetham. She's a cigar roller; works at J. S. Hill in Shoreditch. Here's her address. It's in Shoreditch as well, in Whitmore Ward." He handed Holmes a slip of paper.

Holmes studied it. "Is this in your hand?"

Smith hesitated. "No, sir, it's in his."

"Your employer's?" Smith nodded.

"And here's a picture of her." He pulled a small framed photograph from the pocket of his coat. It showed a pretty woman in her early thirties, dark curls and dark eyes. She sported a fancy hat and a parasol far beyond a cigar roller's wage.

"Do you have a carriage waiting?" Smith nodded again. "Then let us go at once."

The carriage was a well-fitted brougham with a driver. As we rolled away, Smith said, "Have you made any headway on this business?"

"Some," said Holmes. "We have an idea who may have stolen your wallet."

"You do?" Smith's eyes widened. "Tell me who he is."

"No."

"Whattaya mean, no?" His voice rose. "You've been paid good money. I deserve to know."

"Do you want the letter returned?"

"Hell, yes, I want it back. Why else did I come to you?"

"Then allow me do my job. If I tell you whom I suspect—suspect, mind you—you will likely summon your forces and go after him headlong like an alley dog at a rat and scare him into hiding. Then he will not be found, nor will the letter. In order to locate him, I had to give my word that I would not turn him over to the Yard."

"You what?" Smith's eyes bulged now.

"'Who steals my purse steals trash,'" said Holmes.

"Whattaya you talking about?"

"The wisdom of the Bard, my friend. He went on to say, 'but he that filches from me my good name robs me of that which not enriches him, and makes me poor indeed.'" Holmes's tone sharpened. "What is more important to you, Smith? A little money and your pride or your employer's reputation? Vengeance or the return of the letter?"

"The letter, of course," said Smith after a moment's hesitation.

"You feel violated, deceived, victimized, but you shall have to set aside your personal indignation to achieve the more important end. Was there anything of consequence in the wallet itself?"

"A few pounds and some papers."

Holmes nodded. "Enough for someone to deduce your identity and through you that of your employer, if his identity and yours were not already known."

"I don't follow you."

"We must not discount the possibility that the thief was working in tandem with our Miss Sweetham and that perhaps this whole business is a grand plot to bring down a member of Parliament."

Smith's jaw dropped and I knew Holmes's arrow had hit its mark.

"And if he operated independently, we must locate the thief at once before he sets the wheels of a new blackmail scheme in motion. We will know more after we have visited the young lady."

Smith was struck speechless and remained so for the rest of the ride.

Annie Sweetham's flat was a second floor apartment in a building on a crooked little street called Chaps Way. At Holmes's suggestion, the driver let us off two streets beyond to prevent the carriage being seen at the woman's address.

Smith led the way and knocked perhaps a little too insistently on the door. In short order a little man with thick spectacles and an ample paunch protruding from his unbuttoned vest opened it. He peered through his glasses at us and settled on Smith. "So it's you again. Well, Annie ain't here."

"Where is she?" Smith demanded.

"I couldn't say. She left this morning right after you. Took a little carpet bag with her, she did. Said she was going to visit her sister for a few days. I ain't seen her since."

"My good fellow," said Holmes, "it is very important that we find her. Could we perhaps have a look at her room to see if we can determine where she may have gone?"

"See here now," he said. "I don't open my rooms to just any Tom or Robin strolls in off the street. What do you think I'm running here?"

"What is your name, sir?" I said.

"Blankenship. Arthur Blankenship."

"I think you're running a reputable house, Mister Blankenship," I said, "Do you have a room that we could let?"

"No, sir, we're full up."

"Ah," I said, "but you have one room idle tonight. Could we rent it for, say, two pounds?"

A smirk curled one corner of the landlord's mouth. "Ain't you a sly boots?" His eyes slid side to side as he thought it over. "Three pounds."

"Done," I said. I handed him the money and the portly Mister Blankenship led us up the stairs.

Miss Sweetham's flat was more spacious than the house's exterior suggested. It consisted of two rooms, a parlour and a bedroom separated by a pocket door. The flat looked lived in but neatly kept. Holmes paced first around the parlour puffing at his pipe. He moved to the bedroom and continued his examination. He opened drawers of the bureau and found them full of clothing.

"I am of two minds, Watson," he said, picking up a tortoise shell comb from a dressing table. Beside it was a neatly organized array of toiletries, combs and brushes, rouge, and other cosmetics. "Annie Sweetham seems to have left with every intention of returning. There are clothes in the drawers and the closet. Yet I see no truly personal items; no pictures of family or other mementoes of her life. Everything here seems for lack of a better word, disposable."

"A thousand pounds could buy her a whole new wardrobe," I said.

"True." He stood lost in thought for a moment then crossed to the es-

"Do you have a room that we could let?"

critoire. He rummaged through the stationery and pens. "One item in particular is absent, the unicorn seal. She has apparently taken it with her." He turned to Smith. "When you came here earlier today, were you admitted, or did you do your transaction in the hallway?"

Smith said, "I came into the room, but she left the hallway door open."

"Think, man. Is there anything that you can see that appears different from this morning?"

Smith turned full circle. "Nothing that I notice."

Holmes turned his head toward the bedroom. "That door was open?"

"Yes. I could see right into the bedroom. There was nobody else here, if that's what you mean; if so, I would have seen him in the mirror over the vanity table."

Holmes nodded. "Was the bed made up?"

"No, come to think of it, it wasn't."

"Why would a lady allow a gentleman to look into her unmade boudoir? Why would she not close the door?" Holmes crossed to the doorway. A nudge of his finger turned out the handle and he pulled the door closed. "And there, Mister Smith is your employer."

On the panels of the door were tacked newspaper engravings and one photograph of a distinguished looking gentleman with graying sideburns growing into a thick moustache. Written in a neat hand over the pictures were the words "love forever" scratched through by a sharp blade. A broad X was slashed across the face in the photograph. "If I am not mistaken, that is Mister Eli Shepperton, M. P. and member of the Fabian Society."

"My god." Smith turned pale.

"It appears that Miss Sweetham intended this shrine to be found. I do not expect her to return. We can dismiss thoughts of a further blackmail plot. I believe that she fully intended to destroy the man who jilted her after she took his money. Let us search these rooms thoroughly and learn what we can."

It was in a small wastebasket that I found a railway schedule. "Here. Holmes," I said. "This may mean something."

He thumbed through the schedule. "Watson, you have proved your worth once again." He turned the pages in the schedule, examining each one closely. "Interesting," Holmes said. "A circle is drawn around three times and locations. Peterborough, Corby, and Cambridge."

Smith peered over Holmes's shoulder at the schedule. "But which one did she go to?"

"Corby is the furthest destination, Peterborough is the second, and

Cambridge is the nearest." He turned the pages again. "Also, note the times, the chronological order of the departures matches that of the order of distance. Our Miss Sweetham has marked a series of connecting trips, her final destination being Corby."

"But there are direct trains to Corby," I said. "Why so roundabout a route?"

"To prevent being found, Watson."

"Then let's go there," Smith urged.

"Going to Corby will not retrieve the letter any faster. I believe that it is still in London." Holmes pointed to the gallery on the bedroom door. "The knife slashes on his photograph suggest a hatred bordering on mania. It is Miss Sweetham's goal to destroy Eli Shepperton. If she intended further blackmail, she would not have left this shrine to be found. I am now inclined to believe that the pickpocket acted on his own and that you were a random victim."

"I say we thwart her plans here and now." Smith strode to the door and pulled the pictures from it. He crumpled them into a ball in his fists and threw them into the grate. He was about to put a match to them when Holmes stopped him.

"Burning those would be rash," he said. "Should this eventually become a police matter, they may serve as evidence. Further, if you present these to Mister Shepperton as a token of your diligence, it may mollify him somewhat."

"You're right," Smith said and retrieved the pictures from the fireplace. He flattened each and folded them into his pocket. "What do we do now?"

"Watson and I will continue our search for the letter and examine why Annie Sweetham fled to Corby. You shall stay by Mister Shepperton's side in the event contact is made by Miss Sweetham or some other party."

"And since we now know your employer's name," I said, "we might as well know yours as well and stop calling you Mister Smith."

Smith looked sheepish. "Truth be told, Doctor, that is my name: Cornelius Smith. I was so flustered when I first came to you that I didn't think to invent an alias."

The entire next day passed with no word from the Vicar. I waited in our flat in the event the message should come while Holmes canvassed his sources among London's undesirables. He returned just before supper and I could see the frustration on his face.

"No one has seen the Dipper for days, Watson. It is as if he has vanished."

"Perhaps he is lying low and making plans, if he has realized the potential for what he has stolen."

"But we haven't heard from the Vicar either. That suggests that he can't locate him, and his seine is far finer than ours. It comprises every criminal in London."

"Do you suppose the Vicar has reneged?"

"No, Watson, I do not. As inappropriate as the aphorism may be, a gift from the Devil is a debt in the end. The Vicar will keep his word, if only to ensure that if he needs my help in the future, I will not refuse the widow's son."

"In other words, an unholy alliance with a holy man."

"Indeed, Watson. And what have you learned about Corby?"

"Corby is a fair sized town built near the largest ironstone field in England. It is not London, but a big enough haystack for a needle to hide in. The town seems to have its share of general commerce and trades, but iron mining is its bread and butter. As for Sweethams, I would have to consult the Registry."

"No need, Watson; Corby is not Annie Sweetham's place of origin."

"And how do we know that?"

"Because I took the time to visit the J. S. Hill cigar manufacture this afternoon. Mister Wayne the manager was very forthcoming with information, particularly since Annie quit her job three days ago, giving him no notice. Their records show that she was born in Twyckenham, the daughter of William and Dolores Sweetham, listed as her next of kin."

"So what would she seek in Corby?"

"I do not know, Watson, but I intend to find out."

Just before midnight, the Vicar's messenger arrived.

I opened the hallway door to a knock, thinking it Mrs. Hudson and was startled to find myself staring into the unshaven face of a ruffian I recognized from the Saint Dismas Mission. "Mister Holmes?"

"How did you get in here?"

The scoundrel grinned, showing a rank of brown and broken teeth. "We has our ways."

Holmes came up behind me. "I am Sherlock Holmes."

"This is for you." He offered an envelope to Holmes as his eyes swept the room, no doubt scanning for anything of value he might steal.

Holmes took the envelope. He turned it over in his hands. "This is from the Vicar?"

"Yes, sir, it be. From his hand to your own."

"Watson, show the gentleman out, and give him this," Holmes took a coin from his pocket and pressed it into my hand, "when he is out the door."

I escorted the fellow down the stairs and as he stepped outside, I saw Mrs. Hudson peering fearfully through a crack in her door. He held out his palm and as I dropped the coin into it, he tipped his moth-eaten cap. "Evenin', guv'nor."

Back upstairs I saw Holmes stripping off his smoking jacket. "Dress for the weather, Watson. We're going to Cheapside."

"At this hour?"

"The Vicar's note says that Oliver Norwood is indeed on the circuit and has been seen at this address in the last day or so." Holmes tapped the note for emphasis. "If we wait until tomorrow, he may no longer be there."

We hailed a cab and were soon rolling through a chill drizzle.

"What was that business with the messenger? Why did he show up at our door unannounced?"

"A message all its own, Watson, a warning if you will, to keep our bargain. That was the Vicar's way of telling us that he knows where we live and that his people can enter unbidden at any time."

"That's a sobering thought."

"Quite, Watson, but we need have no fear so long as I keep my word. I am sure that the Vicar's men are watching us from the shadows at this moment, and should they think we are bringing the law or any other agency into this business, they will dash ahead and warn Norwood, or do worse to stop us."

"And if Norwood doesn't have the letter?"

"Pickpockets are a close fraternity, Watson. If he does not have the letter, he can surely help us find the person who does."

The cab stopped outside a hostel on a run-down Cheapside street. Three shabbily dressed men stood at the curb passing a bottle among them. Holmes nodded to them as we passed and said, "Give my regards to the Vicar." They eyed us warily as we entered the foyer but said nothing. The lobby was empty, but we already knew that Norwood was staying in room 3D at the back of the building.

The hallway was eerily silent as we approached the door in the dim light of a gas flame near the stairs. Holmes rapped lightly on the door.

There was no answer. He knocked again a little harder this time. From inside the room we heard a groan. Holmes braced his shoulder against the flimsy door and shoved it in with a sharp crack. We stepped inside before anyone could see us and pushed the door shut.

The room was dark but I didn't need my eyes to recognize the stench of vomit and disease. Holmes lit a candle. A leather portmanteau sat open on the only chair in the room. The long overcoat Smith had described hung over the back of the chair.

I didn't see the Little Dipper at first because he was wound in the soiled bedclothes. Then he groaned again and I saw the top of his head, the disheveled sandy hair poking out of the sheet.

I pulled back the corner of the sheet and recoiled as Norwood's head lolled toward me. His face was slick with fever sweat. And then he coughed, a deep wet sound, and blood dribbled from the corner of his mouth.

Holmes started toward the bed. "Watson, is he…"

"Don't touch him, Holmes. Unless I'm mistaken, this man has anthrax."

"Extraordinary." Holmes backed up a step, looking around the room. "The letter, Watson."

"This man may be beyond help, Holmes, but we have to call in the authorities at once. Everyone in this hostel is at risk of infection, as are we."

"But if we notify the authorities, Watson, they will quarantine the place and likely us with it."

"Damn it all, Holmes…"

"Five minutes, Watson. Just five minutes." He didn't wait for my reply but began dumping the valise. He poked through the mound of clothing with the end of his stick. He reached into the bag up to his elbow. "Ah!" He drew out his hand and in it was a small square envelope. "Inside the lining, Watson." It was as Smith described it and slit at one end. "It has been opened."

Holmes was about to remove the letter when we heard footsteps in the hallway. The door burst open and a tall man in shirtsleeves, suspenders hanging from his waist came in holding a lantern.

"What are you about here?"

"I am a doctor," I said. "This man is ill and highly contagious."

The hotelier looked beyond me and saw Norwood. "Blimey," he said and scuttled backward and out the door. We followed him into the hallway. We pushed past him and toward the stairs. "What do I do?"

"Summon the authorities immediately, and under no circumstance let anyone else into that room."

As we stepped out of the building, I noticed that the three men by the door were gone. We had to walk some distance before we found a cab and along the way at my urging, we went into a pub and bought a pint of cheap gin to disinfect our hands.

"Tell me, Watson, how does one contract anthrax?"

"By eating meat from a contaminated animal, contact with the blood or other discharge, or inhaling the spores of the dried bacillus, as do cows or sheep..."

"And which seems the most likely in Norwood's case?"

"I saw no black sores from subcutaneous bleeding, and although Norwood vomited up whatever he ate, the landlord seemed utterly surprised, so it would appear that none of the other residents was ill from eating the hostel food. That leaves inhaling the spores."

Holmes's eyes widened. He drew the envelope from his pocket. He held it slit-edge-down and tapped it with his finger. A fine dust dribbled out and drifted to the carriage floor. "Watson, this plot is darker than I could have imagined. This letter is not an object of blackmail. It is a murder weapon."

"Murder?"

"Annie Sweetham was not content to destroy Eli Shepperton's reputation. She wanted him to die horribly and through contagion, his family as well. There are anthrax spores in this envelope."

"That's a bit far-fetched, isn't it?"

"Is it?" You saw the defaced picture in her flat. We are dealing with a woman crazed with anger who apparently will stop at nothing to achieve her vengeance. The blackmail plot was a sideshow. Shepperton gave a thousand pounds to Smith, who retrieved a sealed envelope. Upon its receipt, Shepperton would open it to confirm the letter's authenticity. Anthrax spores in the envelope or folded in the letter would infect him fatally."

"But he would have to inhale the spores, Holmes."

"Hence the perfume Smith described. The temptation for a last sniff of a mistress's scent."

"But the Little Dipper stole the envelope before Shepperton could open it."

"And if he is not dead already, he soon shall be."

"Thank Heaven you didn't remove the letter, Holmes. What a vicious thing for her to do," I said, shuddering.

"So goes the proverb, 'Hell hath no fury.' We must notify Mister Smith immediately. Shepperton's life may still be in danger if Annie Sweetham realizes her ploy has failed."

"And are you going to return the letter to Shepperton?"

"Once its hazard has been neutralized."

"But where would Annie Sweetham get anthrax spores, let alone know how to handle them properly without infecting herself?"

"I believe we will find those answers in Corby."

"And should we inform the Yard?"

"I am not certain how we may do so without exposing Mister Shepperton, and that was our initial concern. If the hotelier did as he was told, the Yard is already aware of the Dipper's condition and proper measures are being taken to prevent the spread of the disease. Let us wind out this skein a bit further and see where it may lead."

No trains were available until early the next morning, and the sunrise found us rolling northward in an almost empty coach. As we neared Corby, the train passed verdant fields with herds of cattle and sheep. "There, Watson is a source for the spores. The papers report that there have been infections in this region recently."

"That may be so, Holmes, but there is a great leap between their availability and their appearance in that letter."

"Likely our Miss Sweetham had an accomplice. Tell me, Watson, who would be the likeliest person to come into contact with anthrax other than a physician like yourself?"

After a moment's thought, I said, "A veterinarian."

"Very good, Watson. There are two in Corby. We shall visit them both."

Robert Hampstead was away from his office and his home. His neighbors reported that he was attending a conference in Paris and would not return for another week. That left Edward Santer. A two mile walk from Corby in a grey drizzle led us to a gate beside a hand-lettered sign that read "Santer Veterinary". A small farm rested at the top of the hill. We saw no signs of life about the house, the barn, or the outbuildings as we trudged up the rutted lane.

As we came closer, I could hear the lowing of cattle and the braying of a donkey.

"Where there are animals, there must needs be someone to tend them," Holmes said. "Let us hope that Doctor Santer is at home."

The house, like the barn, was rough lumber with a cedar shake roof. The steps and porch were in disrepair, and more than one pane of the windows was missing its glass. Homes rapped on the door with his stick and it shook in its frame. "Hello," he called, and knocked again. No one answered.

"Well, Holmes, what do we do now?"

Holmes tried the doorknob and the door swung inward with a grating of hinges. "We go inside and wait." He stepped across the threshold into the darkened house and I followed. The interior of the house was little better kept than its outside. Water-streaked wallpaper bubbled away from the walls and in places hung in tatters in what once was a parlour. The room had been converted to an office of sorts with a desk and a few mismatched chairs. A shelf held an array of animal skulls. On the wall hung a framed diploma from Lancashire Veterinary School certifying that Edward Santer had completed his studies eight years before.

Holmes stepped behind the desk and froze. "Watson, look at this." He pointed to a framed photograph, a family posed, parents and two teen-aged children. I recognized the daughter at once: Annie Sweetham. It took me a moment longer to recognize the young man. "Good god, Holmes," I said. "I never made the connection. That is Edward Sweetham."

"Someone you know?"

"Someone I've met. He was a young intern at Saint John's Hospital years ago. He was drummed out of the profession when it was discovered that he was addicted to opium."

"So he changed his name and became a healer of beasts. But from the looks of this place, I would say he never shed his addiction." Holmes pushed aside a curtain from a doorway. The room beyond was a crude laboratory, tables cluttered with glassware and vials of chemicals. An old microscope rested in one corner, and beside it lay a small carpetbag.

Holmes opened it and reached inside. His hand came out holding a thick sheaf of banknotes.

"Watson, here is..."

A shrill scream interrupted his sentence as a wild-eyed Annie Sweetham leaped from the doorway behind us with a butcher knife clenched in her fist. She slashed at Holmes, who raised a forearm in defense and the blade bit through his sleeve. He grunted in pain and threw himself backward against a table, shattering vials and beakers.

Annie lunged at Holmes, but her foot caught the hem of her skirt and she pitched forward to the floor. She lay face down gasping for breath, and I could see the tip of the knife protruding through the back of her dress, a crimson stain spreading around it.

I knelt beside her and from the corner of my eye I saw a gaunt, haggard face at the window. The man looked in and disappeared again. Holmes saw him as well and dashed from the room in pursuit. Realizing I could do little to help Annie Sweetham, I followed quickly behind Holmes.

As I rounded the corner of the farmhouse, I saw our quarry run through the open door of the barn with Holmes close behind. As I entered, I saw Edward Sweetham, agile as a monkey, clamber into the loft on rungs nailed between the beams. He turned to look down, and I saw his wild, red eyes glaring with hatred. Sweetham's shabby clothes hung from his frame like an older brother's suit; he had the wasted look of a consumptive, although I realized that it was opium that had eaten him away.

Holmes started up after him and Sweetham hurled a bale of hay from the loft. It struck Holmes a glancing blow on the shoulder and almost took him off the makeshift ladder. "Devils!" screamed Sweetham. Words tumbled out of him in a rapid torrent. "You follow me everywhere I go. You leave me no peace. You've taken everything from me, and now you've taken my Annie. Devils, all of you."

I climbed the ladder and as my head cleared the floor of the loft, I saw Holmes, his stick raised, advancing toward Sweetham. The loft was floored with loose rough planks of odd sizes laid across the joists. Many were warped and they shifted when I trod on them. I had to watch my step in the dim light so that I didn't put my foot between them.

Sweetham groped in the pocket of his coat as he backed away across the loose boards. "Devils! You won't leave a man alone. We were going to go away, Annie and I, and start over. But you came to torment me, and you hurt my Annie. But I know how to deal with devils." Sweetham's hand came out of his pocket holding a glass vial. He pulled the cork with his teeth and poured a small mound of powder into his palm.

He spat the cork away. "You know what this is?" Sweetham's voice rose in pitch. "This is death. Come a step closer and I'll blow it in your bloody face." Holmes stopped his advance, and Sweetham smiled wickedly, sensing the upper hand. "Better still, I'll bring it to you." He took one unsteady step then another. Holmes stood his ground.

I pulled my revolver from my pocket, but before I could cock the hammer, Holmes kicked one of the planks at his feet. Its end slid over the edge of the joist and Holmes leapt on it, his weight sending the other end upward like a child's teeter-totter, and he disappeared through the makeshift floor.

The plank struck Sweetham's hand, and it flew to his face, the deadly anthrax spores along with it. "Aaugh!" He choked and clawed at his eyes. Sweetham turned and staggered backward. His second step put his foot between two of the loose boards and he fell through them to land with a sickening crunch below.

"Holmes!" I cried. Are you all right?"

"Perfectly, Watson," came a voice from below. "Although I can't say the same for Sweetham."

I peered into the near dark and saw two sets of fingers gripping one of the floor boards. Holmes had caught himself before he could fall. "Give me a hand up, would you, Watson."

I lifted Holmes from his predicament and looked through the gap in the planks to the barn below. Sweetham had landed badly on the side of one of the stalls. He was bent backward at the waist over the low wall, and I could see at once that his spine was broken and he was dead.

"I say, that was a near thing, Holmes."

"It was indeed, Watson." Holmes crossed to the stalls and began opening their gates. A slap on their rumps sent the cows and the ass plodding into the yard.

"What are you doing?" I said, although I already knew.

Holmes struck a match and set it to a mound of hay. In moments the old barn was engulfed in flames. "Let us go to the house and finish this business."

I felt at Annie Sweetham's throat and found no pulse. "Should we burn this place as well, Holmes?"

"I fear it is the only way we can destroy the threat of infection." I found a bottle of alcohol on one of the laboratory tables and poured it over my hands. Holmes did as well. He poured the remainder of the bottle onto the tattered curtains at the window. As he lit a match, I said, "What of the money, Holmes?"

He eyed the packet of banknotes where they lay beside Annie Sweetham's corpse. "It is tainted, Watson, like everything in this accursed place. He lit the alcohol and blue fire climbed the draperies.

We stood outside in the grey drizzle and watched the flames climb to the roof of the farmhouse.

"What do we tell the constabulary?"

"We tell them nothing, Watson. What purpose would be served? The perpetrators of this ghastly scheme are dead. Justice is served in a fashion, and we are bound to protect our client." Holmes stared into the flames and said somberly, "*in pace requiescat.*"

"Let us hope that both of those tormented souls have found peace."

"And the Little Dipper as well."

The next evening, Smith came to Baker Street once more, but this time, he was not alone. Eli Shepperton accompanied him. "Smith tells me that you have the letter, Mister Holmes."

"Yes," Holmes said, crossing to a cabinet beside the fireplace. He produced a glass jar and inside it, still in the envelope, was the letter. "I have not yet removed it from the envelope for reasons I am sure Mister Smith has explained."

"Yes, he told me." Shepperton shuddered visibly.

Holmes unscrewed the lid of the jar. He pressed the envelope against the glass with a pen and plucked the letter from the envelope with long tweezers without removing it from the jar. He held it up for Shepperton's inspection. "Is this the letter?"

Shepperton peered through the side of the jar. The relief was evident on his face. "Yes. That is it."

Holmes threw the jar into the hearth. The glass shattered and the paper inside burst into flames. In a moment, it was ash up the chimney.

"I thank you, Mister Holmes. You have rescued me from a difficult situation."

Shepperton left with Smith in tow and Holmes sank into his chair. He stared into the fire for a time, and finally I said, "What troubles you, Holmes?"

"Watersheds, Watson, making the river flow this way or that. You have heard the talk that the Fabian Socialists wish to form a party to represent working people, a Labour Party, if you will. Had Eli Shepperton been exposed and discredited, those plans may have come to naught. I cannot help but wonder what, in saving his career, we may have wrought."

Holmes returned his gaze to the fire and there he sat in silence for the rest of the evening.

The End

The Blackmail Letter

In "The Adventure of the Picked Pocket" I explored a "what-if?" question: what if a pickpocket steals something that is far more valuable than he realizes and is pursued by the victim? What could be so valuable that people might kill to get it back? And why would the victim avoid the police and seek help from a private source?

A blackmail note was an option, but that seemed too simple by itself. So, I started pursuing different lines of thought. What if the pickpocket's victim is not the person being blackmailed? What if he is acting on behalf of someone else and wants to repair the damage before his employer finds that he has lost the incriminating proof?

And what would put Holmes on the horns of a dilemma? Holmes handled a blackmail case in "A Scandal in Bohemia" without involving the Yard, so that was not an issue. Having to strike a deal with the Vicar to not involve the authorities upped the ante. Then when Holmes and Watson find the dying Dipper, he must decide whether to tell the authorities what he knows or continue to pursue his client's interest.

Once Holmes realizes the plot is more than simple blackmail, he pursues the killers without the Yard's involvement, having given his word to the Vicar. In the end, the murderers are dealt with and as Holmes puts it, "Justice is served in a fashion."

Watson is also very important to this story for his medical knowledge, and I thought it was a good bit to have him persuade Arthur Blankenship to allow them to search Annie Sweetham's rooms. In my opinion, Holmes and Smith would have been more direct and forceful and likely less successful.

In many ways an existential side of Holmes comes to the fore at the story's end. The reader realizes that in saving the career of a politician, in this case a Fabian Socialist a few years before the formation of the Labour Party, Holmes has initiated a "butterfly effect" that will shape Britain's history for the next century. Holmes is left to question whether they will in the end have done their nation good or ill.

Sexual scandal and the "politics of personal destruction" are nothing new, and they fit well into the Victorian era. Anthrax in a letter was as viable and dangerous then as it is today.

"The Adventure of the Picked Pocket was a challenge to write, and I hope everyone has as much fun reading it as I did writing it.

FRED ADAMS - is a western Pennsylvania native who has enjoyed a lifelong love affair with horror, fantasy, and science fiction literature and films. He holds a Ph.D. in American Literature from Duquesne University and recently retired from teaching writing and literature in the English Department of Penn State University.

He has published over 50 short stories in amateur, and professional magazines as well as hundreds of news features as a staff writer and sportswriter for the now Pittsburgh Tribune-Review. In the 1970s Fred published the fanzine *Spoor* and its companion *The Spoor Anthology. Hitwolf, Six-Gun Terrors, Co. O. Jones: Mobsters and Monsters,* have been published by Airship 27 Productions, and his novel *Dead Man's Melody* has been nominated for a 2017 Pulp Factory award for Best Pulp Novel of the year.

Sherlock Holmes

in

"The Adventure of the Brazilian Beetle"

By
Aaron Smith

"My name, Mr. Holmes," said our visitor as he settled into the chair I had offered him, placing his brown leather satchel on the floor, "is Harry Lawson, and I am …"

"An artist," Sherlock Holmes interrupted. "That much is obvious by the callus on your finger, clearly the result of sketching with a pencil, which is of a different sort than that which arises from constant writing with a pen. Also, there is a bit of oil paint of a pale blue shade staining the cuff of your left shirtsleeve. And you smell faintly of an alcohol-based solvent used, presumably, for cleaning brushes or erasing unsatisfactory marks on a canvas."

"Yes," Lawson said, shifting in his seat, his face taking on the expression of discomfort I had often seen prospective clients wear as they came to the realization that Holmes could easily detect so much with so little effort.

The name the young man, who I judged to be no more than thirty years of age, had provided jarred my memory, and I quickly realized why.

"Harry Lawson," I repeated. "I do believe I have heard of you. You have a reputation as a painter of strikingly accurate portraits of the notable and famous of England and other parts of Europe, including, if I recall correctly, Her Majesty."

"Yes, Dr. Watson," Lawson confirmed with a satisfied smile, "the queen has indeed sat for me." But the smile quickly faded as the look of desperation he had worn upon his arrival at our Baker Street flat returned. It was a mask of fear and worry, the tired, haunted face of a man who thought he was in dire need of the sort of assistance Sherlock Holmes was known to provide. "But my accomplishments matter little now, for I think a human life is at stake, and I pray I have not come to you too late."

The mention of an endangered life caught Holmes' attention and he sat, leaned back in his chair, and said, "Tell us what has happened, Mr. Lawson. Include all details, for any scrap of information, however inconsequential it may at first seem, can be of the utmost importance."

"I have been most fortunate," Lawson began, "to have not only been able to earn a good living with my pictures, but to have gained a bit of fame as well. However, the soul of an artist is one that sometimes requires solitude and a break from the company of clients and fellow painters. I look forward to those days when no engagements are scheduled, no customers come to call, and I am free to indulge my whims and sketch and scribble at my leisure, answering to no one, being interrupted by no matters of urgency. One of my favorite pastimes is to take a book of blank pages and some pencils or pieces of chalk and make my way slowly and in a carefree state of mind to the Highgate Cemetery. In that great maze of burial sites, I find that the gravestones of varying shapes and sizes, the fortress-like mausoleums, the statues of angels in a multitude of poses, and the postures and attitudes of the mourners and other visitors make interesting subjects for study and sketching. When the sun is at the proper height and the clouds part, the day's brightness creates a striking contrast with the morbid atmosphere of the ..."

"Mr. Lawson," Holmes interjected, "your attention to detail is now becoming excessive. I assume something of interest happened to you in Highgate Cemetery. Please proceed to that part of your story."

"My apologies, sir," Lawson said. "My mind is a tangled mess of emotions and tends to wander into flights of poetry when thus stirred by its chaos."

"Dispense with the apologies," Holmes barked, "and continue your tale."

"It was a warm afternoon," Lawson resumed his narrative, "when I took one of my strolls to the cemetery. All seemed as it usually was and I stopped once or twice to make quick sketches of things or people that caught my eye. I had wandered down one of the paths that wind through corridors of trees with scattered gravestones on either side, knowing that at the end of my short journey would be a stone bench upon which I could rest for a moment and ponder where to go next.

"As I neared the area I sought, a woman passed me, dragging a small boy by the hand. I heard her mutter, 'Shameful behavior in a place of mourning.' I thought she was scolding her son, but as the stone bench came into view, I realized she was commenting on another visitor to the cemetery.

"A young woman had taken the place I had hoped to occupy. She sat cross-legged upon the stone bench. She looked nothing like the properly attired women of London, several of whom I had already seen walking among the graves. This woman was, I thought, in her early twenties. Her hair was long and black, and hanging loose around her shoulders. Her skin was a deep tan, which made me assume she was a foreigner of some sort. Her position upon the bench was oddly casual for such a somber place, and, to make the situation even more shocking—I understood the reaction of the woman with the child—the young woman was barefoot, her empty shoes sitting on the ground before the bench, her eyes were closed, and she was singing, not loudly, but certainly audibly, in a language that most definitely was not English.

"Had I been the same sort of person as the commenting woman, I'd have been horrified indeed to see such a sight in the Highgate Cemetery, of all places. But I am an artist, so my soul does have its wild tendencies, and I am often stricken by awe when I ponder the differences in personality and culture across the human race. So, you see, I was immediately consumed by fascination and curiosity concerning this young lady. And, I must admit, I also found her almost shockingly beautiful.

"I walked closer to the bench. She continued to sing, chanting long notes in a soft, lovely voice; though I still did not recognize words. I moved as quietly as I could, not wishing to interrupt her song. I stopped just in front of her and she must have seen, even through closed eyes, the change in light.

"She opened her eyes and stopped singing. She smiled, and the expression of serenity and happiness was breathtaking to behold. The beauty I had marveled at before was augmented by the surprising color of her eyes. I had expected brown, as light-colored eyes are, in my experience, a rarity among those of darker skin. But hers were of a bright blue, pure, and reminiscent of clean, cool water."

"Facts," Holmes said sharply. "You have made clear that you found her beautiful. Your aesthetic observations are wasting my time."

"Yes, yes, I am sorry," Lawson said. "I smiled back at her, began to apologize for interrupting her reverie, but she motioned for me to sit beside her, as there was more than enough room for two upon the stone seat.

"We spoke for quite some time, and I was captivated throughout our conversation. Her English was quite good, spoken with a lovely accent. She had traveled to London from her home, a small village in Brazil. When she was a child, she explained, a British gentleman had spent several years in her village, where he taught English to the natives. When she had heard of her teacher being gravely ill, she took what money she had and sailed to London to say goodbye to him, such was her gratitude and admiration.

"The teacher had died shortly after the reunion with his former student. My new acquaintance had attended the funeral, and then decided to come back to the cemetery alone several days later, as she liked the quiet atmosphere of the place, much, I suppose, as I have for many years. Unaccustomed to life in London, she had not realized that sitting in such a way, removing her shoes in public, and singing in a cemetery would offend passersby. The song, she told me, was an example of how people of different cultures view death differently. While we have our very solemn

English ways, she preferred to see the end of her teacher's life as a time to remember the good he had done in his days on the earth. And so she sang for him. The language of the song, I learned, had been Portuguese.

"The conversation went on and she told me of life in Brazil, and I told her about my art, showed her some sketches I had with me. She noticed me staring at a beautiful brooch she wore on her blouse. It appeared to be of silver, decorated with several small gems, and in the shape of a winged insect. She explained that it had been crafted by an artist in her home village, a silversmith of some repute, and was a representation of a sort of beetle native to those jungle regions. She claimed to believe that it gave her luck, and said it was her favorite possession. I thought it was a beautiful work of art, though not quite as beautiful as she who wore it.

"I asked her how long she intended to stay in London, and she admitted to not having decided yet. I summoned the courage to ask if I could see her again and if she would do me the great honor of posing for me. She smiled her wonderful smile and promised to consider it. I gave her my card. We said our farewells and parted ways.

"It was only after the glow of my delight at happening to meet such an intriguing woman had begun to fade ever so slightly that I realized, to my great shame, that I had somehow, in all that long, wonderful conversation, neglected to learn her name!"

Sherlock Holmes interrupted again, this time raising his voice in a loud warning, "Mr. Lawson, you stated moments ago that a life may be at stake. That is what caught my interest. If that was a lie and you have come here to ask me to find this woman simply because you were too absent-minded to ask her name, I must refuse. She knew your name and would have sought you out already had she so desired! How long ago was this chance encounter?"

"Ten days, Mr. Holmes," Lawson answered. "But it is not only my wish to see her again that has brought me here to seek your help."

"Then what has occurred since that day?" Holmes asked.

"Yesterday," Lawson said, "I happened to be walking along the street not far from the east end of the Highgate Cemetery. I had just received payment from a client and was on my way home, in no particular hurry. I glanced down at the ground and saw this!"

Lawson reached into his shirt pocket, produced a small object, and held it up for Holmes and me to see.

"The silver beetle," I said. "And you found it abandoned on the street?"

"Let me see it," Holmes said. Lawson handed it to the detective.

Holmes turned the piece of jewelry over several times, his sharp eyes taking in every detail.

"Interesting silver work," Holmes said. "The gems that were here have fallen out and left small impressions where they had been attached. Other small markings indicate a number of impacts to this brooch."

"Yes, of course," Lawson said. "I suppose it was kicked and stepped on by those walking too quickly to notice it where it lay."

"That is true," Holmes continued, "although it may have been struck in other ways as well. You said, did you not, that the woman who wore this brooch referred to it with great affection, as if she valued it highly?"

"Yes, Mr. Holmes, and that is what has me so afraid for her safety. From what little I know of her, she did not seem to be the sort to carelessly lose an object of such beauty and value. I dread to think what may have happened to her! Will you help me, Mr. Holmes?"

"I will certainly try to help this woman," Holmes answered, "if she is indeed in trouble of some kind, as this discovery of yours seems to indicate."

"But how can you," Lawson asked, "if we do not know her name or how to find her?"

"There are ways," Holmes assured him. "First I will need you to provide as detailed a description as possible of this woman. Watson, will you please take down the notes?"

"Of course, Holmes," I said.

"Dr. Watson, that will not be necessary," Harry Lawson said. He opened the satchel he had brought with him and took out a thick bundle of papers. Dividing the stack into halves, he handed one to Holmes and one to me. "I saw her only one time, but her face remains burned into my memory."

Lawson had drawn dozens of sketches of the Brazilian woman. He had not exaggerated when he had spoken of her beauty. She was indeed a striking vision to behold, even if she was now only lines on paper.

"This will do nicely," said Holmes. "We will have to be permitted to borrow these drawings."

"Of course," Lawson said.

"Then leave us your card, Mr. Lawson, and we will contact you as soon as we have information regarding this case," Holmes said. He then bellowed, "Mrs. Hudson, come and see our visitor out!"

"Holmes," I asked after Lawson had left, "how can we possibly find one young woman in a city the size of London, when we do not even know her name? We have these drawings, but I doubt they are enough to work with. We would have to show them to every man or woman in the streets, and even then we have no guarantee the subject would be recognized."

"Watson," Holmes replied, "when will you cease to have so little confidence in my methods? Yes, to ensure that many eyes see these depictions of our mysterious woman will aid our cause, but that is only one limb of the investigation I am about to begin. In a day or two, you will see, we will know, at the very least, the Brazilian woman's name and where she has been residing."

I knew from years of experience that Holmes would not be dissuaded by my doubts. I was, as always, ready and willing to be of assistance.

"How may I help, Holmes?" I asked.

"Make haste to the nearest shop that offers stationary supplies, Watson! Purchase thirty sheets of the thinnest paper you can find, and a dozen pencils."

As I went for my coat and hat, Holmes threw open the window, put his head out into the air, and shouted, "Wiggins, fetch Henry and Alexander and report up to my rooms at once! There will be coins for all!"

"Yes, Mr. Holmes," the voice of a young boy shouted back. Holmes had summoned several of the Baker Street Irregulars, a band of street urchins who had often been of great assistance to us. Holmes paid them what amounted to small fortunes in the minds of children, which made them all the more happy to be of help. The three he had called for this time, Wiggins, Henry, and Alexander, were, I knew, among the more intelligent of those boys, even capable of reading, a rare skill among the poorest of London's residents. Wiggins, among the older of the boys Holmes often employed, was the unofficial leader of the Irregulars.

I hurried off on my errand.

By evening, the factory Holmes had set up in Mrs. Hudson's kitchen had produced twenty copies of what we had decided were the three best of Harry Lawson's drawings of the unnamed Brazilian woman. The method of reproduction was simple. Our three Irregulars sat at the table and traced, as precisely as they could, the lines of Lawson's sketches onto the thin paper placed over the originals. The remaining ten sheets I had purchased were the unfortunate victims of mistakes that had gone beyond hope of salvation. The work progressed quickly as Holmes' promise of payment was added to by Mrs. Hudson's feeding pie to the boys. Our long-suffering landlady seemed to enjoy having mouths other than mine and Holmes' to feed, though she tried to hide her delight by grumbling about the dirt the urchins had tracked in and the fact that none of them seemed to have had a good hot bath in quite some time.

When Holmes felt we had sufficient pictures of the person we sought to find, he handed money to our three young helpers and instructed them to distribute the images to their friends at first light of morning. They were then to spread out and traverse as many streets as they could between Baker Street and the Highgate Cemetery, asking any passerby who might be willing to look if they had seen or knew anything, however trivial it might seem, about the woman.

After a breakfast expertly prepared by Mrs. Hudson, Holmes and I made our way to the administration office of the Highgate Cemetery, where we were let in by a secretary. Following a wait of some thirty minutes, during which Holmes paced impatiently, the head of the cemetery staff, a Mr. Snow, arrived. Snow was an elderly man, with tufts of hair sticking out around the edges of his head, pure white to match his name. He coughed several times before finally demanding, in a rough voice, what Holmes and I wanted from him so early in the day.

"You would, I assume," Holmes said, "be aware of all recent burials in this cemetery."

"Not only the recent ones," Snow responded in a tone that suggested he felt insulted by Holmes statement, "but of all the corpses encased in this place for the last twenty-three years! I never forget the dead!"

"That is most impressive, Mr. Snow," Holmes said, dismissing the man's bragging, "but I am only concerned with a new addition to your collection of the deceased."

"Tell me the name," Snow said.

"That is what you must tell us," Holmes explained. "The man we wish to know about was English, a schoolteacher, who traveled and died recently after an illness. He was not a young man. That is all the information we possess, but it should be enough for a man of your excellent knowledge to recognize whom we speak of."

"Carlisle," Snow said. "Ambrose Carlisle was his name. Aged sixty-six, buried a fortnight ago. A schoolteacher retired to London after many years abroad, in some warmer climes if his tanned face was any indication."

"An excellent and logical assumption, Mr. Snow," Holmes said. "Had life not brought you here to keep account of the dead, perhaps you would have made a fine detective. Now, tell me this: were you present at the funeral of this Ambrose Carlisle?"

"I was not!" Snow snapped. "I have no time to attend all the services in a cemetery as vast and important as this!"

"Then can you tell us the name of the clergyman who officiated at the funeral?"

"Of course I can. It was Father Dalton."

"And at what church would we find this Father Dalton?"

Snow scowled at Holmes, clearly growing tired of the interrogation. He turned to his secretary, barked, "Miss Jackson, look up Father Dalton's address so these gentlemen will let us get on with our day's work!"

Holmes and I found Father Dalton sweeping the floor of his church, thoroughly whisking away every bundle of dust and debris that had accumulated between and under the pews.

"Can I be of help to you gentlemen?" the minister asked as he looked up, his solitude broken by the sound of our shoes upon the hard floor.

Holmes wasted no time on pleasantries. "I understand you recently spoke at the funeral of one Ambrose Carlisle."

"I did," Dalton confirmed. "Were the two of you there? I do not remember you."

"We were not," Holmes said. "But we hope you might tell us something about a person who did attend the service. Do you recognize this young woman?"

Holmes took from his pocket one of Harry Lawson's sketches, unfolded it, and handed it to Father Dalton.

"She was there," Dalton said. "But I had never seen her before, and have not seen her since."

"You did not learn her name?"

"No, I only remember her being present ... oh, and something else!"

"What have you recalled?" Holmes asked, and I could hear the hope in his voice.

"The young lady carried on a short conversation with Professor Winbolt."

"Who is Professor Winbolt?"

"An old acquaintance of mine," Dalton explained. "He teaches anthropology at the King's College. I have never met another man so fascinated by the peculiarities of human behavior. Several years ago, I assisted him by answering some questions about the religious habits of my congregants, for a book he was writing."

"And he knew Ambrose Carlisle?"

"He was at the funeral. I assumed they were colleagues, both being members of the educational profession."

"And what did Winbolt discuss with the young woman?"

"I am not in the habit of eavesdropping. Perhaps the professor found her interesting because she was clearly not a native Londoner. She is, I would guess, a Spaniard?"

"Brazilian," Holmes said.

"Is she a criminal?"

"Not to my knowledge. We simply wish to locate her. I thank you for your help, Father. Perhaps Professor Winbolt can shed more light on this matter."

With that, Holmes darted for the door.

"Good day, sir," I said to the minister as I followed my friend out.

As much as he disliked the notoriety my written accounts of his cases brought him, Sherlock Holmes' celebrity occasionally had its uses. The young clerk who received us at the King's College muttered some kind comments about his fascination with Holmes' methods and was supremely happy to be of assistance to the detective and me. He led us down a long corridor to a door upon which was nailed a placard designating it as the entrance to the office of Professor Bartholomew Winbolt. Our guide knocked, waited until the occupant had called for us to enter, and then stuttered out a string of expressions of joy at having had the chance to meet Holmes. I thanked him for reading my work and he hurried down

He led us down a long corridor to the office of Professor Bartholomew Winbolt.

the hall, doubtlessly to tell the next several people he saw of the delightful encounter he had just had.

Holmes, having heard enough from his admirer, pushed open the door and went through. I followed and, perhaps purely by instinct, but more likely because of some observation reaching my brain in a way I could not precisely understand—and I imagine Holmes' mind works in that way often and successfully, though for me it is a far less frequent oc-currence—instantly disliked Professor Winbolt. He had an air about him that suggested great conceit, strong opinions, and a merciless determina-tion to allow nothing to alter those ideas.

Winbolt looked down at the card Holmes handed him, sneered as if our visit was as distracting as a sudden earthquake, and barked, "What is it you want?"

Holmes wasted no time on pleasant introductions. "I understand, Professor Winbolt, you were in attendance at the recent funeral of a schoolteacher called Ambrose Carlisle."

"Yes," Winbolt snapped. "Ambrose was a colleague. What of it?"

"My sympathies on your loss, if Carlisle was a friend," Holmes said, his voice softening as he tried to calm the professor's annoyance.

"I did not say he was a friend," Winbolt insisted, "though he had my respect, at the very least."

"Sometimes," Holmes said, "that is worth even more than friendship."

"What is it you want with me, Mr. Holmes?"

"I have been told, Professor," Holmes said as he took Lawson's drawing from his pocket, "that you were seen at the funeral conversing with this woman."

Winbolt snatched the paper from Holmes, glanced at it, and, handing it back, replied, "Yes, I remember her. We spoke briefly."

"Of what did you speak?"

"I asked her some questions."

"For what purpose, Professor, did you question her?"

"Scientific curiosity," Winbolt said.

"Was her name among those queries?"

"It was ... but I do not recall it now."

"I see," said Holmes. "And what is this scientific curiosity of which you speak?"

"I am an anthropologist, sir, and that does not mean I am only in-terested in the various human cultures of the past. Indeed, I am just as fascinated by the numerous cultures of the present world and, specifically, how they often merge, or, in more unfortunate cases, clash with one another."

"So you spoke with this young woman not because you knew her previously, but because she was not English?"

"I could tell immediately upon seeing her that she was a foreigner."

"You say that as if you found her presence at the funeral offensive, yet you must know that Ambrose Carlisle taught in many parts of the world and would have had students of many nationalities."

"Of course, but that does not mean I approve of their kind coming here!"

"Quite a closed-minded attitude from a man of science," Holmes said, and it was clear to me that he was now intentionally pushing at the professor with his words, trying to test the limits of Winbolt's strong opinions on the subject of foreigners.

"It is not closed-minded, Mr. Holmes, not at all. As an anthropologist, I appreciate the myriad differences between peoples! And I most surely do not approve of those differences being lost by migration, interbreeding, and the mingling of cultures and races! It will, I am convinced, lead to the rise of chaos and anarchy in the lands that were once our colonies in North America, and I shudder to think of the same degradation occurring here in England!

"I say we let the English have England, the French have France; the Spaniards and natives have already become a mixed race in the South American nations and so they should stay there to prevent further corruption of the world's unique bloodlines! Leave the African continent to the backward black races, allow the Asian nations and islands to be the provinces of their yellow-skinned people, and let the Arabs have their sands!"

"But, Professor Winbolt," Holmes argued, "the world continues to shrink as progress occurs with each passing year. Ships sail at greater speeds and less and less time is needed to travel from one nation or even one continent to the next. There is nothing you or I or any man can do to prevent the cultures of the world from interacting with each other. These developments you so loathe will only increase in frequency as time passes and improvements are made to our means of getting from one place to another."

"I concur, Holmes, and it is for that reason that I fear the future."

"Is that fear, Professor, powerful enough that it might tempt you to do harm to a foreign visitor to this city, one such as the young Brazilian woman you encountered at Carlisle's funeral?"

"Certainly not," Winbolt protested. "I am shocked that you would make such an accusation!"

"I am accusing you of nothing," Holmes said. "I simply wish to understand the facts."

"Then understand this, Holmes! I am a man of science, of intellect, and have earned the respect of my colleagues over the many years I have been an observer of the world and a teacher of facts. I am no criminal. Although I do not approve of the natives of lesser nations invading our shores, I will not stoop so low as to engage in barbaric behavior more suitable for less civilized parts of the world. I have much work to do, so I will bid you and your friend good day!"

With that, Professor Bartholomew Winbolt pointed to the door.

Holmes and I exited the office.

"A pompous, foul, opinionated man," I said in regards to Professor Winbolt as Holmes and I rode back to Baker Street. "Do you think he is telling the truth in his denial of having done anything other than speak with the missing woman?"

"I do not know, Watson," Holmes admitted. "Our dislike of the man cannot be taken as evidence of any wrongdoing, though it would be wise for us to learn more of this professor before reaching any definite conclusion. As it stands, we have made no progress as yet, for we still do not even know the name of the Brazilian woman."

"Perhaps news awaits us at home," I said, hoping to counter Holmes' frustration with an ounce of optimism.

My hope was rewarded as we disembarked in front of our flat to find young Wiggins of the Irregulars sitting upon the front stoop.

"One of the boys came through, Mr. Holmes," the lad said excitedly.

"Then come upstairs, Wiggins," Holmes said, "And tell us what you have learned!"

Once inside, Wiggins handed Holmes one of the copies of Harry Lawson's sketch of the Brazilian woman. Under the portrait had been written, in a wild scrawl, a name and address.

"Mrs. Margaret Soames," Holmes read, and then said, "This cannot be the name of a Brazilian."

"It's not," said Wiggins. "Alexander showed the picture to a lady on the street and she said she knew the girl, said she'd rented her a room but hadn't heard a word from her nor seen a sight of her in days. By the time Alexander reported back to me—he'd written the name and address as he was running to get me—he'd plain forgotten the name of the girl in the drawing."

"Still," said Sherlock Holmes, "your friend has done well. Here is a bonus for you and for Alexander." He took out a few coins, gave them to Wiggins. Turning back toward me, he said, "Come, Watson, our day's journeys are not yet concluded."

Mrs. Soames was an older woman, though not quite elderly, still robust for her age. She greeted Holmes and I warmly and invited us to sit in her small parlor.

We were soon served tea and Mrs. Soames finally sat with us. Holmes showed her Lawson's drawing.

"I believe you told one of the boys who work for me that you know this young woman," Holmes said.

"Her name," Mrs. Soames said, "is Benedita Costa. She arrived here last month and came to me in response to an advertisement I had posted in the newspaper. I rented her the room upstairs. The money was useful, though renting the room was more so I would have some company, someone to talk to since my Henry is gone. And she's such a lovely girl, and speaks such good English for a foreigner. We had some superb conversations over tea ... and then one day she disappeared, went for a walk and never returned. I have been keeping her things here for her, and hoping she is well."

"Why did you not report her disappearance to the police?" Holmes asked.

"But I did! And they told me they would make some inquiries, but that it was likely just a case of an alien to London deciding on a whim to wander elsewhere. I supposed I wouldn't get much more help from them after that dismissive comment."

"May I see Miss Costa's belongings?"

"Yes, Mr. Holmes, as I cannot see what harm it will do."

We followed Mrs. Soames upstairs, where she let us into a small bedroom. Holmes went about the routine of digging through the tenant's clothing and other items, but finally put down the last of them, turned to me with a bored expression, and said, "Nothing, Watson!"

He then faced Mrs. Soames, said, "Thank you for your time," and marched down the stairs and out through the door.

"And thank you for the tea!" I shouted as I followed.

"Do inform me if you find her," Mrs. Soames called after me. "Please!"

"Confound it, Watson!" Holmes shouted as we walked along the street "There are times I cannot bring myself to forgive the laziness and incompetence of Scotland Yard!"

"At the very least," said I, attempting to encourage my friend, "we now know her full name."

"For all the good that does us!" Holmes continued his tirade. "But hope is not lost, Watson, for something occurred to me shortly after we left Professor Winbolt's office several hours ago."

"What is it, Holmes?"

"It is the reason we must divide our resources. I have an errand to ask of you, Watson."

"You have only to name it."

"Go to Scotland Yard and enlist the help of one of the inspectors whom we have trusted in the past. Lestrade, Bradstreet, Gregson—it matters not which of them it is, for we need a man who can discreetly look into records of recent calls and complaints to the department."

"What, precisely, am I seeking aid in finding?"

"Any report of a woman being accosted or otherwise molested in the vicinity of the place where Harry Lawson claims to have discovered the battered silver beetle."

"Which was, if I recall, near the east end of the Highgate Cemetery," I said.

"Indeed, Watson, indeed," Holmes confirmed. "Now hurry, for it grows late in the day and you must catch one of our frequent allies before his shift has ended and his home and supper beckon to him."

"And where will you be, Holmes?"

"I must look into a matter that I hope will be related to this investigation, for it occurs to me that a certain surname is not nearly as common as Smith, Johnson, or, for that matter, Watson! I shall see you tonight back at Baker Street!"

It happened to be Inspector Bradstreet that I found first. A tall, stout man with a full beard, Bradstreet had been involved in several previous cases with Holmes and I, perhaps most notably the bizarre affair in which the unfortunate young engineer, Victor Hatherly, had lost his thumb.

"Digging through reports is not something I do lightly," Bradstreet said, "especially when such a task is at the request of amateurs. No disrespect to you and Holmes intended, but perhaps matters are better dealt with when brought officially to police attention."

"But the case we are investigating was indeed brought to the attention of the Yard," I protested, "and promptly ignored!"

"We are busy," Bradstreet countered, "and there are times when certain matters are too trivial to have our full attention devoted to them."

"And that, Inspector, is why men like Sherlock Holmes are necessary. I ask again, will you help us?"

"Come along then," Bradstreet said with an exaggerated huff.

I followed him into a room filled with cabinets, each of which featured drawers containing written reports of matters called to Scotland Yard's attention in recent weeks or months. I knew from previous visits that older reports were sent to another floor, but it was only in newer information that I was interested on this evening.

After having given Inspector Bradstreet a brief account of what I sought, I watched him rummage through several of the drawers before he finally pulled out a thin document, only two sheets thick, held together by a Gem clip.

"Seems there was an incident reported that fits your description, Dr. Watson," Bradstreet said as he looked over the report. "Four nights ago, a man walking along the same stretch of road you designated claimed to have seen a young lady being grabbed by two men, screaming while the assault was taking place, and being rather rudely shoved into a cab, which then sped off after the driver laid a cruel strike of the whip upon the horse's back. The witness, it says here, was reluctant to interfere due to the fact that he walks with a severe limp and doubted his ability to hurry across the street and face a possible physical confrontation. Instead, he went as fast as he could, supported by his cane, to fetch the closest constable. By that time, the carriage had long since vanished. So you see, Doctor, there was nothing we could do, not having any idea of the identity of the woman or her abductors, if indeed that is what they were."

"Thank you, Inspector," I said. "Did the witness describe the victim in any detail, other than to say she was a woman of youth?"

Bradstreet glanced down at the report again, laughed, and looked up at me. "Luck is not on your side tonight, for the witness to the scene not only had trouble with his leg, but was nearsighted as well!"

"Thank you for your help," I said. "It was indeed valuable, although I wish it had been more so. Good night, Inspector."

I hurried back to Baker Street after my meeting with Bradstreet, eager to tell Holmes what I had learned. When I entered our rooms, I found him seated in his favorite chair, a cloud of pipe smoke swirling above his head, and a bright smile across his face.

"Watson," he shouted, "when memory serves, it serves well!"

"What have you discovered, Holmes?" I asked.

Holmes turned his head slightly toward the door and bellowed, "Mrs. Hudson, a fresh pot of coffee, if you please!"

I declined to join Holmes in drinking coffee, as I intended to sleep that night, electing instead to enjoy a glass of brandy.

After stirring a bit of sugar into his beverage, Holmes looked at me and inquired, "Did the name Winbolt not stir your memory as it stirred mine, Watson? You are, after all, a more thorough reader of the daily papers than I, as I tend to confine my attention to the crime section."

"I must confess it did not," I said, "but I do not possess the often-seemingly supernaturally sharp capacity to recall minutiae that you do."

"There is nothing supernatural about it, Watson, for it is merely a matter of practice. One must hone the memory as one might slide a knife along a sharpening block until it is as keen as its potential allows. But no more digressions; let us return to the matter of the missing woman."

"The name Winbolt, then …"

"It belongs not only to our professor of anthropology, Bartholomew, but also to his brother, Horatio."

"That name, Horatio Winbolt," I admitted, "still means nothing to me. Is he a man of some note?"

"Music boxes!" Sherlock Holmes shouted, so loudly that I thought the vibrations would cause several trinkets to fall from the mantle.

It was then that I recalled the name.

"The Winbolt Toy Manufacturing Company," I said, "is responsible for the very ornate mechanical music boxes that have been so fashionable among London society the past several Christmas seasons."

"Yes, Watson, yes," Holmes confirmed, "with one even being presented to Her Majesty last Christmas."

"And this company is headed by the brother of Professor Winbolt?"

"Indeed it is."

"But what has this to do with the apparent abduction of Benedita Costa?"

"Oh, Watson, I had hoped you would ask that! Am I to understand that you have ascertained that indeed she was taken against her will?"

"It seems that way, Holmes, although there is no solid proof beyond a reported event concerning which the police were unable to pursue a proper investigation due to lack of information."

"Tell me what you learned at Scotland Yard, Watson, and we will see how it relates to the Winbolt brothers!"

I gave Holmes as full an account as I could of the report Bradstreet had shown me. When I had finished, Holmes stared at me for a moment, then said, "Rest, Watson, while I ponder the facts, incomplete as they may be. Tomorrow, we shall continue upon what I suspect has become a strange and perhaps sinister trail."

Curious as I was, I did not ask Holmes to clarify what he meant, for I knew from experience that he would reveal that to me only when he was ready. I went to bed.

It was the smell of yet another pot of coffee that woke me, and this time I was drawn to the hot drink like a man in the desert who spots merciful, lifesaving water.

I dressed quickly and ventured out of my room to find Sherlock Holmes still in the chair he had been in when I had retired, still with a haze of smoke like a halo over his head.

"Good morning, Watson," he said.

"Have you been awake all night, Holmes? Lack of proper rest can take its toll on even the heartiest of men …"

"Spare me the lecture, Doctor. Drink your coffee and eat your breakfast, for we have a long day ahead of us."

"You have reached some conclusion in your meditation upon the Costa problem, then?"

"I have theories, and that is all I have, but perhaps they can be proven or disproved by means of a bit of espionage."

"Then your long night was not wasted. You have conceived plans."

"I have, and I have already sent Wiggins to fetch Harry Lawson."

"Why do we need Lawson?"

"To gain us admittance to the Winbolt Company, of course," Holmes said, as if I would immediately understand the particulars of his scheme.

"Winbolt," he began to explain when he took notice of the confused look upon my face, "more than tripled production of its music boxes two years ago. The company's owner, Horatio Winbolt, claimed, when quoted in a certain newspaper article, that such an increase in manufacturing was due to a machine he had installed at the factory. He declined to provide the interviewer with the particulars of the equipment's design, saying that he wished to guard his secrets lest they fall into the hands of competitors."

"I had no idea," I remarked, "that the music box industry was so mercilessly competitive."

"I would not expect it to be. Such secrecy is an oddity worth investigating, do you not agree, Watson?"

"I suppose so, but I still do not see the connection between this and Miss Costa."

"Perhaps there is none, but I must know for certain before other avenues can be explored."

"I see," I said as I attacked my breakfast with fork, knife, and the sort of great hunger that comes after a night of peaceful slumber.

As I finished my meal and poured my second cup of coffee, Mrs. Hudson opened the door and announced our visitor.

"Mr. Lawson to see you, Mr. Holmes," she said.

Lawson entered, sat down without so much as a proper greeting, and stared hopefully at Holmes. "Have you found her?"

"Not yet," Holmes answered.

"Then why have you summoned me here?" Lawson asked.

The young artist looked terrible. He had not shaved, his skin had taken

"Have you found her?"

on a sickly gray color, and his words were slightly slurred as if either by drink or tiredness.

"Are you ill, sir?" I asked.

"Only an illness of the heart," Lawson said. "My head is heavy with worry and I have been unable to sleep, eat, or even paint. Please tell me you have learned something … anything about what has become of her! I beg you!"

"We have discovered some pertinent information," Holmes said.

Holmes and I related what we knew so far: the young woman's name, where she had been staying, her appearance at the funeral and her encounter with Professor Winbolt, and the report of what we thought had been her abduction.

"Is that all you have summoned me here to tell me?" Lawson asked when Holmes had finished his story.

"I have also called you to ask your assistance," Holmes said.

"What could you possibly need of me?" Lawson asked, and it was evident from the tone of his voice that his patience had worn thin as the paper the boys had used to trace his drawings. But he took in a deep breath and, more calmly, assured us, "If my being here helps bring Benedita to safety, then I am, of course, more than willing. Benedita! Finally, I have a name to put with her face."

"What I want," Holmes explained, "is to investigate the activities of one Mr. Horatio Winbolt, brother of the anthropologist and owner of a large manufacturer of music boxes and other trinkets. Judging by the quotes attributed to Winbolt in various newspaper articles, he is a man with a high opinion of himself, and thus would be likely, given a bit of encouragement, to deem himself worthy of having his portrait made by a painter of great renown."

"I am grateful that you think so much of my work, Mr. Holmes," Lawson said.

"I have never seen your work," Holmes replied coldly, "but I am aware of its reputation. And that reputation will, I hope, be enough to make Winbolt wish to sit for you. He will then be persuaded that the portrait be painted not at his home but at his place of business. He will be advised that it is best to capture his likeness at the place that defines who he is as a man and a magnate."

"How will that allow you and Dr. Watson admission to the factory?"

"You will require your agent and assistant to be present."

"I see," said Lawson with a nod. "But you are something of a celebrity too, Mr. Holmes. What of the chance that Winbolt will recognize you?"

At that, I began to laugh. "Mr. Lawson, I assure you that Holmes is quite capable of rendering himself unrecognizable to me, let alone a man who has seen his face only in, perhaps, the illustrations that have accompanied my accounts of his cases. Holmes is as much an artist with disguise as you are with brush and paint!"

"All right," Lawson said. "But how shall I approach Winbolt? I have only ever been commissioned when it was the subject's idea, including the occasion on which I was honored to have the opportunity to paint the queen."

"Allow me to see to that small detail," Holmes insisted. "Return here tomorrow morning, nine o'clock, and bring the tools of your trade."

"Will I begin this job that soon? I must rest if I am to paint tomorrow, and I do not know if sleep will come, no matter how desperately I desire it."

In response to Lawson's worry, Holmes turned to me.

"Watson, will you provide our friend with something to put him to sleep?"

"I should be happy to do just that," I said, and reached for my bag.

A moment later, Harry Lawson shuffled slowly to the door and left us. I hoped the pills I had placed in his hand would be sufficient to give him some peace for the hours of sleep needed to renew his energy. When he had gone, I questioned Holmes.

"How do you expect to convince Horatio Winbolt to commission Harry Lawson to paint his portrait, especially by tomorrow morning? From what I have read in the articles you showed me, Winbolt is an obstinate man, and I doubt very much it will be easy to talk him into doing anything, much less something like paying for a portrait and putting his other obligations on hold while sitting for it. Why should he listen to you, me, or any ally we set to such a task?"

"I have, of course, thought that very problem through quite thoroughly, Watson. Horatio Winbolt, you see, is a member of the Diogenes Club. As such, he is well acquainted with my brother Mycroft. I shall let my brother do the work this time. Mycroft can be quite convincing when arguing a point. He will make Winbolt want—no—need to have his portrait painted immediately!"

The remainder of the day went by uneventfully, with Holmes leaving for several hours on errands of which I did not ask the details. I spent the afternoon reading, and then joined Holmes for a meal of Mrs. Hudson's roast beef. The late evening found me trying to finish the novel I had begun hours earlier, while Holmes sat silently and smoked.

But the quiet of the night was shattered by a loud pounding on the door at nearly eleven.

"Aha!" Holmes shouted. "I knew he would not fail, and he has gone so far as to leave his usual haunt and confirm his success to us in person! Mrs. Hudson! That will be my brother knocking. Please see him up!"

Heavy footsteps shook the stairs, the door opened, and Sherlock Holmes' older brother entered our flat, threw off his overcoat, and stood there like a giant of a man as Mrs. Hudson shut the door behind him.

It had been some months since I had last seen Mycroft, but he had not changed. Tall and massively built, with a head that seemed impossibly large, he bore some resemblance to his thinner brother, and had an intense piercing stare that seemed to suck in all the details of his surroundings in a way that was much more intimidating than that of Sherlock.

"All accomplished?" the younger Holmes asked.

"Indeed," Mycroft answered as he lowered himself into a chair. "Horatio Winbolt heeded my advice immediately and will display the utmost willingness to sit and be immortalized on canvas by the brush of Harry Lawson tomorrow morning."

The two Holmes brothers working together was always an interesting phenomenon to witness. I could not contain my curiosity. "How did you convince him so quickly?" I asked.

Mycroft laughed. "Lies and forgery," he said. "Horatio Winbolt is aware that I work for the government in some capacity, though he, of course, is unaware of the particulars. With that fact at my disposal, along with some documentation I had manufactured specifically for the occasion, I congratulated Winbolt and informed him that he has been chosen to have some sort of official recognition from Her Majesty for his, as I put it in my story, contributions to the wellbeing of British industry. I hinted, though did not go so far as to say as much in my collection of lies, that a knighthood may be in his future. Of course, he believed me, due to the weight of my reputation at the club. I then strongly suggested he have his portrait prepared at once, as we may want to hang it among the images of some rather notable Diogenes members should the honor from the queen be as momentous as it seems it might. He did protest a bit, complaining of the time and expense that might be wasted on having his likeness thus captured, but I assured him that the work could be done—and would perhaps serve him better if done—at the building containing his factory and office, rather than his private estate. He then, as I predicted he would, since he has little to no knowledge of the arts, asked me if I had an artist to recommend. I told him he had better contact Harry Lawson at once, for who better to paint Horatio Winbolt than the man who had not so very long ago painted the queen!"

Sherlock Holmes clapped his hands together loudly, said, "You have my thanks, Mycroft!"

"And you, Sherlock, have, I assume, the twenty pounds I owe the forger of Winbolt's letter from the queen?"

"Yes, just a moment," the younger of the brothers said as he walked into his bedroom to retrieve the money.

I took the opportunity to ask a question that seemed quite vital at the moment.

"Are you not worried, Mycroft," said I, "that Winbolt will discover your deception?"

"I am betting, Dr. Watson, that Sherlock has stumbled upon something quite nefarious, and that soon it will not matter what Horatio Winbolt says or does, for he will have matters to worry about that far outweigh any little trick I subjected him to!"

It was clear to me that Mycroft knew more about what his brother suspected than I had been told. Whatever the reason for that, I knew all would become clear in time, perhaps even the very next morning.

Harry Lawson was in much better spirits when he arrived at precisely nine in the morning, just as Holmes had instructed.

"Good morning, Dr. Watson," he said. "Your medication has allowed me to rest, and I feel wonderful, though I am still deeply worried about the safety of Benedita. I am ready to paint as I have rarely painted before! A cab waits outside with my equipment inside. Where is Mr. Holmes?"

At that moment, Holmes emerged from his room, barely recognizable. He had dressed in an old pair of trousers and a well-worn shirt. A false moustache adorned his face and he had added a hint of gray to his hair and applied a mole to his left cheek.

"Hello, Harry," Holmes said, his voice already taking on an accent, which shifted slightly from word to word as he perfected it. "I shall be your assistant, and my name will be Bruno. Watson, who shall require no disguise, will act as your agent, and we shall call him Mr. Hampton. Let us be off, then. Hampton, you will provide the driver with directions to the Winbolt Company."

Holmes shoved a sheet of paper into my hand. I looked down to see that it featured an address and a description of our route. The three of us departed together and took our seats inside the carriage, among the easel and cases of brushes and paint.

As we rode, Holmes explained to me exactly what I was to do once we arrived at our destination.

The building housing the Winbolt Toy Manufacturing Company was a large structure sitting in an otherwise sparsely populated region outside London's busier sections. The carriage stopped on the grounds and I instructed the driver to return for us in eight hours' time. I carried a notebook Holmes had given me, along with a dozen pencils. Also, under Holmes' advice, I had concealed my revolver within a pocket of my coat. I walked up to the doors of the building with Lawson and Holmes following as each of them carried a portion of the artist's supplies.

I knocked upon the door and waited for a response from within. In less than a minute, the big wooden doors opened toward the interior and we were met by two large men in identical suits, each of whom bore the telltale bulge of a pistol strapped to his side under his jacket.

"Good morning, gentlemen," I said. "My name is Hampton. I represent Harry Lawson." I turned halfway back toward my two companions, waved my hand in their direction as I introduced them. "He has an appointment with Mr. Horatio Winbolt. And this is his assistant, Bruno."

"Yes, sir," said one of the armed guards. "You are expected. Mr. Winbolt will see you straightaway."

We were led inside by one of the guards, while the other remained near the doors. We climbed a staircase and were deposited in a waiting area outside a door upon which hung a nameplate identifying it as the office of Horatio Winbolt. A moment later, a small man with spectacles emerged from the office and greeted us in a voice that was, to put it as politely as possible, severely lacking in masculinity.

"I am Geoffrey," he said, not volunteering a surname, "Mr. Winbolt's personal secretary. Which of you is the artist?"

"I am," said Harry Lawson. "Allow me to introduce my agent, Mr. Hampton, and my assistant, Bruno."

Geoffrey made a little bowing gesture toward me, but looked suspiciously at Holmes. For a moment, I worried that he had recognized the detective despite his disguise, but I then realized it was more a look of scornful disapproval, perhaps at the state of Bruno's attire.

"Will you all be present as the portrait is painted?" Geoffrey asked.

"I should like to meet Mr. Winbolt," I said, following Holmes' instructions, "after which point I shall excuse myself. After that, while Mr. Lawson works, I wonder if I might be given a tour of the factory, if that would not be too much trouble?"

"That would be my pleasure," Geoffrey said. "But what of *him?*" he asked, looking yet again, with hostility, at Holmes.

"Bruno is quite indispensable to Mr. Lawson," I explained. "It would be helpful to have him there … unless, of course, there is some objection."

Geoffrey snorted, almost spoke, then stopped himself, and finally said, "I shall leave that decision to Mr. Winbolt. Come, gentlemen, and meet your client."

Horatio Winbolt bore some resemblance to his brother, but was larger. His mostly brown hair was streaked with white and his cheeks ruddy. He wore an expensive suit, expertly tailored to fit his bulky frame.

He looked the three of us over as we entered, and then shot a look of dismay at Geoffrey, who shrugged.

"Sir," said Geoffrey, "This is Mr. Harry Lawson, his agent Mr. Hampton, and his assistant."

"You shall make a fine picture," Lawson said.

"I am pleased to meet you, sir," said I.

"*Buongiorno,*" said Sherlock Holmes in an excellent Italian accent.

"He must leave," Winbolt said.

"But he is my assistant!" Lawson protested.

"I have commissioned *you* to paint my portrait, Lawson. I did not agree to the presence of foreigners. Do you want your money or not? There are other painters in London!"

I stepped between the angry businessman and the young artist.

"You are the customer, Mr. Winbolt," I said. "If you wish Bruno to leave, I will see to it. Mr. Lawson shall have to do without assistance just this once. Harry, set up your things and decide where you would like Mr. Winbolt to sit. Geoffrey, is there someone who might escort Bruno outside? I am sure he will be content to wait there for us, as it is a pleasant day with few clouds and a fine breeze."

"Come with me, Bruno," Geoffrey said. "Mr. Hampton, I will see him out and return for you. I have not forgotten your request for a tour of the facility."

Geoffrey and Holmes departed, with Holmes keeping his character up by muttering Italian profanities.

Horatio Winbolt was much more polite once the room had been cleared of the man whose presence he found so offensive. He complimented Lawson's previous work, agreed to sit in a chair against a wall that Lawson had designated as being the best reflector of the natural light that streamed in through the office's large window, and even offered us tea. By the time Geoffrey returned, Lawson had begun his work, having drawn a few preliminary lines in light pencil upon the fresh, new canvas.

I followed Geoffrey out of the office as he began to explain the layout of the building.

"There is very little that will be of interest to you on this floor, Mr. Hampton, for it is only clerical work which takes place here. You have seen Mr. Winbolt's office. Mine is over there, and behind that other door is our records and filing room, but those places are quite dull compared to the marvels to be found in the heart of this castle of ours. Come along and see the wonders of the Winbolt music box manufacturing method!"

What Geoffrey showed me was truly amazing. We went first to a small room wherein two men selected various objects, including gears, screws, and the round cylinders that produce the notes while turning inside a music box, as well as the pieces of wood and cloth that would go to make the exterior walls, bottom, and lid of such a box. These things were then dropped into separate tubes that led into the wall at a slight downward angle.

"These two workers," Geoffrey explained, "are feeding the machines."

"You mean to tell me," I asked, "that some sort of contraption will now put the pieces together?"

"Yes, Mr. Hampton," Geoffrey said, his voice rising in excitement. "In most of the civilized world, man is just beginning to understand the possibilities inherent in the harnessing of electricity to make our lives easier and lessen our workload. Hotels and residences now boast electric lamps, and other uses have been found for this mighty natural force that can be trapped and run through wires to do our bidding, but here at the Winbolt Company, we are many steps ahead of the rest of the world!

"Few men have seen what you are about to see, Mr. Hampton. Mr. Winbolt has a firm policy of keeping journalists out, for he does not wish the secrets of his manufacturing process made known to his competitors. He will also not allow scientists or engineers within the works, for he dislikes other men meddling with his inventions. But you, I feel, can be considered a friend of the company, for you have brought your artist here on short notice and charged a reasonable fee for a portrait that must be done quickly.

"Let us now descend one level further into the factory and witness the wonder of assembly!"

What I saw on the next floor down from the level where the components were dropped almost literally made me unable to breathe. It was a vast chamber containing equipment that seemed fit for a novel by Jules Verne rather than for the real world. Long rubber belts ran along the length of the room and seemed to move by themselves. They carried half-finished music boxes, neatly spaced, from station to station, where they would run downward, disappear into a hole, then reemerge when the moving track sloped upward again and brought them back to visibility. On each return to sight, another part had been added until, finally, at the very end of the room, which is where Geoffrey and I stood, the music box was complete and a man, one of only two workers in the room, took each one, looked it over, and placed it in a slightly larger wooden box. The other employee would walk up and down the tracks and write something in pencil upon the pages of a small notebook, as if inspecting the works and checking the speed of the wondrous machine.

"Good lord!" I shouted, sincerely shocked by what I saw. "Is that all it takes to create such exquisite items, two men and this machine?"

"Indeed," Geoffrey said. "A larger crew, composed of seven gentlemen, arrives early each morning to oil the gears and pulleys of the machines, and make certain all is well. Once they are finished, these two fine workers run the operation for the remainder of the day, often turning out as many as fifty music boxes by late afternoon."

"Bravo," I said, clapping my hands together thrice.

My outward joy, however, was but a mask; my true attention was focused on certain questions Holmes had directed me to discover the answers to.

"Do you mind terribly much if I make some rough sketches of this incredible device?" I asked. "They will merely be a keepsake of this experience, and you have my word as a gentleman that they shall never be published or shown to any member of the press or academic community."

"That will be acceptable," Geoffrey said. "I am most happy you have enjoyed the tour, Mr. Hampton. Are you hungry? Perhaps you would join me for tea and biscuits while we wait for Mr. Winbolt's portrait to be completed."

"I would be glad to," I said as I scribbled some notes to refer to later when I talked with Holmes.

"If you wish, I will have one of the men bring food outside for your Italian," Geoffrey offered.

"No," I said. "Bruno will be fine. He is probably enjoying the warm afternoon and amusing himself by watching the birds and listening to their songs. He is a rather simpleminded fellow, though he is useful to Harry."

During tea with Geoffrey, who was such a perpetually nervous man that his manner began to fray my own nerves, I inserted into the conversation several questions designed to unearth information I thought Holmes would find pertinent. After my time with Winbolt's assistant, I spent the next several hours waiting for Harry Lawson's session with Horatio Winbolt to end. When the door to Winbolt's office finally opened, Lawson stumbled out carrying his canvas and bag of brushes and paints, looking quite exhausted. I hurried over to help him, taking possession of the bag and letting the artist retain his hold on the canvas, which was surely the more valuable of the two items.

"Did it go well?" I asked.

"He is an arrogant, conceited windbag," Lawson said, keeping his voice low to avoid Geoffrey's overhearing his remarks. "But I will admit he knows how to keep still."

"The painting?" I inquired.

"Rough, but with all the essential lines in place," Lawson answered. "I shall have no difficulty finishing it in my studio, with the aid of the reference sketches I made before applying much to canvas."

"Excellent," I said. "You appear to be tired. You will be home and at rest within the hour. Our driver should have returned by now, so go and seat yourself in the cab while I find Bruno."

Geoffrey saw us out. Our carriage had indeed arrived, and Holmes, still bearing the mannerisms he had created in order to portray the Italian, stood petting one of the horses.

As evening darkened London, Holmes, Lawson, and I sat at Baker Street, eating a meal prepared by Mrs. Hudson. Holmes had shed his accent and disguise and donned his usual sort of attire.

I took the first turn at revealing what I had learned at the Winbolt Company.

"A most extraordinary operation, this Winbolt Company is. A great machine, churning forth dozens of musical boxes, with a minimum of employees to be paid. Truly an efficient business."

"How many workers?" Holmes asked.

"Winbolt himself," I replied, "the assistant, Geoffrey; the two doormen we met today; two men to feed parts to the machine; seven men, I was told, who maintain the machine; and, as Geoffrey revealed over tea, three watchmen who guard the place by night."

"Are these men armed?" was Holmes' next question.

"Indeed they are," I said. "While Geoffrey did not specifically say so, I had the impression that Horatio Winbolt is adamant that no journalist or industrial spy should ever witness the automated miracle he has created."

"Watson," Holmes said, with his voice low and deadly serious, "do you believe in this, as you called it, miracle?"

"Holmes," I admitted, "I am at a loss as to what to believe. It seems highly improbable that such a marvel of machinery could have sprung from Winbolt's imagination into reality when lesser devices are the recent product of some of the world's leading inventors. Yet I saw it at work!"

"You saw, Watson, but did you hear? Tell me, how loud was the dynamo that produced the electrical power necessary to the manufacture of all those music boxes?"

"Not—" I was startled by Holmes question, as I had managed to overlook, in my dazed awe, what so easily occurred to him. "Not nearly as loud as one would expect! What should have been a thunderous roar was no more than a steady, pleasant hum. Holmes, what the devil is really happening in the Winbolt factory?"

"A most extraordinary operation, this Winbolt Company is."

"I have theories, Watson, and I hope they are not accurate, though I fear they are. If I am correct, we have uncovered an evil as foul as any I have seen, a disgusting abuse of power fit for the likes of such evil men as Professor Moriarty and Baron Gruner!"

I shuddered to hear Holmes speak those two names. For him to compare whatever he suspected to the schemes orchestrated by those men, the theories he spoke of must have been monstrous indeed.

"Will you share these ideas with us?" I asked.

"Not yet, Watson. Our own eyes and ears will tell us if I am correct, perhaps as soon as this coming night."

"And what were you doing," I inquired, "while banished from the interior of the factory?"

"Sniffing around outside, making a mental picture of the exterior of the Winbolt grounds and building, and guessing at some irregularities in what I observed. All will be made clear soon, Watson, and I fear we are to unveil a great ugliness, a true horror."

Following that foreboding statement, Holmes turned to Harry Lawson.

"And did you, Mr. Lawson, perform the one small task I assigned you, beyond, of course, the beginning stages of the portrait?"

"Yes," Lawson answered. "As I packed up my brushes, I dropped my watch onto the lowest shelf of Mr. Winbolt's bookcase."

"Excellent," Holmes said. "Then we have our reason to revisit the place! You will, of course, Lawson, project a great need to retrieve the watch at once, for it must seem truly valuable to you if our ruse is to be a convincing one."

"When will we go?" Lawson asked. The eagerness in his voice was obvious.

"Between ten and midnight should be the best time," Holmes said. "The guards will be tired, the darkness covering the land, and the presence of most of us concealed."

"There will be more than the three of us involved?" I asked.

"Yes, Watson, we will need assistance. Would you be as kind as to go yourself and fetch Inspector Bradstreet and several constables?"

"Of course," I said as I stood and reached for my hat and coat.

At eleven that night, Holmes, Lawson, Bradstreet, and I sat in a carriage, its horses at full speed, and a young constable holding the reins. Behind us were two more carriages driven by policemen. The passenger seats of those vehicles were empty, in anticipation of our having to bring various people away at the conclusion of our expedition.

As we rode, Sherlock Holmes counted off the ideas and events that had led to his theories on what we might soon discover.

"The extraordinary reports of Winbolt's machine, coupled with his fanatical desire to keep its supposedly technological secrets concealed from the prying eyes of any man possessing expertise in the mechanization of industry; the notably small workforce employed by the Winbolt Company; the attitude of Horatio Winbolt toward the non-English, as evidenced by his treatment of poor Bruno; the similar attitude found in his brother, the anthropologist Professor Bartholomew Winbolt; the fact that the young Brazilian woman, Benedita Costa, vanished in what was possibly a violent incident, as indicated by the damaged state of the beetle brooch and the witness account found in the files of Scotland Yard; and our knowledge that Miss Costa had recently encountered Professor Winbolt.

"Lawson came to us, we met Professor Winbolt, I recalled the existence of his brother the manufacturing magnate and read of the peculiarities of his success—and suddenly a nightmarish set of circumstances formed in my imagination, a dark dream of greed and hate that I am now almost fully convinced is no fantasy, but a wicked, brutal reality which must end this very night, even if we must risk our lives to see it ceased!"

With that, Sherlock Holmes stopped speaking, turned his head slightly to stare out the window into the passing night, and spoke not again until we reached our destination.

He was truly infuriated by whatever he expected us to find as our investigation progressed.

Our three carriages halted on a dark road a short distance from the Winbolt grounds. In hushed voices, we discussed our plan. Though Bradstreet was the ranking police officer present, he stood aside and allowed Holmes to instruct the constables.

"You three will remain here with the two empty carriages. You," he pointed to one of the young, uniformed men, "lend me your whistle.

Should you hear its siren, you are all to come at once. Inspector Bradstreet, you will drive our carriage onto the grounds. Lawson, your task is to disembark and knock upon the door of the factory building. When one of the guards opens it, you will insist that you be allowed to enter to retrieve the watch you left there this past afternoon. Do not allow them to refuse your request. In this way, at least one, and perhaps all of them, will be distracted. While that is happening, Watson and I will try to gain access to the building by means of a small rear door I discovered while investigating the exterior today. Bradstreet, if I blow this whistle, you must run to find us, for it will mean either danger or an important discovery. Do you all understand your roles?"

We all nodded.

"Bradstreet, are you armed?" Holmes asked.

"Of course I am—and I would like to go with you and the doctor when we arrive. Is it not better that three of us face potential danger than just the two of you?"

"I am grateful for your willingness, Inspector," Holmes said, "but if I am wrong, it is better that the scandal of this unsanctioned search fall upon my name rather than smear the reputation of Scotland Yard. Rest assured that I will call you at the first indication that I am correct in my assumptions. In such an event, your first responsibility must be to see to Lawson's safety, and then you will find Watson and me."

"Very well."

"And you, Watson, I trust, have brought your revolver?"

"Holmes," said I, "judging by the state of agitation your theory about this case has given you, I would not dream of leaving Baker Street without a weapon."

"Let us go, then, gentlemen."

Bradstreet pulled the reins to stop the horses in front of the entrance. Holmes and I crouched down in the carriage to avoid being seen as Harry Lawson stepped up to the door and pounded loudly upon the sturdy wood.

The door swung open to reveal two large men. They looked angrily at Lawson. The taller of the two spoke.

"It's the middle of the night, you idiot. And even in daylight, the management here does not take kindly to soliciting! Get out of here!"

"Wait," Lawson implored. "Please, before you shut the door in my face, allow me just a moment of your time."

"Then say your piece and make it fast!"

"My name is Harry Lawson. Earlier today I was here to paint the portrait of your employer, Mr. Winbolt. I seem to have accidentally left my watch behind and I am terribly worried about it. I must have it back at once, for it belonged to my father and holds great sentimental value for me. I beg of you, let me in for only as long as it takes to retrieve what is mine."

"Bloody hell! That's all you're here for? A watch? Come back in the morning, you daft fool!"

"Wait! I will give you two excellent reasons to let me in."

"All right, give us your reasons, and then we'll happily shut the door in your face."

"First, because I was here to paint Mr. Winbolt, I am, just as you are, his employee. And, I dare say, a more valuable one than you two brutes, as my job requires rare skills possessed by very few men in any given generation. How do you think Mr. Winbolt would react if told how badly you have treated me thus far tonight? Second, I will gladly provide you with a small reward for admission to the building."

"Reward?"

Lawson reached into his pocket and produced something. From my vantage point, I could not see the contents of his hand as he held it out for the guard to see, but, judging by the change in the man's expression, I guessed that it was money.

"Listen," the guard said, his voice far less aggressive now, "how about we make us all happy? If you'll just tell me where you left your watch, I'll send Barney here up to fetch it. When you have the watch, I'll take my reward."

"I would strongly prefer," Lawson said, "that I am escorted in to find the watch myself. It is an antique and quite delicate. Barney has hands better suited for pugilism than the handling of precious objects."

"My job is to keep people out of here at night," the guard countered.

"I will double your reward," Lawson said.

At that, the guards parted like the Red Sea, and Harry Lawson entered the building. As the doors began to close behind him, we could hear the guard say, "Barney and me are both going with you, just in case you try anything."

The door closed and we heard the lock turn.

"Excellent work by the artist," Holmes said. "Perhaps he should have been an actor. Two of the three sentries are now distracted. Come, Watson!"

Holmes and I climbed out of the carriage, using the door on the side opposite of that facing the Winbolt building. We walked in a half-bent manner, as low to the ground as we could, until we slipped around the edge of the building where the shadows were deeper.

We stayed close to the wall, moving by feeling our way around the stone exterior, guided by the light of the moon, which was, fortunately for us, quite bright in the night sky.

As we reached the end of the wall and turned left to explore the rear side of the factory, Holmes whispered, "We are nearly there."

Holmes stopped, ran his hands along a section of the wall. I could just see the outline of a door. Holmes tapped on the surface, which sent back an echo indicating it was made of metal. He tried the knob, found it locked.

"A bit of light, if you would, Watson."

I took out some matches, struck one. There, in the glow of the flame, Holmes took out his lock picks, expertly tricked the mechanism behind the doorknob, twisted it, and pushed the barrier inward, admitting us to the rear of the Winbolt factory.

We were in a long corridor. When the first match had burned down, I began another. We passed several closed doors as we moved slowly down the hall, our footsteps as quiet as we could keep them. We finally reached a staircase that led down into darkness. I lit yet another match and we descended. At the foot of the steps, the narrow passage opened into a much larger space. Several electric lamps hung above us, dim and providing just the minimal light we required to see our surroundings, but cancelling the need for matches. I knew immediately where we were.

In front of us were many tables, each of which bore various types of tools. Several chairs stood at each station. Stretched across the room, its track suspended by thick cables several feet above the tables, was the long belt I had seen in action many hours earlier. Occasionally, it rose upward on the track to vanish into an opening in the ceiling, only to reemerge several feet later, reminding me of train tacks that arched heavenward to disappear into and reappear from holes in the sky. The slope of the track had been precisely measured to prevent objects from sliding off if the climb was too sudden or steep. Turning where I stood, in order to view all regions of the room, I could see two large hand cranks, one at each end of the chamber, which were connected to the belt.

"This is the machine, Holmes, the apparatus used to manufacture the music boxes—but it is no machine at all!"

"Precisely, Watson! There was never a machine. Had a man of Winbolt's ambition and greed truly devised such a wonder, I have no doubt he would rather have sold its design and made an even greater fortune replicating it than to settle for the mere position of being England's greatest maker of music boxes! It was all a trick, a legend cultivated to hide the terrible truth behind the manufacture of his trademark toy!"

"But how does this…this false miracle really work, then, Holmes? How are the music boxes truly manufactured?"

"Watson, more and more I fear all my theories will be proven correct this night. Truly, the hellish depths of the evil side of the human imagination have no bottom. Let us proceed through that next door," he pointed to an exit from the factory floor, "and witness perhaps the greatest collection of suffering we have ever seen in one place."

We took several steps toward the door, but stopped when the door opened from the other side.

"Who the devil—" said the man who stepped over the threshold, but he decided in mid-sentence to speak with his gun instead. He raised a pistol, took aim at Holmes, who stood slightly in front of and to the left of my position.

I moved as quickly as I could, drawing my revolver and managing to pull the trigger first. My shot was good, striking him in the chest. He fell backward and did not move again.

"I have killed him, Holmes," I said, my mind a mixture of relief and guilt. I have never enjoyed violence, though I have not hesitated to fight when no other course is possible.

"If you had not, he would surely have slain me. Come, now that he has opened our way for us."

Holmes rushed through the doorway and I followed. What we saw upon our arrival in the next chamber filled my eyes with tears and my heart with rage.

Cages lined the walls. Iron boxes with thick bars, containers perhaps fit—and even then quite cruel—for animals in a zoo. But this was no menagerie, for inside each cage stood, sat, or slept a human being, most of them now having been roused by the sound of the gunshot and rising to their feet to look through the dim light at the two strangers who had entered their prison. None of them spoke, and I could see by their expressions that it was fear that kept them silent.

Holmes and I walked slowly along the room, stopping for a moment to look into each cell. They wore tattered clothing, most looked unwashed, and the smell of the place was rank. Judging by their features, there were Chinese, Hindus, Arabs, Africans, and an assortment of others not of typical English, Irish, or Scottish stock. Men and women, young and old, and even several weeping, shivering children were among the captives.

As we stopped before one cage, its occupant stared back at us, her long black hair cascading down around her shoulders, snow white teeth and bright, still hopeful eyes glowing from within a face covered in the grime and sweat produced by hard labor and filthy conditions. I knew that face, for I had seen it brought to the likeness of life in dozens of sketches.

"Miss Costa?" I asked. "Miss Benedita Costa?"

"You know me?"

"My dear young lady," I said, "It is because of you that all these unfortunate people here will now go free."

At that moment, she smiled at me, and I understood why that smile had made our friend Harry Lawson go to such lengths to find her after a chance meeting among the graves and the accidental discovery of the silver Brazilian beetle.

"Watson!" Sherlock Holmes barked. I had been aware of his moving away from me as I spoke with Miss Costa. Now his footsteps drew near again and I turned to see him standing there jingling a set of keys. He threw the ring to me. "Let them out, Watson, while I go to find Bradstreet. Give me your matches, so I may navigate the dark corridor."

Moments later, I heard the shrill sound of the borrowed whistle.

The two guards who remained alive were placed under arrest. One of the constables went to collect more policemen and several more carriages with which to transport the slaves of Horatio Winbolt to hospital. When last I saw Benedita Costa, she was being carried toward one of the wagons by the young artist who had come to us for help and initiated the case. Judging by the expression upon his face at that moment, he did not at all mind the burden in his arms.

As the area was evacuated, Holmes recited the facts of the nefarious plot once more for the benefit of the report that would have to be written for Scotland Yard's files.

"Horatio Winbolt wanted a way to produce his music boxes without having to pay the wages of the large number of workers needed to manufacture enough of them to meet the demand. As he and his brother held the same low opinion of anyone not born in this land, they took to assembling a force of slaves. Professor Bartholomew Winbolt, during his researches into the immigrant population of London, would identify those foreigners whose disappearances would not be noticed: the widowed, the orphans, the refugees, and the lone travelers. He would then inform his brother of their whereabouts and men would be sent to abduct them and transport them to the factory where they would be caged and let out only to work.

"Taking advantage of the fact that the use of electrical machinery has advanced considerably in recent years, though not yet to the extent that a process such as what Winbolt seemed to possess is possible, he created a false mechanism, to be put into action using a minimum of electricity and a complicated series of pulleys, wheels, and belts which were cranked by hand. This show was put on only when visitors were present at the factory. The men he employed to supposedly maintain and run the machine were, in reality, slave drivers!

"Horatio Winbolt is a brilliant criminal, and among the cruelest men I have ever been made aware of. Had he treated his prisoners and slaves kindly, his actions would still be of the utmost evil, and his making them live in chains and filth elevates his status to that of a true devil among men. Whatever charges you will bring against the fourteen men involved, including, of course, the two sentries who still live, accessory to murder must be included. While I roamed the exterior in the daylight to look for indications of hidden areas in the factory and entrances alternative to the front doors, I also happened upon a section of the grounds where the soil had been disturbed many times. When digging occurs there, as now it must to gather all information needed for prosecution, you will surely discover the remains of the many unfortunates who did not survive their enslavement. Truly, I have rarely encountered such an ugly set of events, even in my profession."

When all had left the grounds save for me, Holmes, Bradstreet, and one constable, the inspector suggested we go straightaway to arrest the man responsible for the terrible evil we had just put to an end.

"We shall wake the wretched bastard and have him in irons before he knows what is happening."

"No," said Sherlock Holmes, "I think not. I beg you to indulge one wish of mine, Inspector Bradstreet, and allow me to wait here until morning. When Winbolt arrives for his day's work, I should like to have a brief conversation with him, after which I assure you he will be dealt with in a way far more fitting of his crimes than any prison you can send him to."

"If you intend to execute the man, Holmes, you know it is my duty to stop you. I agree the scoundrel deserves to hang, but we are not the court."

"You have my word I will not kill him. If it is any consolation, I will allow you the satisfaction of going to arrest his accomplice, Geoffrey, as well as his brother, Professor Bartholomew Winbolt of the King's College. But I will be in your debt if you leave the lord of this castle for me to deal with, and I never forget to repay what I owe a man."

"All right, Holmes, have it your way."

"Thank you. Watson, let us go to Winbolt's office. There, I will write a note for you to deliver to my brother Mycroft. Do not worry about the hour, for he rarely sleeps. The message will make little sense to you, but he will understand. Once you have done that, you may retire to Baker Street for the night, or, should you prefer, rejoin me here."

I did not even consider the first option. "I shall return as quickly as humanly possible, Holmes."

I stood in the lobby of the Winbolt building at just past seven in the morning. I heard, first, a knock upon the door, followed by a string of profanities with a questioning tone behind the words, and then a key turning in the lock.

Horatio Winbolt did not see me immediately upon entering.

"Geoffrey!" he called out.

"Geoffrey will not be coming here today," I said, startling Winbolt.

"Hampton! How did you get in here?"

I drew my revolver as a precaution. "Hampton was merely a guise," I said. "My name is John Watson. It is my pleasure to inform you that Geoffrey, as well as your night watchmen and the crew of men who tend to your manufacturing process, have all been placed under arrest. If you will please proceed up the stairs to your office ..."

I walked behind Winbolt, urged him onward through the door on the upper floor.

"Who in God's name are you?" Winbolt shouted as he found Holmes seated behind his desk.

"Yesterday, Mr. Winbolt," Holmes said, "you thought I was an Italian and had me ejected from this very room. As you can now see and hear, you were mistaken. I am as English as you are. My name is Sherlock Holmes. You are, I believe, acquainted with my brother, Mycroft. You are also, I suspect, aware that Mycroft holds a rather special position in Her Majesty's government, although you may not know the details of that arrangement. Furthermore, being a man of some intelligence, even if that intellect is prone to be used for less than honorable purposes, you will have heard tales of certain places utilized by our nation as prisons to which are sent those criminals judged to be too vile, too dangerous, or otherwise unsuited to the more traditional penitentiaries. In those places, there is no chance of parole and no possibility of release, and suicide is carefully guarded against. In approximately one minute, several men sent here by my brother will arrive to escort you to one of those exclusive prisons, where you will spend the remainder of your natural life in a manner very similar to that in which your workers suffered until this past night. I hope that life is a long one, Mr. Winbolt. If he runs, Watson, resist the urge to shoot him, for such mercy is unfit for his kind."

The End

Collision

Sir Arthur Conan Doyle's stories of Sherlock Holmes and the stories of his successors in writing about the Great Detective (at least the ones who follow Doyle's lead faithfully) have a very strong current or theme at their core. That theme is friendship.

The relationship between Holmes and his chronicler and companion, Dr. John Watson, was adult friendship at its best, a wonderful example of mutual respect and willingness to help each other in the direst situations. Holmes accepted Watson as a loyal and intelligent (by normal standards) man with a good heart and adventurous spirit and indulged Watson's desire to keep a written record (sometimes too embellished for Holmes' liking) of the cases they worked on together. And Watson accepted Holmes' many eccentricities and occasionally rude and abrupt behavior while remaining, throughout their many years of acquaintance, truly in awe of his friend's genius and the special skills that made him perfect for the role of the world's first consulting detective. The two often risked their lives for each other, although they rarely expressed the depth of their admiration in words (which is true of most male friendships).

Two especially potent examples of the way Doyle brilliantly portrayed the Holmes-Watson friendship come to mind for me as I write this essay. In "The Adventure of the Three Garridebs," when Watson is shot (though not seriously), Holmes' reaction speaks volumes. First, the detective knocks the shooter out by slamming his pistol down upon the man's head. He then rushes to Watson, saying, "You're not hurt, Watson? For God's sake, say that you are not hurt!" Then, when the shooter comes back to consciousness, Holmes warns, "If you had killed Watson, you would not have got out of this room alive."

In a much earlier story, "The Final Problem," there occurred the scene (one of the most famous in the canon), where Watson arrives at the Reichenbach Falls to discover that, apparently, Holmes and his arch-foe Moriarty have gone to their deaths together after fighting and plummeting over the falls. At the very end of that story, Watson's conclusion reveals the degree of admiration he feels for his (he thinks) lost comrade: "If I have now been compelled to make a clear statement of his career, it is due to those injudicious champions who have endeavored to clear his memory by attacks upon him whom I shall ever regard as the best and the wisest man whom I have ever known."

Ha! I know Holmes isn't really dead at the end of "The Final Problem." I've read all the great stories that came after his return in "The Empty House," and yet that passage still brings me almost to tears.

Yes, Holmes and Watson are among the most famous friends in popular fiction. I'd put them up there with the Lone Ranger and Tonto, the Star Trek trinity of Kirk, Spock, and McCoy, and, especially, a pair that was certainly inspired by Doyle's work and might be viewed as the next generation of detective and partner, Agatha Christie's Hercule Poirot and Captain Arthur Hastings.

So why the thoughts of friendship to open this essay? Because that subject has an importance to how the story you've just read, "The Adventure of the Brazilian Beetle," came into being. It's because two people suddenly collided and their lives became connected in one of the best of all possible ways.

I have never been the sort of man who has an abundance of close friends. That's just not the way I am. I have many friendly acquaintances, but not many people who I can share my deepest feelings and opinions with and not be looked at like I'm crazy. I'm naturally an introvert and I'll admit I have my eccentricities, so I can be hard to understand and get along with (those traits do help me as a writer, though). It's rare that I really, truly connect with someone.

Then I found Samara! A few years back, I took a part-time job to supplement the pay from my regular day job (yes, writers tend to be poor!). I'm now back to just one day job, but I got something out of that temporary gig that is much more valuable than a paycheck. About an hour into my first day there, I walked into a room to find a woman loudly arguing with a coworker. The argument was philosophical in nature and I was impressed by the vigor with which she was stating (or, rather, screaming) her case! I was intrigued and we soon became friends. I could tell a thousand stories about little incidents that took place over the next year: comments exchanged, conversations, laughter, memories shared, excursions together to places outside work, etc, etc, etc, but those accounts could never mean as much to anyone reading this as they do to us, so I won't bore anyone. Suffice it to say that she became one of the best and closest friends I have ever had. We don't see each other every day anymore, but when we do meet (and I wish that was more often), the friendship keeps its strength, and I suspect it always will.

A year or so ago, Samara took a trip to Europe and wandered around Italy, France, and England for a few weeks. She gave me two gifts from that trip, two things that mean more than any souvenir or trinket she might have brought back. First, I now have a picture of her reading one of my novels as she sits in Buckingham Palace, of all places, which I think is pretty cool! And, second, the first time I saw her after the trip and she told me some of what it had been like, she inadvertently started the ball rolling on the story I wrote for this anthology. Samara grew up in Brazil, and she visited the Highgate Cemetery while in London and told me about some of the strange people she saw hanging about there. So that account, twisted about a bit, inspired the premise behind this latest Holmes mystery, except it was now an English artist having a chance encounter with a Brazilian woman in that very famous cemetery. Close enough. Samara also suggested the name Benedita for the Brazilian character.

So that's the story. A very important friendship that I am eternally grateful to be a part of inspired my latest story of the detective and the doctor who make up the two halves of one of the greatest friendships in all fiction. It seems like an appropriate circle of events. Thanks, Samara!

AARON SMITH - thrilled to now have had eight Sherlock Holmes stories published, and still enjoys every visit to the Baker Street in his mind. His short stories have appeared in many anthologies and magazines and fall under genres including mystery, fantasy, horror, science fiction, and even a western. He is the author of the zombie horror novel *Chicago Fell First*, and the Richard Monroe espionage novels *Nobody Dies for Free* and *Under the Radar* from Pro Se Press. More information about Smith's work can be found on his blog at www.godsandgalaxies.blogspot. com He invites readers to follow him on Twitter as @AaronSmith377

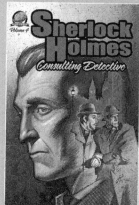

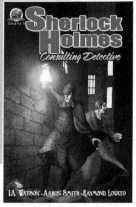

From Out of the Past

The year 1885 finds Doctor John H. Watson down on his luck. His prospects look bleak until a chance encounter leads him to a meeting with another literary-minded young physician named Arthur Conan Doyle. Together, they hatch a plan for a series of works based on the adventures of Watson's roommate, the Consulting Detective Mr. Sherlock Holmes.

Then a very attractive young lady, Mary Morstan, arrives at 221 B Baker street seeking help. Soon Holmes and Watson are drawn into the dark world of the Sholto brothers, a web of blackmail and murder. Even with the assistance of a rising playwright named Oscar Wilde, Holmes finds himself taxed to the limit of his powers when his own darkest secrets are exposed. What truths lie beneath the surface of the *Picture of Innncence*?

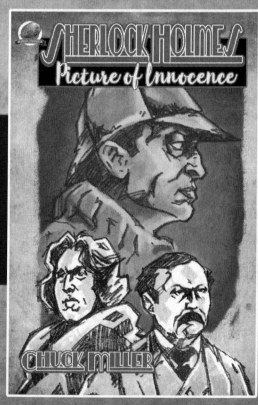